MW01537518

Molly Marple Mystery

Carolyn Haynes

ADDICTIVE GRACE PRESS

Copyright © 2024 by Carolyn Haynes
Molly Marple Mystery
Los Angeles, California

ISBN #979-8-9990385-0-0
Printed in the United States of America
All rights reserved under International Copyright Law.

The use of any part of this publication, reproduced, transmitted in any form or by any means, electronic, mechanical, photocopying, recording, AI, or otherwise, or stored in a retrieval system without the author's prior written consent, is an infringement of the copyright law.

Molly Marple Mystery/Carolyn Haynes
Published in the United States of America

This is a work of fiction. Names, characters, businesses, places, events, and incidents are either products of the author's imagination or used fictitiously. Any resemblance to actual persons, living or dead, or real events is coincidental.

Some names and identifying details have been changed to respect the privacy of individuals.

While historical figures, locations, and events may be referenced, this story remains a work of fiction. The characters' thoughts, actions, and beliefs do not reflect the author's personal views nor serve as an evaluation of actual historical figures, movements, or events.

This novel is meant to entertain, not to assert conclusions about real people, past or present.

13 % of royalties are advanced to local & worldwide charities.

Dedication

To my beloved daughters—Linda, Jennipher, Jill, Jessica, my first-fourth, Cathy—and my incredible sister Gloria. To my precious grandchildren, who fill my heart with endless joy.

I lovingly dedicate this book to you. You are my inspiration, my greatest gift, and a blessing beyond measure. More than I could have ever dreamed, you are the beautiful story God has written into my life.

Table of Contents

1

Love, An Act of Courage

A glass of wine, a plate of hot, spicy chicken wings, and the rain hammering against the rooftop—I was lost in an Agatha Christie mystery. What could be lovelier? For a while, her brilliant prose drowned out the horrors of last spring. Then, a flicker of light caught my eye, faint but familiar. My breath hitched. Was it just a trick of the storm... or something more? I peered into the dark corner of the garden, my heartbeat quickening. Suddenly, I was transported back to the memory of that night, the moments of almost unbearable beauty with Daniel, the breeze of intoxicating fragrances of orange blossoms and honeysuckle, and the warmth of his presence.

"Is everything alright, Molly?" His grounding voice echoed in my memory.

I laughed, brushing it off. "I'm just overwhelmed by the beauty of the evening, Daniel... and a curious sparkle of light in the garden."

The following morning, the world felt almost normal again. Daniel slept late while I walked to the village bakery, returning with warm pastries and two rich, comforting cappuccinos. The sun had burned through the fog, filling the garden with golden shards of light. I stepped outside, and the air was drenched in perfume—sweet, warm, unforgettable, as if the garden remembered love—until I saw it—a familiar glint. I moved closer, and a gold and silver antique locket was tangled on a broken branch. My heart quickened. Had someone been in the garden last night? I picked it up, feeling the weight of its history. Inside was a crumpled, marred photo of an unrecognizable man on one side, and on the other, the torn remains of an image someone had removed. A single familiar engraving on the back sent a chill through me: "Always and Forever." Where had I heard this? Was it connected to a recent crime? A forgotten secret? I rushed inside, placing the locket

under a magnifying glass, until I heard the shower running. Daniel was up.

As a lieutenant in the Los Angeles police department, he was brilliant at solving mysteries. And I was anxious to see his reaction to what I'd found. I tucked the locket into the drawer and began preparing our favorite French scrambled eggs/Oeufs Brouilles, guaranteed to elevate breakfast and set the stage for my discovery. The rush of his footsteps as he ran down the stairs thrilled me. He kissed my cheek with an exuberant,

"Good morning, my beautiful Molly Cleary. Breakfast smells amazing. Oh, and you've been to the bakery, just what I needed."

Daniel paused, opened the bag, and inhaled dramatically, closing his eyes as if savoring the scent of freshly baked muffins and croissants.

"Molly, these pastries are wonderful! How about we eat in the garden?"

"Perfect," I said, slipping my curious find into my pocket as he carried the tray outside.

The warmth of the morning sun made the garden feel almost surreal, a cocoon of beauty shielding us from the outside world. With each delicious bite, the weight of my discovery pressed against me, burning in my pocket. I couldn't wait any longer. I reached for the locket, held it up for Daniel to see, and blurted out,

"Daniel, I found this tangled in the honeysuckle bush. It might be the flash of light I saw last night. What do you think?"

He stilled. Lifting his coffee, he took a slow sip, his gaze fixed on the locket. Silence stretched between us, the birdsong and distant hum of morning traffic fading against the sudden heaviness of the moment. A troubling shadow passed over his face.

"Is everything okay, Daniel?" I asked, my pulse quickening.

He set down his cup. "Yeah. Let's go inside; I'm cold."

Cold? The sun was already warming the garden. Did he recognize the locket? A chilling suspicion clawed at me—was he hiding something? The thought struck hard, stealing my breath. Could this locket be tied to another woman? Another life? But I hesitated, recalling the man I married. Daniel's childhood dream of becoming an officer had shaped him into someone both admired and loathed. His commitment to justice had made him a hero to many, yet an enemy to a few in power. He'd learned to separate work from home, leaving little room for probing questions.

"Let's take a walk on the beach," I suggested.

I'd hoped to break whatever held him in its grip. He nodded, albeit reluctantly. The day was perfect. The sun hung low, casting golden light across the ocean. We kicked off our shoes, letting the cool sand soothe our feet. The rhythmic waves seemed to slow time, yet Daniel's grip on my hand was firm, almost desperate. Then, without warning, he stopped. Turning to face the horizon, he inhaled deeply as if trying to draw strength from the sea air.

"What's bothering you, Daniel?" I asked, my voice softer now. "Can I help?"

His response was a burst of frustration, his eyes locked on the skyline.

"Molly, something's not right. It's more than just criminal threats—this feels bigger, deeper. I think it's coming from within the department, someone with power and influence. But I can't prove it yet. And the thought of you… or a child… being caught in the middle of this—it's tearing me apart. I hate that this is our reality. I'm so sorry about our dream of having a family."

Sadness etched across his face as he closed his eyes, struggling to find words.

"What dangers, Daniel?"

He shook his head, then looked at me, tears threatening to spill over. He shrugged, unable to explain—the

question about the locket burned on my tongue, but I couldn't bring myself to ask. I held his hand close to my face and looked into his troubled eyes.

"Daniel, if we're meant to have children, we will. But we have each other right now—and you have a mystery to solve."

As he held me in his arms, the sun's calming brilliance shimmered on the water, casting a serene glow as it moved over our feet. The tide gently pulled at the shore, gathering the unspoken fears and cares between us, then swept them away to the vast, waiting sea. Daniel's tormented words softened, and the ocean breeze seemed to whisper resolutions, coaxing his troubled thoughts toward a more hopeful horizon. Daniel's words settled over me like an encroaching storm— "something bigger, something deeper." The weight of his unease pressed against my chest, but I wasn't ready to let fear take hold. I squeezed his hand, grounding us both.

"Let's go home," I whispered.

The walk back was quiet, the rhythm of the waves filling the silence between us. When we reached the house, a breathless hush had settled between us, a fragile peace waiting to be broken. I turned to him, searching his face.

"I don't want to think about any of this tonight," I said, barely above a murmur.

"Just you and me."

A flash of hesitation crossed his eyes, but he pulled me close, his warmth seeping into me like a shield against the unknown. His strong arms enveloped me like an unseen fortress, a refuge to escape all care. His eyes filled with a love that words could never express and time would never erase. Love stretching beyond all measure passed through us, and his kiss echoed our first many years ago. An incomprehensible passion, eclipsing limitation, opened a treasured door that night to the sublime, an Eden-like universe with promises of indescribable bliss that will reside with me forever.

The Night That Changed Everything

The morning after was painted in mist and memory. A soft ache of contentment lingered beneath my ribs, the residue of our exquisite night together, continued whispering promises and fleeting bliss that silently warmed my skin. But as dawn crept into our little corner of Brentwood, reality returned with the hush of fog pressing against the windows. I woke before Daniel, my heart knotted with the weight of his suspicions from the evening before. The questions he'd raised—half-formed, edged with fear—clung to me like the heavy marine layer settling over our street. I slipped from the warmth of our bed, padded across the cool floor, and wrapped myself in Daniel's robe. He stirred but didn't wake. I kissed his shoulder, then went to the kitchen, needing coffee and answers.

Outside, the town seemed to hold its breath. Porch lights blurred in the fog, casting halos over the slick pavement. The distant clock tower, normally a cheerful sentinel, groaned its morning chimes like a warning carried through cotton. The silence was not peaceful—it was expectant. I stood at the window, coffee in hand, watching the mist thicken like secrets in the air. Daniel's strange reaction to the locket looped in my mind, refusing to settle. And then, unexpectedly, uninvited, the image of a local girl returned. Young. Beloved. Murdered. Her name had once been easily spoken in every café and yoga studio in Brentwood. Her death, a slow burn of mystery and media frenzy, had left the town scorched. Could there be a connection between her and the locket? Her husband, an affable actor, a rising star with a golden smile, had been the only real suspect—but never charged. The headlines had faded, but the unease hadn't. It lived on in the pauses between conversations, in the way people changed the subject too quickly, in the way that locket had made Daniel look like he'd seen a ghost. I hoped, rather than believed, that Daniel's frightening suspicions would reach a conclusive resolution.

11

For the most part, Brentwood's streets and homes are lovely—some even charming with their white picket fences and flowering vines. But seeping through the gloss, a quiet strangeness sometimes lingered, subtle and unsettling. You'd never guess that behind one of these pristine facades might lie something as curious—and charged—as an antique gold and silver locket. Mysteries surrounding it were growing. My thoughts spiraled as I stared into my coffee. What would Miss Jane Marple do with something like this? She'd study the details, watch the players, and ask the question no one else thought to ask. I smiled faintly. I could almost hear her voice encouraging me to do the same. Outside, the village was beginning to stir. Shops would soon open, and the air would fill with the buttery scent of croissants, fresh bread, and dark roast coffee. As the fog clung to the hedges, it lifted enough to make the day feel possible again. Ideas began to form: I'd ask Daniel about the locket on our morning stroll. Casual, conversational, while browsing heirloom tomatoes or lingering by the cheeses in our cozy English-style market. His voice was warm and eager when he awoke, as if last night's shadows had never touched him.

"Ready for our Saturday morning adventure, Molly?" I nodded, slipping the locket into my coat pocket. I was ready and hoped I'd have more than bread and brie by noon. Outside, the fog dissolved into honeyed sunlight. The morning air was crisp, the street glistening, and the church bell tolled as birds began their tentative morning song. Daniel and I walked hand in hand to the farmer's market, the scent of warm pastries and ripe produce drifting toward us on the breeze. Neighbors greeted us with smiles and waves, their faces glowing in the soft morning light. The market buzzed with life—a comforting constant, even as Brentwood grew more affluent, private, and guarded. Somehow, despite the gated homes and whispered scandals, the wholesome heart of Brentwood still beats here. Farmers offer fresh eggs and handpicked greens with the pride of generations. Customers can still wander into the fields,

connecting with the land that makes this place feel less like Los Angeles and more like a storybook. Mrs. Thompson, our local baker, handed us warm blueberry muffins while waiting for our approval to prepare our favorite Greek olive bread.

"The usual?" she grinned. We nodded, already taking a bite—the tangy sweetness grounding us in something real. At the butcher's stall, Jake Harris waved us over.

"Morning, Daniel! Morning, Molly! Daniel, I hear your boss just moved into our neighborhood?"

"Yes," Daniel replied. "Chief Bates and his wife arrived yesterday."

"Well," Harris said, lowering his voice slightly, "we could use more good people around here."

Daniel nodded politely, but I caught a brief, disturbed look in his eyes. I forced a smile, but my mind was already elsewhere. Chief Harold Bates. His name had surfaced before, more than once, buried in stories that never made the headlines but left trails in hushed conversations and suppressed files. That he now lives just blocks from us didn't feel like a coincidence. It felt like the tightening of a noose I hadn't known existed. We smiled, made our purchase, and moved on. Mrs. Clarke pressed a small bouquet into my hands at the flower stand.

"For you, my dear. A little something to brighten your day."

I thanked her, touched and unsettled by how perfect it all felt. As we reached the end of the market, a local band played under a striped tent. Daniel slid his hand in mine, and we swayed to the music. Though ecstasy surrounded us, I couldn't shake the weight in my pocket. The locket felt heavier than it should. I wanted to ask him about it, but something held me back. A hush inside me, like the one that had blanketed our street that morning. And then it came to me—not in words, but in knowing. This wasn't the resolution of anything. It was the beginning. The fog may have lifted, but I was already stepping into a valley of shadows.

Shattered Morning

The following week, Los Angeles basked in a warm kiss from the sun that reminded Daniel of his old rookie beat—a patch of the city filled with grit, promises to friends, and memories that still brought a smile to his face. True to his word, he returned to those congested sidewalks, nodding to familiar shop owners, letting the rhythm of the old neighborhood wrap around him like a favorite jacket. Eventually, he found himself at Maria's Flower Shop. Family-owned for over a century, it remained the heart of the neighborhood. The brass, flower-shaped doorknob felt warm in his hand. Inside, the shop greeted him with its usual exquisite fragrance and color, and Maria's familiar, uplifting smile. Customers buzzed in and out, their arms full of tulips and lilies, and for those precious moments, time stopped. But the sun was setting, and it was time for Daniel to leave. Maria approached, holding a beautifully wrapped bouquet. Her smile faltered just slightly, her voice muted.

"This was ordered for you earlier," she said, eyes searching his. "They asked to remain anonymous."

Daniel raised a brow but chuckled as he took the bouquet.

"It's probably Jake and Alice Harris—the butcher and his wife. They send Molly anonymous flowers and silly notes all the time."

Maria hesitated.

"It didn't sound like Alice."

Daniel, smiling, shrugged it off, said his grateful goodbyes, and moved toward the door.

"I'd better leave before traffic gets impossible!"

Slipping back into the main roads and highways' usual chaos, he called me, laughing about the overwhelming fragrance filling his government-issued car.

"It's strangely relaxing," he said.

We laughed about his day—his voice warm, full of life. I was just about to remind him that Jake and Alice always sent flowers to the house, and to ask about the locket, when he suddenly gasped.

"I almost ran a red light. I love you, Molly Cleary. I'll be home soon."

Then the call ended abruptly. I lingered, the phone still pressed to my ear, his voice echoing in my mind. For a moment, the world felt perfectly still. Eventually, I set the phone down, trying to shake the feeling that something had shifted. While his favorite meal simmered in the oven, I slipped into a hot bubble bath, letting the scented water relax me. My thoughts drifted to the day we met—he, with the LAPD; I, with the *Los Angeles Times*. Our shared love for volunteering at the local soup kitchen drew us together almost instantly. I smiled, remembering his heart-melting grin and how it could calm the angry, desperate, and lost. He was a reassuring presence on the streets—his quiet strength like sunshine for the weary shopkeepers navigating life's daily chaos.

Emerging from my reverie and wrapped in my soft white robe, I set the table—white linen, flickering candles, everything perfect. Then, I slipped into my black cashmere dress, added a spritz of Chanel No. 5, uncorked the Châteauneuf-du-Pape—Daniel's favorite—and waited. Then came the knock. Three familiar taps—Daniel's signal when he had a surprise. I laughed, heart fluttering, smoothing my dress as I rushed to the door. But when I opened it, the air turned cold. Officer Ciara Conway stood there, her eyes wet, lips pressed into a thin line. Behind her, Officer Kyle lingered in the shadows, holding something in his hands. A wave of familiar perfume—sweet, floral, impossibly strong—washed over me. I gasped. My joy evaporated. My breath caught. They asked to come in. I didn't move. Didn't answer. I stood there, blocking the doorway, clinging to one last moment of not knowing.

"I thought it was Daniel," I said, my voice strangely light and bright. "He had a surprise planned... something special tonight..."

They said nothing. And I said nothing more—because deep down, I already knew. Kyle stepped from the shadows, extending a large, stunning bouquet. The scent hit me like a wave. I felt myself floating outside the moment, watching from somewhere far away. My hands flew to my chest as the room spun. I collapsed. Ciara caught me, guiding me gently to the couch. I couldn't speak. Couldn't think. My mind rejected everything I knew was coming. She knelt beside me, her voice soft but unshakable.

"Molly... Daniel was in an accident."

Kyle handed me a glass of water. I couldn't take it. He quietly stepped aside, dialing my family. Ciara's following words broke through like shattering glass.

"He didn't make it, Molly. Did you hear me?"

I blinked, trying to make sense of it.

"No... no, I just spoke to him."

"An accident," she repeated, her voice already drifting away.

Then, there was another knock at the door. I ran to answer it, knowing it was Daniel, and called his name, only to find my mother and sister. Their sorrow broke me, and I sank into their arms, tears flowing uncontrollably. Ciara and Kyle quietly said goodbye.

"Justice will be served," Ciara said, her voice firm. "Especially for one of our own."

The door clicked shut behind them. For days, I drifted through grief's haze, clinging to anything that remotely resembled normal. But Ciara's parting words kept pressing in—*justice would be served?* Why did they leave me unsettled, as if there was more beneath them than comfort? But before I could unravel her cryptic words, I first had to get through Daniel's funeral and past the headlines dominating the front pages of every newspaper and blaring news broadcasts. They

announced that it was a hit-and-run, and the public was invited to show their support along the procession route. Thousands lined the streets, and Los Angeles County Police Chief Harold Bates spoke at the memorial. As I slowly regained my strength, Ciara gently revealed more of her suspicions and Kyle's conviction that Daniel's death was not an accident. He recorded Daniel's last words that life-altering evening, then treated the incident as a crime and demanded that proper protocols be observed. My mind raced with a searing intensity. Part of me longed to hear Daniel's voice again, but I feared what his final words might reveal. Despite my doubts about my ability to face the truth, I was driven to piece together the mystery for the love of my life, my husband, and my best friend.

As the months passed, the painful injustice gnawed at me, growing stronger each day. Grief would strike with a frightening intensity, leaving me gasping for breath, my vision blurred from burning tears. Before Daniel, I thought I understood love—knew its depths. But our love was profound, beyond words —a connection unlike anything I'd ever known. Now, standing in that fateful, shadowy valley of unanswered questions—Daniel's concern for my safety, his secrecy, the stark reality of our shattered dreams—I felt the threat of devastation emerging, lurking to consume me. Though I am forever grateful to have loved and been loved so deeply, the price is a loss that feels like an invisible amputation, something that will forever alter me. In the days that followed, the outside world pressed in, arriving in an overwhelming mass of condolence cards and phone calls, while I drifted in a fog of mixed emotions. However, much to my relief, my cousin Claire Moore came to help. Her presence brought much-needed comfort and stability, guiding me through the worst of my loss before she returned home.

Vivid dreams of Daniel haunted me nightly—romantic getaways and long conversations, all ending with him trying to answer my question about the locket, leaving me waking in

confusion and panic. But one evening, many months later, as I drifted to sleep, I felt a familiar, comforting touch on my face. I turned, and Daniel stood beside our bed, more handsome than ever. He gently brushed my hair back, and at that moment, our love was as fierce as ever; no words were needed. He sat beside me, his soul-piercing gaze stripping away every distraction; this wasn't a dream, but what was it? As our eyes locked, a profound sense of peace washed over me, filling my heart with relaxation and a flicker of joy I hadn't felt in months. Daniel silently rose, his eyes never leaving mine, and with a longing smile, he slowly backed away, stopping at the door with a look of unspoken reassurance before leaving. I was enveloped in contentment beyond description—soothing, heart-mending peace that assured me I would be okay, that love would endure. Courage entered my life that night. Although deep valleys lay ahead, I felt safe and connected to something greater. Life, though changed, would continue. I felt the first stirrings of hope returning to my life.

But as the days passed, my journalistic instincts stirred beneath the surface, casting doubt on that dreamlike encounter with Daniel. Trusting something so intangible began to feel naïve and unrealistic. My rational mind labeled it a fairytale spun from grief and shock. The peace it brought dissolved into a familiar fog of confusion—something I could at least explain. As a journalist, I couldn't afford to cling to what felt like delusion. It was dangerous. Might be even a little mad. With my return to work looming, I had to anchor myself in what I did trust: the facts. It was time to investigate Daniel's death—and the truth behind the locket.

2

Unsettled Truths

A brisk morning wind swept through Los Angeles, setting the white birch branches tapping against my bedroom window. I pulled the covers tighter, savoring one last moment of warmth before reaching for my bathrobe. Downstairs, the ritual continued: I curled up on the couch with a steaming cup of tea in hand, letting the rustling leaves soothe me. I opened *A Murder is Announced* and followed Miss Marple through her clever twists and turns—until something stirred. An idea. A spark. I closed the book. In the office, I approached Daniel's desk. My heart pounded as I unlocked the file drawer and began to sift through his notes. Then I saw it—the locket. I hadn't laid eyes on it in months. My hand hovered before I picked it up, the cool metal anchoring me as Daniel's troubled expression, the last time he saw it, flashed through my mind. This locket held secrets. I was sure of it. A shiver ran through me, and the locket slipped from my fingers, landing on the desk with a soft clink. I gently placed it back in the drawer. His handwriting stared up at me from the pages, raw and intimate. Tears welled up. It felt like trespassing. But before diving in, I thought of Miss Marple's quiet strength—and her habit of taking care of herself before a case. I showered, dressed, and made a healthy breakfast. Then, with a clearer head and steadier heart, I returned to the desk—ready to begin.

Daniel's notes revealed two heavily lined words: *Hampton Fife* and *GRB*. Daniel had never mentioned either, and GRB—was it someone's initials? The pressure of the pen strokes suggested anger or perhaps... a breakthrough. I spent the weekend sorting through every note, desperate for answers. My efforts felt fruitless until I stumbled upon a barely legible entry, one that suddenly stopped me. It spoke of a man in authority who overtly profiled those different from himself, refused to acknowledge police brutality, and made a foolish

and dangerous demand that officers be immune to the laws governing the rest of society. Daniel's notes revealed he had double-checked his source and that the information was valid. Daniel gathered further confirmation and planned to take his findings to Internal Affairs. I paused, gaining a deeper understanding of Daniel's suspicions. His words were there, a murky puzzle slowly coming into focus. But what did the locket have to do with this puzzle? The further I read, the more elusive the answers seemed. Then, Agatha Christie's words suddenly echoed:

"Many answers are revealed while washing the dishes."

There was something disarming, even charming, about the idea that truth could emerge between soap suds and quiet routine. However, the air in the house felt too still. I stepped out, took a short drive, and without meaning to, passed Daniel's old precinct. The memory of Chief Bates' declaration of support resurfaced, with a gentle nudge to accept the offer. Nostalgia? Or the hope of finding something new? I parked and entered, stepping into a world that felt both familiar and unnerving. The comfort I sought was interrupted by an angry voice in a distant room, shouting vile things—classist comments that made my blood boil. As the shouting moved closer, an officer friend of Daniel's caught my eye and hurried toward me.

"It's not a good day for a visit," he whispered, gently guiding me back to my car.

"Who was that?" I asked intently.

He only shrugged, his expression grim as he ushered me away. I drove off, not finding a sanctuary in the precinct or memories but in the thought of Agatha Christie's Miss Marple, ever observant, quietly collecting details like Daniel's note on the man who profiled those different from himself. Was he the man I just heard, and was he a criminal or an officer? Maybe, like her, I needed to be patient, to let the pieces fall into place on their own. But as the precinct faded in my rearview mirror,

I knew one thing for sure: *answers were waiting*, and I had to keep searching.

As the weekend approached, I received a letter from my cousin Claire Moore. She asked if I could help with preparations for the birth of their first child. My heart soared at the thought of seeing them again—and perhaps there I would find some answers. It would also be my chance to see the Rose Haven community Claire had described in such mesmerizing detail. It sounded like *St. Mary Mead*, straight from a Miss Marple novel. This could be the fresh start I needed— an escape into quiet, natural beauty and the perfect place to further my investigation. Charged with anticipation, I confirmed I'd be there the following week, extended my leave of absence from work, and prepared for my first solo adventure.

The day had come. I was nervous, but also strangely excited. Stepping out alone felt monumental. I brought my neatly packed suitcase downstairs—complete with the locket and my Miss Marple novel—and set it by the door. But as I paused, a wave of fear gripped me. Daniel wasn't here to hold me, kiss me goodbye, or drive me to the station. That realization knocked the breath from my chest. I tried to push it away. I was a capable journalist. This tragedy couldn't paralyze me. Still, when I opened the door, the outside world hit me like a spotlight—too bright, loud, and strange. Panic swelled. My head spun. The thought came like a scream: *How can you let go of Daniel and grab hold of life again, Molly? You're deluding yourself.* I slammed the door shut, my back pressed against it, shaking. Even the short ride to Union Station felt impossible. I told myself I could always turn back, but the comfort was hollow. I closed my eyes and breathed deeply, summoning the inexplicable peace I'd felt with Daniel that night—the dream, the love, the sense that something unseen had reached me. *Would it meet me again if I moved toward it?* Slowly, breath by breath, courage returned. *You have nothing to lose,* I whispered. Tears blurred my vision as I gripped the suitcase

handle and opened the door again. The sun touched my skin, warm and steady, like a gentle escort forward. I didn't look back. I couldn't. The tears still came, but each step toward the waiting taxi felt like defiance—and hope. A peaceful three-day train ride lay ahead—hopefully, the first step toward something new.

I entered the grand old Union Station, an architectural gem in the heart of Los Angeles. Regarded as "the last of the great train stations," I gazed at the expansive beauty while marveling at the history surrounding me. I wondered about the countless people who passed this way and walked these beautiful floors. For a moment, a subtle appreciation of the richness of life tugged at my heart, melting that sickly feeling. I felt a subtle peace as I moved past the bench where Daniel and I had sat, waiting for his mother long ago. A lovely, cheery family now occupied that evocative space. With a lump in my throat, I smiled as I passed them, took a deep breath, and continued to the train.

Emanating somewhere within me, I heard a faint whisper. A phrase Daniel would softly say to me when I was overwhelmed. "Hold your head up high, Molly-girl; remember how much you are loved." It was just the encouragement I needed, calming my heart as I walked through the long, deserted passageway. Tears came and went until I finally stepped into the sunshine again and saw a massive, streamlined, gleaming-bright, silver train before me—a Camelot Coach to carry me away from pain with its powerful engines roaring. As I stopped and looked for my car entrance, a skilled, amiable porter must have noticed my confusion and asked if he could help. I silently nodded yes. He checked my ticket and pointed me in the right direction. The steady rumble of the engine stopped, and the air became still. My heart raced as I unsteadily stepped aboard and into the romance of trains. I was momentarily captivated by the thoughts of Miss Jane Marple's final goodbye to the love of her life as he boarded the train, leaving for the war.

22

Interrupting my daydream was a neatly dressed and distinguished-looking porter who greeted me. He removed the stub from my ticket, introduced himself as Alfred, and explained that he would be my attendant for the duration of my trip. He helped me with my suitcase and escorted me to my private dwelling for the following three days. He graciously opened the compartment door, revealing the view of a welcoming room with all the comforts of a five-star hotel. I entered wide-eyed, pleased, but a bit dazed! Alfred kindly pointed out all the amenities and explained their functions. While opening the fold-down table beneath a landscape window, Alfred announced I could dine in my room or the dining car, then brought my attention to a button by my table if I needed assistance. I was awkwardly speechless but managed a genuine thank you while standing in appreciation. Alfred smiled and handed me a menu, advising me to mark my food requests and attach them to the clip outside my door.

"Do you have any questions, ma'am?"

"No. Thank you, Alfred."

He turned and quietly closed the door behind him. The train whistle pierced the air as I reached for my suitcase to unpack. I froze, breath catching as the engine roared to life and the train began to move. A thrill of excitement and uncertainty surged through me. I closed the suitcase and sat at the table, watching people wave goodbye from the platform. *Goodbye*, I thought—a fitting farewell to what once was. Turning back to the quiet of my cabin, I observed every detail, then closed my eyes in a silent prayer. A gentle calm stirred within me, unlocking a new sense of resolve wrapped in a smile. At that moment, I decided to eat in the dining car. Fear lingered, but courage was beginning to take root. I unpacked slowly, my hand still trembling but no longer paralyzed.

The three days passed quickly. The train's rhythmic hum soothed me, offering space to breathe, grieve, and adjust. As we pulled into Rose Haven, I felt well-rested, heartbroken, but grateful. The engine's familiar drone quieted, replaced by a

stillness that signaled something new. Drawing the curtain aside, I gasped. The station looked like a rose garden sprung to life—blooms in every hue spilled from clay pots, ivy trailing around a carved sign: *Haven's Railway Boutique*. A rose-covered trellis in shades of salmon framed the view like a painting. The entire platform welcomed me—a warm, rose-scented breeze wrapped around me as I stepped off the train. The engine hummed softly behind me, then slowly faded, carrying the past with it.

I followed a few passengers through an archway to the back door of the magical-looking boutique. A wave of velvety rose scent stopped me—a rich, intoxicating fragrance that filled me like miraculous medicine. Then, like a hug from Daniel, I noticed the rose-shaped brass doorknob—the same as Maria's in Los Angeles. Giddy and in awe, I reached for it tenderly and stepped into what felt like a page from a fairy tale. Inside, the air shimmered with scents of plumeria, lavender, lemon, and peppermint. Gorgeous, high-quality items filled the shop. Laughter floated through the haze of my wonder, drawing my attention to the front—a vintage sandwich counter with gleaming chrome stools topped in deep red vinyl. Behind it, a cheerful couple served exquisitely prepared culinary offerings while chatting warmly with customers. I felt I'd gloriously stepped back in time.

I wandered slowly through the aisles, savoring the elegant displays and island paradise fragrances, drifting closer to the friendly conversation. Reaching the front door, I stepped out into a childhood dream—the aptly named village of Rose Haven. Each storefront was graced with at least one blooming rose bush. At first glance, the town looked like a storybook come to life. It was more than I'd imagined—so far from the clamor of city life, the secrets behind opulent doors, the locket mystery—yet I felt closer than ever to my beloved Daniel. Enchanted and energized, I fervently hoped the locket wouldn't reveal my worst fear. Passing the country cab, I decided to walk to my cousin's cottage just a few blocks away,

to savor every inch of this Miss Marple town. The gently curving sidewalk led me past quaint shop windows, while the soft calls of nautical horns and bells from the glassy sea urged me to slow down. While held in captivated awe, my focus sharpened on the flower-draped benches and café tables, wrapped in a tranquil and fragrant breeze. Finally—blissfully—at the town's edge, tucked beneath ivy and sun-faded brick, was a storefront so unexpected, so utterly cinematic, it felt plucked from a dream. *Bookstore and More.* It could've been a cousin to Shakespeare and Company in Paris. I didn't dare go in—*not yet.* But I knew I'd be back. Just beyond it, the harbor shimmered like a spilled secret, and there—unfolding like a ribbon from its edge—was Abbey Lane. The road to Claire and Steven Moore. It seemed to be waiting for me, inviting me to enjoy the beauty of enchantment.

I entered Abbey Lane, a shaded country road dotted with streams of sunlight peeking through the branches. Rambling alongside this beguiling road, a rushing freshwater stream splashed over the cobblestones. *This must be paradise,* I thought. As I strolled along, my weary body reminded me that it had been a long journey from Los Angeles, and this was more exercise than I'd had in months. Thankfully, as Claire had described in her letters, the entrance to Moore Cottage lay just ahead: a century-old, charming covered footbridge, steeped in history. She'd written of Steven's fierce devotion to saving it from demolition, and how, once rescued, he lovingly restored every beam. I longed to see the bridge that had carried so many footsteps—and stories—across the years.

As I continued walking, my heart was touched when the bridge came into sight. The charm and history encouraged me to walk faster to reach the entrance. With my first step upon the squeaky boards, I passed into the realm of history, spellbound by a world of wonder. How many people tread these same boards, and what agonies and ecstasies flowed through this space? I stopped at the crest of the bridge, enraptured. I gazed over the railing at the passing brook

beneath me. The echoing bird songs swirled gracefully through the air as brightly adorned birds sat on swaying branches, seeming thrilled by the spectacle. *Could there be a more beautiful place than this?* I thought. I grasped my suitcase and descended to an open gate leading to their garden. Before me lay a wide, meandering gravel path, surrounded by more glorious roses, gardenias, lavender, rosemary, and countless fragrant flowers, leading to their thatched-roof stone cottage. The sound of gravel beneath my shoes brought memories of the beautiful English walkways I'd seen in movies and longed to visit. As I continued, a booming sound that vibrated beneath my feet jarred the clinging mist of tranquility. Startled, I froze to see a massive cow thundering toward me. In a state of breathless shock, I was unable to move. Breaking through the dust-filled thunder somewhere close, I heard Steven's commanding voice,

"Quickly, raise your arms, Molly!"

I dropped my suitcase, and my arms shot up as if by magic. Steven ran before his 1200-pound producer, grabbed my case, and pressed it over his head. The wayward Holstein came to an abrupt standstill, creating a smothering blanket of dirt and gravel swirling toward me. Overcome by the haze and sudden gravel pelting, I turned away, coughing and covering my face.

"Oh, my sweet Molly Cleary. Are you okay?

"Yes, a little shaky, but okay."

"I'm so sorry, I must repair this old bridge gate. Essie enjoys a run for the exit now and then. Let's put her in the barn and dust you off. It's so good to see you; how was your trip?"

Still coughing and brushing the dirt from my face,

"It's good to see you, too, Steven. The train ride and a change of scenery are just what I needed, I think." Steven laughed.

"Well, let's get you inside for a cup of tea. Claire is anxious to see you."

I carefully stroked Essie and laughingly said to her,

"What a frightful storm you create, my girl. If I recall correctly, your name means 'star.' I need time to see if it's appropriate for you."

"Does it really mean star, Molly?"

"Yes, I think so."

"Hmmm, I think I've made the right choice in names. I'm beginning to believe that naming a cow and using her name as I speak to her will cause her to produce more milk. Someday, people will know this to be true!"

"Do you seriously think so, Steven?"

"I do!"

While guiding her to the pen, Steven enthusiastically patted Essie's massive Holstein face, saying,

"A true beauty you are, my Essie! Molly, milk production is up 30 percent, and I expect it to increase."

"I can't imagine, Steven. However, she's quite an impressive animal. So tell me, how is Claire feeling?"

"She's tired most of the time now, but I'm sure the sight of you will brighten her spirits."

Steven secured Essie in her pen, then abruptly stopped and lowered his head.

"Oh, Molly, forgive me for not immediately considering what you're going through."

"It's okay, Steven. It completely disappeared with Essie's greeting."

Steven hugged me compassionately, and then we left contented Essie and entered the cottage hand-in-hand through the kitchen's back door. Claire had the kettle on and was preparing finger sandwiches when I entered.

"Molly, my dearest cousin, it's so good to see you! Hugging me, Claire asked,

"How are you? How was your trip here? I can't believe you've agreed to help me, given what you've been through. Come, sit down. I'll pour a cup of tea, and Steven, dear, will you bring Molly's bag to her room?"

"Right, I'll take it up now!"

"Claire, I need to keep busy. What can I do to help?"

"Oh no, not now, Molly, please make yourself at home, catch your breath. I can see by your clothes you've met Essie!" Looking down at my dust-covered coat, I laughed.

"I confess I have."

"Here, give me your coat and sit right here."

I embarrassingly sighed as I sat down to Claire's thoughtful preparations, placed beautifully on their inviting country table.

"I want you to relax, Molly, for at least two days; there's plenty of time to help me."

"Well, maybe just today, Claire. Tomorrow morning, I will take care of whatever needs doing."

"Okay, Molly, if you're sure!"

"In the meantime, Claire, thank you for this lovely welcome."

"Molly, your kind offer of help is a priceless gift. I don't think I can manage this last month by myself."

"By yourself!"

Steven said as he thundered down the stairs in a shocked but joking tone, then sat down to tea. Claire smiled, closing her eyes in regret,

"I'm sorry, dear...not well said." Steven put his hand on hers,

"I know what you meant, and I'm happy you're here too, Molly. I don't want Claire alone in the house, particularly when I make deliveries. But is this too much for you?"

"No, I need the diversion, and I promise I'll let you know when or if it's too much."

We finished our tea and a pleasant visit, and then I retired to my room to rest before supper. Weariness enveloped me; unpacking would have to wait. I happily collapsed across the luxurious-looking bed. Like being suspended on a cloud, I sank into the most lavish, deep feather bed and instantly fell asleep. My next memory was a gentle knocking and Steven's calming voice at the door.

"Molly, supper is ready."

I didn't want to awake from this exquisite escape. Trying to open my eyes, I faintly said,

"Hmmm...thank you. I'll be right down, Steven."

The food smelled tantalizing as its fragrance slipped beneath the door, making me eager to get up and eat. Descending the stairs and enjoying the smells of home cooking, I asked Claire if I could help.

"Nothing, dearest Molly, come and sit by me and relax; Steven is taking care of everything."

He proudly placed two glorious bowls of beautifully presented food on the table, and Claire and I began to serve. Steven had prepared a beef stew with various vegetables from their garden, fresh-baked rolls, and a mound of butter from Essie. Then, with a flourishing gesture, he placed a small covered bowl with a beautiful hand-carved wooden spoon and proudly announced,

"This is our first batch of honey; I hope you enjoy our newest venture."

I couldn't help but feel admiration and awe at their accomplishments. The food was exceptional, and sitting at their table offered a welcoming comfort. Ever the storyteller, Steven regaled us with the tale of raising a particular calf—an achievement widely celebrated in Rose Haven for its charitable contributions to those in need. With a nostalgic gleam, he described how his father had taught him to butcher, package, and store the meat for their family —a tradition passed down through generations. His vivid descriptions left no detail spared as he named every part of the animal, recounted its various uses by past generations, and proudly shared how this legacy had shaped the community. Then, with unmistakable pride, he began to speak of his most recent animal conquest.

Although I admired Steven's passion and devotion to family traditions, a sense of discomfort began to grow. My history couldn't have been more different. Raised in the city, shaped by journalism, I'd witnessed the darkest corners of

humanity. Steven's story brought back a flood of remembrances. Daniel's accident surged to the surface. The memory was like a shadow I couldn't escape. The hit-and-run, the locket, the questions still unanswered—they pressed down, warping everything around me. Steven's cheerful stories began to feel like chains, each tightening around my chest. Then came the thought I couldn't unthink—that the meal before me might once have had a name. Nausea rose hard and fast. Claire must've noticed the color drain from my face because she gently interrupted, steering the conversation away.

"Steven," I asked, barely keeping my voice steady, "did you name the calf? Is that... what we're eating?"

A heavy silence settled over the table. Steven blinked, hesitated, then nodded. The room spun. A rush of heat—shame, revulsion, grief—swept through me. I stood abruptly, knocking my chair over, and fled outside. I barely reached the porch's edge before I lost my dinner. Moments later, Claire quietly appeared at my side, her hand resting gently on my shoulder. She handed me a glass of water, her voice soft as she apologized for Steven's candid storytelling. Embarrassed and still reeling, I muttered with a slight laugh,

"Growing up in the city, I never considered exploring the details of how food gets to the table. However, an opportunity to broaden my perspective is now before me."

"Molly, don't trouble yourself. Life on a farm has been our dream. An exciting, rewarding, and occasionally challenging way of life for us, but it's not for everyone."

Claire had a gift for easing tension. Her calm simplicity carried a quiet wisdom that felt ancient. We were the same age, yet she seemed to hold the insight of generations. Back at the table, Steven was overly apologetic, his concern genuine. He'd brewed a cup of mint tea using leaves from their garden, and within minutes, the warmth settled my stomach. Laughter slowly returned as we shared childhood memories, the evening softening into something almost sweet. Soon after, I said goodnight and retreated to my room to unpack. My computer,

a well-worn Miss Marple novel, and the locket were tucked between my clothes. I held the locket in my hand; Its cool weight reminded me of the mystery still waiting. I wasn't sure what to do with it yet... but I intended to find out who it belonged to.

From beneath the warm cloud of a feather comforter, my clear vantage-point spotlighted Claire's rare gift for making her home a sanctuary. My eyes took in every detail of this simple yet elegant room. Something extraordinary happens when kindness and love are foremost in preparing a humble room. It becomes a nurturing, safe space. Covered in well-crafted Knotty Pine, each thick wall surrounded me like strong arms. An inviting stone fireplace warmed the room, providing a relaxing ambiance and shadows that danced along each wall. Steven built a fragrant cedar closet and a well-designed en-suite with heated, ocher-colored stone floors. Claire crafted floor-to-ceiling drapes of lined tan velvet framing the view-clad windows. They generously pooled on the stone floors, enhancing the elegant country look she designed.

I wrote in my journal, "Love emanated through and around me, delighting my eyes with beauty as it began a shift in my heart, mending the loss of my lovely times with Daniel." With a prayer for restoration and enlightenment to begin within this safe space, I drifted into a most relaxing sleep. The following sunlit morning, I awoke laughingly to the sounds of a zoo. But the smells of glorious bacon, eggs, biscuits, and coffee pulled me out of bed and helped me quickly dress, run downstairs, and into the kitchen! Finding Claire hard at work, I said,

"Good morning, Claire."

"Good morning, Molly. How did you sleep?" Claire sang out.

"Not one dream; I don't think I even moved. The bed barely looks slept in. Where is Steven?"

"He's been up since 5 a.m., milking the cows and goats. I'm surprised they didn't wake you; they're quite noisy." Claire laughed.

"Claire, please sit down and let me finish."

"I absolutely will; thank you, Molly."

Claire put her feet up as I set the table, pulled food from the oven for a dozen people, called Steven, and then placed this hearty breakfast in the center, surrounded by brightly colored plates. Steven entered the back door, looking famished.

"Good morning, Molly. Did the animals and I wake you up?"

"I never heard a thing until a few marvelous minutes ago."

Steven kissed Claire and took hold of her hand as he sat down, uttering a simple prayer over the food; then, we began to eat. I'd never seen anyone eat as much food as Steven did that morning. Still in awe, I couldn't help but comment on the strawberry jam Claire made from their berry patch, the butter from their cows, and fresh golden honey collected that morning. Then, taking a breath between a mouthful of food, Steven said,

"Molly, wait until you taste the goat cheese. We're thinking of selling it along with the milk and butter. Claire's developed a few interesting flavors using herbs from our garden."

Spellbound, not only by their enthusiasm but also by their creativity, I entered into their world's attractive passion. They managed to make a profitable living while enjoying the process. But my excited thoughts were interrupted by a loud, sharp knock at the back door and the abrupt entrance of a tall, imposing man! I was terrified, but no one seemed surprised. Smiling and looking pleased, Claire said,

"Molly, this is David Donegal; he owns Donegal's Market in town and often joins us for breakfast before returning with supplies for his shop."

David said with a loud, commanding Irish/Scottish accent,

"Nice to meet you, Molly lass. Don't move; I'll get meh plate."

Grabbing a plate and flatware, he crudely pulled the chair out beside me, sat with a thud, piled a mound of food upon his plate, and, through non-stop conversation, finished two helpings of food. He had a shocking appetite; no morsel was left on the table. The need to escape this seemingly angry man threatened to overpower me. I jumped up and asked if anyone wanted coffee. Steven, Claire, and David all answered yes. After serving coffee to everyone, I considered placing the pot next to David, but I reconsidered in disgust. Half standing, David downed his coffee, banged his fist on the table, expressing his appreciation for a grand feed, and then exclaimed he must start packing his truck and return to the market.

"Goodbye, mo chara Claire, see ya next week! Claire smiled warmly and welcomed David as he bounded out the door. Steven kissed Claire, grabbed the empty plates, put them in the sink, and followed David to help fill his weekly order. An irritating, palpable cloud remained inside the cottage after David's abrupt exit. Dazed, I returned to the table to quietly enjoy coffee with Claire and asked,

"Mo chara? And why is he so angry?"

The words spewing from my mouth intensified the persisting rage I felt.

"He's infuriating!" I said in disbelief.

"Don't let his gruff mannerisms bother you, Molly; he has a good heart, though badly damaged."

"Truly? I can't imagine!"

"Mo chara is an Irish term of endearment, meaning my friend. Listen, I know I can trust you with information that only David, Steven, and I know, so please keep what I'm about to tell you to yourself."

Not wanting to hear about him, I reluctantly nodded in agreement. Claire, smiling, continued,

"David's discovered he has quite the lineage. His bloodline traces back to a powerful third-century group in England. Steven thinks there may be titled relatives—even a king—in his ancestry. But wars, betrayals, and endless feuds shattered the line of succession. The weight of all that history clings to him. He came here hoping for peace, but centuries of brutality and unanswered questions follow him like a shadow. When he first bought the local market, he hosted small gatherings—cards, drinks, and some laughs. By day, he ran the store. By night, he hit the Irish whiskey hard. Those card games often turned into arguments. Steven convinced him to try trail rides on our dapple-gray Appaloosa. Mama's an unusually intuitive horse—we hoped she might be able to help. And she did. After a few rides, David said he was finally feeling calm. He's cut back to just a few beers a night, but it's still a daily fight."

"Thanks, Claire. I never would've guessed. I felt his anger and matched it, but… knowing this helps. Doesn't make me like him, but it softens my reaction." I paused.

"One thing, though. He's got an Irish name, but his accent slips between Irish and Scottish. And now he might have British royalty in his blood?"

Claire nodded. "There are conspiracy theories he's been digging into. It's possible that even his name isn't real. He's hoping to find the truth—soon. But if it helped your anger, that's all that matters, Molly. Oh, by the way, I'm going to my book club tonight at 7. We'll meet in *The Harbor Bookstore & More*. Would you like to join me?"

"That sounds interesting. What are you discussing?"

"Tonight's topic is a good mystery plot."

"Ooh, I'm in!"

Returning to the kitchen sink, I saw David's truck leaving as Steven entered and sat beside Claire. Holding her hands in his, he said he'd be out making deliveries and would

be home for dinner. He hugged her, talked to their incubating baby, and then kissed Claire like a man who had just met the love of his life. An unexpected wave of crushing grief washed over me as I filled the dishwasher. I missed those heavenly romantic moments with Daniel, our daily conversations, and those incredible laughs. But as I reminisced, the locket seized center stage, jarring my heart, igniting a sense of purpose. Not wanting to spoil their moment, I kept my back to them, fighting back my tears and praying this pain would quickly leave. While Steven and Claire said their goodbyes, I said I needed to make a phone call, managed a cheery goodbye, and went upstairs. I called the precinct and was transferred to the person in charge of Daniel's case, Detective Jake Johnson. He reassured me that officers Ciara and Kyle were investigating leads, and he felt certain an arrest was imminent. But why wasn't I reassured? As I thanked him, I had a perplexing feeling that the puzzle was becoming more intricate; I wanted to tell him about the locket, but didn't feel comfortable disclosing more concerns. Descending the stairs, consumed by who I could trust, I was drawn to read more of Agatha Christie's Miss Jane Marple.

Sensing something was wrong, Claire asked if I'd like to go into town, meet a few locals, and stop for lunch. It sounded pleasant, and I agreed. I quickly finished cleaning the kitchen, and we left for the town in their baby-ready car. Claire pulled onto the main road, stopping just before their bridge entrance. With the windows open, the pine and lavender-scented air rushed into the car. Claire, enraptured, deeply inhaled the intoxicating fragrance and then exclaimed that this was her favorite spot. The scents and sounds of rushing water splashing over the mounds of stones had an immediate soothing effect on me as well. Claire smiled and suggested a boat cruise around the harbor, and hopefully, we'd catch a glimpse of the wildlife and a few hidden coves only known to the locals. It sounded like heaven to me. So we continued our short drive through the tree-lined, enchanted street until the

grand reveal at the harbor. Claire parked at a dock close to the impressive Catamaran Charter Vessel with people filing aboard.

"What do you think, Molly? Want to join the crowd?"

The atmosphere was uncomplicated and compelling.

"Yes, absolutely, let's go!"

We left, but Claire didn't lock the car. Concerned, I mentioned it, and she laughed, explaining that no one in Rose Haven needs to lock their vehicle. Astonished, I joined her laughter as we hurried aboard and found a bench on the top deck. A gentle breeze swept across my hands as the catamaran left the dock and headed toward open water. The haunting memories receded for a moment, replaced by the cries of seals and seagulls echoing through the air. We passed elegant homes tucked among towering trees, their vibrant gardens spilling toward private docks and canvas-covered boats. In hidden inlets, grand mansions rose behind sweeping lawns, yachts moored beside boathouses like scenes from a painting. With every turn, the beauty pulled me further from the weight I carried. Near the end of our tour, Claire pointed toward a quiet channel. The catamaran slowed as a white English Tudor mansion came into view—majestic, with leaded windows, tan shutters, and a three-tier fountain commanding the front lawn. Surrounding it, a riot of flowers in vivid bloom. But what made me gasp was the two tan Great Danes romping behind a white split-rail fence.

"Claire, everything is so coordinated—the dogs even match the shutters!"

She laughed. "I know. And there's more."

She gestured toward a sleek yacht and dinghy beneath towering pines, beside a dock house—a miniature version of the mansion. Then, in a quieter voice, she shared the story with me.

"The house was built in the early 1900s by Christine and Anthony Wise. They asked that it stay in the family—and so far, it has. Their four granddaughters—Linda, Jennipher,

Jill, and Monique—inherited it three years ago. Jill and her husband restored the yacht, which now hosts weddings half the year. They've already been booked out for two years. The dock house is now a high-end Airbnb, complete with small boats. The other sisters built successful businesses in town— our local legends."

As Claire spoke, the calmness unlocked something that had been hindering me. The soft rhythm of water beneath us, the sun dancing across the deck—it felt like stepping into a different life. The fear the locket carried loosened its grip, just slightly. In that quiet moment, I let myself believe that love, even unseen, could still protect and guide. Tears slid down my cheeks as if some confined part of me had been set free. I felt the wind, not just on my hands, but washing over me, clearing the fog. The numbness of grief lifted. I felt life emerging. I hugged Claire and thanked her for being a light in the darkness. When we disembarked, Claire suggested we leave the car and walk through town for lunch and shopping. I happily agreed. As we slowly strolled into town, I told Claire about my walk on the beach with Daniel, my unique evening in the garden, and the locket. It was the first time I'd spoken about them, and Claire listened without comment. With each worry laid bare and my burdens shared, we reached the library. Claire, aglow with enthusiasm, introduced me to her longtime friend and librarian, Margot.

"It's so nice to meet you, Molly. Are you living in Rose Haven?"

"No, I'm helping Claire for a few months, then it's back to the city."

"Why don't you join us for a poetry reading this Friday evening? Claire, are you and Steven coming?"

"Yes, I wouldn't miss it. Besides, this may be the last one until after the baby is born."

"What do you think, Molly?" Margot asked.

"Yes, I'd love to join the reading!"

"Great! I'll look forward to seeing you three on Friday."

"Oh, by the way, Margot, Molly, and I are going to *The Bookstore & More* tonight for mystery night. Are you going to be there?"

"Are you kidding? I wouldn't miss it!"

"Wonderful, see you tonight!"

"Bye, Margot. It was lovely meeting you, and I'll see you tonight."

"Bye, Molly, you're one of us already."

A comfortable blending into paradise began as Claire and I left and crossed the street to a cottage-looking café. We passed beneath an arched lattice opening covered in pink roses, which led to an outdoor dining area, and then through a half-opened white Dutch door. The intricate hand-carved sign above the door read Hanna's Café. A tall, young, and beautiful girl met us with a warm greeting.

"Hi, Claire! You're looking awesome, our mother-to-be!!" The girl hugged Claire, then extended her hand to me and said,

"Hello, I'm Hanna. Are you new to our town?" Surprised, I said,

"Yes. And is this your café?"

As Hanna walked us to a comfortable booth by the window, she said,

"Yes, and I hope you enjoy every moment here."

Between each delicious bite of food, I learned of the master woodworker who supplies the town with signs, furniture, cabinets, figurines, and a growing school for eager students. The people of Rose Haven had an infectious enthusiasm for town events, and I was beginning to feel its pull. After lunch, Claire and I strolled next door to Le Bon Boutique—partly to browse for something to wear for Mystery Night, and partly to meet her longtime friend, Monique. At the front desk, we were greeted not by perfume but by the rich aroma of freshly ground Arabica beans. Behind the counter,

Monique was animatedly demonstrating the art of perfect coffee, her hands dancing over a gleaming brass cappuccino machine that looked like it belonged in a Paris café. She finally turned, lit up with recognition, and hugged Claire warmly before turning to me with equal warmth. After introductions, she ushered Claire to a chic French country-style sofa and served her a dreamy cappuccino. Claire melted into the cushions like she'd found heaven. I wandered the boutique in quiet splendor. The space was small but opulent; every corner was filled with stunning French designs. I'd covered fashion shows in New York, written countless articles on couture… but being *inside* it like this—touching it, possibly *wearing* it— felt surreal. Elegance had always lived in a world just beyond my reach. Eventually, I returned to Claire's side, still buzzing with wonder.

"Molly, want a coffee?" she asked, eyes half-closed in bliss.

"No thanks. These designs have already energized me."

Claire laughed, then turned to Monique.

"Do you have a blouse that would work with her jeans for Mystery Night?"

Monique gave me a thoughtful once-over, then disappeared into the back. Moments later, she returned with a silk blouse in hand. She smiled, holding it up as if it were a secret that had been revealed.

"This," she said, "matches your green eyes."

I could hardly believe it.

"Monique, this is the blouse I saw in that Paris fashion magazine—the one I fell in love with! It's perfect. I don't even need to try it on. Thank you!"

The three of us laughed in delight. Claire beamed, thrilled for me, but her pregnancy had taken its toll. She needed rest before the evening's event.

"Stay and enjoy your cappuccino, Claire." I clutched the blouse. "I'll get the car."

She handed me the keys with a smile of gratitude. "Wonderful idea, Molly. Thank you."

I floated out the door, carried by the kind of happiness that feels borrowed from a dream. Back home, as twilight settled in, I lingered in my room, holding the silk blouse against me. The day had been charmed—until a familiar ache tugged at the edge of it. The locket. Daniel. And the fear that I may have loved a version of him that never really existed. I steadied myself, exhaled, and forced a smile into place. Then I headed downstairs, each step a quiet act of resolve.

"Hey, you two—I'm ready!" I called, more brightly than I felt.

"We are, too," Steven replied, as Claire lit up.

"Oh, Molly, that blouse is stunning! It makes your eyes sparkle."

"Thanks, Claire. Monique is magic. I hope she'll be there tonight."

Steven dropped us at the entrance of *The Harbor Bookstore & More*, its glass-paneled doors veiled in vintage lace. Shadows of guests moving behind them, voices blending in a happy hum. As Steven parked the car and rejoined us, we stepped through the doors and into the buzz of *Mystery Night*—rows upon rows of books from every genre, cozy sofas and armchairs atop worn Persian rugs, and side tables with glowing lamps. The air carried hints of bergamot and history—tea and parchment steeped together in quiet conspiracy. Toward the back, a hand-carved counter anchored the space, a Victorian-style silver samovar, polished to a mirror sheen beside the register. Above it, a railed mezzanine office overlooked the entire store, doubling as a stage. This was my sanctuary—thousands of books, each holding secrets and adventure. Claire led me toward the front, where Steven had saved three seats. She introduced me to the elegant and poised store owner, Jennipher Talia, who greeted me warmly before glancing at the clock.

"If you'll excuse me," she said, ascending the stairs to the mezzanine, "it's time to begin."

The lights dimmed, leaving the room aglow in a soft, amber blush. Instantly, the store transformed into a literary hideaway.

"Well, everyone," Jennipher announced, "tonight we're diving into Agatha Christie's 50th book. Any guesses which one?"

A beat of silence, then Margot called out, "*A Murder is Announced?*"

Jennipher smiled. "Spot on, Margot. Would you care to come up and share a synopsis?"

Margot joined her, standing in the warm light above us.

"It's one of my favorites," she began. "Set in the quiet village of Chipping Cleghorn, a murder is announced in the newspaper's small ads. Miss Blacklock's friends gather, expecting a parlor game—but what unfolds is anything but. The plot is cunning, the clues masterful. It's one of Miss Marple's finest hours, wrapped in the atmosphere of post-war Britain—dark, precise, unforgettable."

As the room leaned in, a chill ran down my spine. Something in what she *announced* struck a nerve—murder cloaked as a game… clues hidden in plain sight. The locket in my purse seemed to burn through its boundaries. Then, suddenly, as if on cue, the front doors flew open, and a strong gust of cold air rushed in, blowing over one of the small lamps. Everyone gasped as a six-foot, dark-haired man with his black trench coat blowing in the wind entered. With every eye on him, he silently closed the doors behind him. Eyes widened, with more gasps filling the room! I pulled my coat tightly around me in chilled fright, gripping the collar as though it might shield me. Claire stifled a laugh behind her hand, her eyes dancing with amusement. Leaning in, she whispered,

"He's Frank Pierce—a mystery writer and tonight's reader."

My grip on my coat loosened, but my gaze remained locked on him. With a mix of awe and disbelief, I breathed,

"What an entrance!"

His violet eyes immediately grabbed my attention while I tried hiding my fascination from everyone. As Frank began, I inched my way to the edge of my seat. Each word he spoke was riveting, and his captivating, deep voice drew me into the intricate world of Agatha with each passionately shared phrase. I'd never heard a more commanding, masterful storyteller. He brought Christie to life with unmatched brilliance, painting her world in vivid, unparalleled dimensions. Each terrible incident unfolded with gripping intensity, and the characters' confusion and fear were palpable. Through his masterful delivery, Frank wove together the complex clues Miss Marple meticulously left behind, captivating the audience with his narrative sleight of hand. I was utterly entranced, hopelessly swept into the journey. As he turned the last page, fear gave way to reassurance; with evil defeated, all is well again. Ninety minutes had passed, but it seemed like a moment. I couldn't believe it was over. Thunderous applause rose amongst the shouts of appreciation. Frank stood with a broad smile of gratitude, ready to meet his public. The story strangely ignited the path to solving my mystery. I desperately wanted to follow my convictions. Daniel's death would be resolved if I didn't give up. Finding the person responsible was possible, but my mind reeled with the previous suspicions I had harbored. I needed the courage to accept the truth, no matter how heartbreaking, and I believed I could learn from the process that Agatha penned as she created Miss Marple. Deep in thought, I felt a tap on my shoulder.

"Did you enjoy the reading, Molly? Claire said.

Within the thunderous applause, I haltingly said,

"More than you know, Claire, more than you know!"

Jennipher resumed her center-stage position, inviting everyone to help themselves to tea, refreshments, and copies of Frank's latest book on the counter. As the crowd dispersed,

I stepped forward, introduced myself to Frank, and thanked him for a reading so riveting it felt as though Christie herself had whispered the tale—then, heart pounding, I asked if he might spare a moment. He graciously responded, waiting for me to ask my question.

"Mr. James, do you believe that with diligent efforts, say like Miss Marple, a person could solve an actual case?"

"Well…please call me Frank. I'm not sure, Molly. I've read that these are more of a fairy tale for adults, especially for puzzle lovers. They may also help in dealing with fears or traumas."

Though my heart sank a bit, I held to my conviction.

"Yes, I've read that too. However, considering Agatha Christie was a research master, I find truth and hints of usable ideas in her brilliant writing. What do you think?"

He paused, then, looking bewildered, said,

"I'm embarrassed to say I've not given that angle a proper thought. But I will now."

"Thank you, Frank. I want to run a few thoughts by you in the future if that's okay."

"Yes, that would be fine. I'll ask Jennipher to give you my contact number. Oh, by the way, I live in Los Angeles. If you're ever in the area, we can get together for a chat."

Gazing into his gorgeous violet eyes, I couldn't find the simple words to say I live in Los Angeles, too.

"Okay, that would be great, Frank."

We shook hands, and I left a little breathless, eager to find Claire and Steven. After warm goodbyes, we made our way home beneath a sky already hinting at change. By morning, something within me had shifted. I swung my legs out of bed with purpose, threw open the window, and called a bright hello to Hamish, the rooster—my unexpected ally in this new chapter. I was gathering a circle of helpers now, fueled by a fierce resolve to seek justice for Daniel. Today, Claire could rest easy. I had a mission. Slipping past their bedroom with

quiet care, I flew down the stairs, ready to greet Steven—and the day.

"Well, good morning, Molly sunshine! How are you this fine day?"

"Steven, I'm finally able to say I'm good, thanks!"

"It sounds like Rose Haven is working its restorative powers on you."

"I think so. I am beginning to feel alive again."

"You've been through a lot, Molly, and I'm that pleased to see you smile again."

"So am I, Steven, so am I! What can I do to help?"

"Nothing here, but I'm ravenous. When will breakfast be ready?"

"I'll get right to it, cousin!" I laughed, remembering how he could clear a plate.

"Oh, by the way, Molly—David's joining us for breakfast. Ring any bells about how much he eats?"

My smile vanished.

"Yes, I remember that and more! The feast will be ready soon."

Dreading David's arrival, I busied myself in the kitchen. Steven had gathered a basket of eggs that morning, so I made a golden frittata, added warm biscuits, fresh berries from the garden, Essie's butter, and brewed a large pot of coffee with a pitcher of hot milk. As I set the table, the quiet hum of domestic peace clashed with the storm in my mind. Last night's reading wouldn't let go. Daniel. Justice. His face floated in my memory with a clarity that ached. Claire's voice called down the stairs, breaking the spell.

"Good morning, Molly!"

"Morning, Claire. Sleep well?"

"Like before I was pregnant!" she said, entering with a glow. "And whatever you're cooking—it smells divine."

She wrapped me in a hug.

"You even warmed the milk? I feel like a princess!"

We laughed, enveloped in priceless, cousinly joy, as we returned to childhood.

BANG

A loud, jarring knock rattled the back door like a thunderclap.

"Sounds like David," we said together. I rolled my eyes. Claire chuckled, then called out,

"Come in!"

The door flew open with an explosive crash as it slammed into the wall behind it. David burst in, voice echoing like a stage actor's,

"Good morning!" he bellowed while marching in and dropping into a chair like a king claiming his throne, eyes locked on me. My stomach tightened. I turned away, pretending to tidy the already clean counter, determined not to let him rattle me.

From outside came Steven's easy voice, a perfectly timed rescue.

"Molly, breakfast smells amazing! I'm on my way!"

"Okay!" I hollered back, more grateful than I could say.

Steven stepped inside moments later, kissed Claire's cheek, and calmly took his seat. His presence eased the edge in the room. I joined them, forcing myself to stay present. No drifting to Los Angeles. No Daniel. No Frank. No case files or conspiracies or grief. Just this moment—Claire, peaceful and glowing, leaning back in complete relaxation. I clung to that image like it might steady me. She enjoyed every mouthful of food, declared hearty compliments to the chef, and seemed utterly at ease with David. Steven was pleased to see his beloved Claire radiating with contentment and relieved of her chores. David, enjoying the meal, paused for a moment.

"Is somethin' wrong, Molly?"

"Why do you ask?" I snapped, sharper than intended.

"Ye've got that faraway look in yer eyes."

I hesitated, weighing the risk. Then, deciding honesty was worth his unpredictable reaction, I said,

"I haven't had an update on Daniel's case. But I've decided—I'm strong enough now. I'm going to pursue it further."

Claire and Steven exchanged glances, then Claire said gently,

"Molly, you know his case is a priority. He was a ranking officer."

Steven nodded. "They wouldn't let it fall through the cracks."

I heard them. I even believed them. But I wasn't convinced.

"I still need to ask more questions."

To my surprise, David didn't interrupt. He paused, and for a fleeting moment, I caught something I never expected—concern. Genuine, unguarded concern. Then, just as quickly, his bluster returned. A joke, a subject change, and breakfast rolled on without another word about my resolve. Afterward, Steven hugged me.

"Thanks for everything, Molly," he said, his voice quietly sincere. "We're so glad you're here."

David, unusually subdued, didn't meet my eyes but said,

"Delicious, that. Much appreciated."

I looked at him, uncertain, and reluctantly lying, replied quietly,

"My pleasure."

As the three of them stepped into the garden, I lingered at the table, a quiet sense of triumph secretly unfurling. From the open door came their laughter, twining with the low murmur of animals. Claire, serene on the carved bench, watched Steven in the stalls and David hefting crates into the truck. A flicker of warmth spread through me. Maybe…I was gaining the strength I'd need for the shadows waiting in the dangerous valley ahead.

3

What He Knew

Minutes after breakfast, I was at the dishwasher, hands busy but mind sharp. All those hours with Miss Marple had finally paid off. Agatha Christie hadn't just given me comfort—she'd given me a compass. A door had opened in my mind somewhere between her knitting needles and sharp intuition. Not just curiosity now—this was war. I wasn't playing detective. I *was* one. Fueled by Jane Marple's quiet brilliance, I vowed: I would outwit my husband's killer. But instinct alone wouldn't be enough. Claire had reminded me of that. Prayer had become more than ritual—it was armor. So, with one hand on the sink and the other steadying my breath, I prayed—not for peace this time, but for courage. The courage to follow every thread, no matter how twisted. I needed to think. David and Steven were saying their goodbyes. I wiped my hands, grabbed my bag, and approached the open door.

"David, mind if I catch a ride into town?"

To Claire, I added,

"I'll be back in an hour. Need anything?"

She shook her head with a smile. I didn't tell her I was chasing shadows.

"Oh, thanks, Molly. I've got everything I need—enjoy yourself!"

On the ride into town, David peppered me with questions about Daniel. I deflected each one, too tired to spar and unwilling to share what I didn't trust him with. When we arrived, I thanked him and declined his offer to drive me back. Though I was full from breakfast, I made a beeline for Hanna's Café. Hanna's was the perfect place to gather my thoughts: the low hum of conversation, the scent of cinnamon and coffee, the faint sounds of the harbor beyond the patio. I found a quiet table outside. Hanna spotted me at once.

"Just made a fresh pot, Molly. Want a cup?"

"I'd love one, thanks."

As she set the mug down, I hesitated.

"Do you have a minute?"

"Sure, it's slowing down. I could use a break, too."

She poured herself a cup and pulled up a chair. I told her everything—my doubts, my drive to keep digging, my fear that this wouldn't be easy. Hanna listened without flinching. Her support was immediate and steady.

"You're doing the right thing," she said, then added with a wink, "Want to use the office phone?"

"Seriously?"

"Seriously."

After a grateful hug, I cleared our mugs and headed to her office. Five minutes later, I returned with a grin and dropped onto the counter stool.

"Hanna, can I have another cup of that amazing coffee? I've booked an appointment next week!"

She clapped her hands. "Yay! Celebration time! Want cake with that coffee?"

I laughed. "Yes—and I'll walk off the calories back to Steven and Claire's. Hanna, you're a born psychiatrist."

Back at the house, Claire was still outside, feet up, bottle-feeding a lamb. She looked up as I approached.

"Molly, you're beaming!"

"Claire—I'm on to something."

I scooped up a bleating lamb of my own while updating my glowing cousin. She listened closely, eyes narrowing with concern.

"I'm worried, Molly. There's always more to these things than the public ever hears. It could be dangerous."

"I've thought about that," I said. "But I'm starting small. A few quiet, unassuming questions."

Claire paused, then said,

"This reminds me of David Donegal's past. Steven and I have always found it odd how little people know about him.

And, honestly, we've both wondered—how is it possible there still aren't any solid suspects in Daniel's case?"

"Yes, exactly! I've wondered about that too."

Claire usually needed a nap by noon, but not today—these twin mysteries had sparked something in her. After feeding the lambs, we huddled close, tossing theories back and forth like detectives at a war table. Her eyes gleamed with determination.

Suddenly, she called out, "Steven, I think we need internet service."

Steven looked up from the pasture.

"Right now?"

"Yes! Molly and I can use my last month of pregnancy to research... interesting information."

Steven blinked.

"Okay. I'll call when I'm done feeding."

"I'll do it!" Claire said, already halfway to the house.

We returned to the kitchen, our steps charged with purpose. What began as a gut feeling was evolving into something more profound—something bigger. Within two days, Wi-Fi at Moore Cottage had opened a digital rabbit hole of forgotten names, shadowy documents, and unanswered questions. Then Claire, clearly unsettled about my upcoming appointment in L.A., finally shared what she'd been holding back.

"I need to tell you something about David," she said, lowering her voice to a near whisper, as if the walls might be listening. My breath caught.

"It starts long before us—before America, even before modern England."

Her gaze went distant, her voice taking on the cadence of memory passed through generations.

"It began in the mid-1400s, during the reign of Edward IV. He had two sons: Edward, the heir to the throne, and Richard, Duke of York. When the king died in 1483, their uncle, Richard, Duke of Gloucester, was named Lord

Protector. But he wasn't the kind of uncle fairy tales are made of. He locked the boys in the Tower of London and declared them illegitimate. Days later, he took the crown for himself as Richard III."

I knew this story. Everyone did—the Princes in the Tower. But Claire wasn't telling it like a legend. She was recounting it like a warning.

"The boys were never seen publicly again, but whispers spread. Not just in England. Across Europe. Rumors said they were murdered—or escaped. Generations later, descendants of the original Tower staff passed down a different tale."

Claire leaned in closer, her voice a thread.

"Some believed the princes survived. And Molly…" She hesitated, searching my eyes,

"There's compelling evidence David Donegal is a direct descendant of that bloodline."

I was so taken aback, I couldn't speak right away.

"You're telling me that loud, rude man could be royalty?"

"Very likely, Molly."

I shook my head in disbelief.

"That's hard to accept. Sure, he has a commanding presence, but what about his manners? Far from princely—let alone royal."

Claire gave a knowing smile and let out a soft, measured laugh, watching me wrestle with the idea. I was transfixed, lost in thought. Before I knew it, I was standing at the refrigerator, mechanically pulling out ingredients for lunch, my hands working on autopilot. The days that followed blurred into a swirl of revelations and preparation. Life at Moore Cottage shifted to welcome its newest member, while I focused on my trip to Los Angeles. Claire and Steven moved between decorating the baby's room and their newest culinary experiment: homemade goat cheese.

When the day of my appointment finally arrived, so did a creeping sense of danger. Still, I clung to my purpose. The

locket was tucked securely in my purse—the mysterious piece I planned to show Detective Johnson. Whatever secrets it held, I was ready to confront them. Steven dropped me off at the train station, his steady presence offering a brief moment of reassurance.

"Good luck, Molly. I'll be here when you get back."

As the train pulled away from Rose Haven, its quaint charm and safety receding into the distance, a heavy quiet settled over me. My carefully planned questions dissolved into a fog of uncertainty. Grief, that familiar shadow, rose again like a tide, pressing against my resolve. Tears welled unexpectedly. I turned to the window, embarrassed, trying to hide the flood from strangers. But in the reflection, I didn't just see a widow—I saw a woman in motion. A woman choosing courage over fear. I thought of Miss Marple—her quiet strength, her unwavering sense of justice. And I remembered that evening at The Harbor Bookstore & More… Frank's reading of *A Murder Is Announced*, his voice carrying Agatha Christie's words with reverence. That night had planted the seed of conviction. I *had* to uncover the truth about Daniel's death. The tears slowed. My breathing steadied. I could do this. I replayed Daniel's accident again—how sudden it had all been, how little we knew about the driver. A phantom, still unnamed. Still unpunished. The mystery clung to me like mist as the train rolled into Union Station. I was one of the first to step off. Crossing the threshold of the station's back entrance, I realized how far I'd come. Just a month ago, I had fled to Rose Haven, shaken and broken. Now, I walked with a different rhythm—more grounded, more certain. Gratitude welled as I stepped out into the sunlight and hailed a cab to the police station. I was still grieving. Still afraid. But I wasn't running anymore.

Crossing the threshold of the police building, I muttered a silent prayer that this would not be a wasted effort. I found Detective Jake Johnson's office with little trouble. The room was bleak—windowless, cramped, and thick with the scent of stale coffee. An abandoned brewing pot sat in the

corner like a forgotten relic. His desk was a cluttered landscape of paperwork and empty plastic cups. Two battered chairs faced him, worn by time and use. I stepped in. A man hunched over the desk looked up.

"Detective Johnson?" I asked, voice steady. He stood and extended a hand.

"You must be Mrs. Cleary."

"Yes. Daniel's wife."

"Please—have a seat. Coffee?"

I glanced toward the dusty pot.

"No, thank you."

He snickered, pouring a cup for himself.

"Probably smart. This stuff could peel paint." He dropped into his chair and got to it.

"Officers Ciara and Kyle took Daniel's case as far as possible. They hit a wall. Sorry—bad phrase under the circumstances. Since it's an officer's death, the case landed on my desk. But I'll be honest—it looks like a straight hit-and-run."

He paused, watching for my reaction, then continued.

"A witness in a café saw a dark car speed past. Couldn't see the driver. No plates, no distinct markings. We pulled camera footage, but there's not much to go on. It was quick. Messy."

He reclined back, the chair groaning under the motion. "I wish I had better news."

I leaned forward, a calm, polite smile fixed in place—a perfect Miss Marple facade hiding the storm beneath.

"Detective Johnson, as you may know, Daniel was firmly against the chokehold. He often said he wouldn't use it on animals or people. He believed putting an arm, flashlight, or anything else across someone's throat until they couldn't breathe was unacceptable. And he didn't judge based on race, gender, or orientation. That stance earned him criticism. His fellow officers distanced themselves—but Daniel never wavered."

I let that settle before asking, unemotionally.

"So, Detective… did he pay the price for his beliefs?"

His expression shifted—first a hint of discomfort, then frustration, then something close to contempt.

"Are you implying," he said, voice tight, "that one of our own was behind the hit-and-run…some sort of conspiracy?"

Miss Marple's gentility slipped. My spine straightened, my voice sharpened.

"I'm not implying anything. I'm asking—could it be possible?"

Silence fell, thick and hostile. The room, already claustrophobic, seemed to shrink around us. He grabbed his cup, took a gulp of bitter coffee, coughed, then snapped,

"It's *improbable*. Everyone respected Daniel. I can't imagine anyone doing this."

Then, narrowing his eyes, he added, "Let me ask you something, Mrs. Cleary. Do you think grief has clouded your—what's the word?… *imaginative* thinking?"

For a beat, I couldn't breathe. But I summoned Miss Marple again—her poise, her steel—and let my silence speak louder than his outburst. When I finally answered, my voice was even.

"No. I think grief has clarified it. Why not consider my question, Detective? It's a fair assumption."

He rose slowly, placing both hands on the desk, his glare radiating heat. Silence thickened between us. I swallowed hard, willing myself not to flinch.

"Mrs. Cleary," he said, voice clipped and deliberate, "leaving the scene is a crime. We're committed to finding the perpetrator. But beyond that—frankly—it's a ridiculous assumption."

I stood, the chair squeaking beneath me, and extended a hand. He didn't take it. Instead, he stepped around the desk, gesturing stiffly to the door.

"Do you watch a lot of police dramas? Or maybe you're just an enthusiastic mystery reader?" His sneer was unmistakable. Anger surged, hot and immediate—but I caught it, barely. Miss Marple's voice flickered in my mind, 'let them underestimate you.' I turned, breath shallow, a bitter taste rising in my throat.

"Thank you for your time, Detective. I look forward to our next update."

Behind me, he sighed long and frustrated. I didn't look back until I was almost at the door. He was already pacing, muttering, retreating to the comfort of his desk—a small victory. The train ride back to Rose Haven provided a welcome respite. As the city blurred past, I reclined slightly, savoring the quiet. The memory of our exchange replayed in my mind—his unwillingness to see what was before him, and my growing certainty that he was missing or concealing something. What would Miss Marple do now? I already knew—she'd let him talk. Let him bluster. She'd find the truth, one subtle clue at a time. I had planned to show him the locket, but one look at his eyes told me it would be buried in paperwork like everything else. So, I kept it to myself. The train arrived, and Steven was waiting on the landing, chatting with a store owner.

"Welcome back, Molly! How did your meeting go?"

"It was a modest beginning."

"Well, a beginning is better than nothing. Come on, Claire's been glued to the computer all day."

"Really? That doesn't sound like Claire."

As we left the station, I told Steven about the meeting and shared my growing suspicions. He listened quietly, nodding, though concern lined his face.

"I'm still not sure this is wise," he said finally.

"You and Claire chasing this… whatever it is. It feels risky."

"I don't know either," I admitted. "But something's wrong, and the feeling won't leave me."

He looked over at me, his voice soft.

"Just… be careful, okay?" I didn't answer. I couldn't bring myself to say I was scared, too. When we reached the cottage, Steven pulled up to the back entrance.

"Tell Claire I've got a few deliveries. I'll be back before dinner."

"I will, and thanks for the ride, Steven."

"Anytime, Molly girl. See you tonight."

Inside, I found Claire exactly where I'd left her that morning.

"Claire, have you moved at all?" I teased.

She laughed.

"I made lunch! But the stuff I'm finding is too good to step away from. It reminds me of when I interned in Nottingham. I've always loved the business side of my animal science degree."

Curious, I leaned over her shoulder.

"What have you found?"

"I started a family tree from King Edward IV. Then I detoured into the disappearance of his sons. Molly—what if we could connect this to David?"

I stared at her, realization hitting hard.

"Claire… do you realize our whole course has changed?"

"Yes! Isn't it amazing?" Claire beamed. "The doctor said I need to take it easy this last month, so this research is perfect. I'll be back to farm duties soon enough."

A week passed in a blur—painting the nursery, unearthing more about David. But the unease inside me kept growing. I couldn't shake Detective Johnson's dismissive glare, the way his words cloaked contempt in politeness. I picked up the phone and called the precinct and was routed to Johnson.

"Mrs. Cleary," he answered, tone clipped and cold, like he was already bracing for battle. "Every officer's aware of the search. We've got two men under surveillance, but no conclusive evidence yet."

I bit back a retort, breathing in slowly before answering.

"Thank you, Detective." I hung up before he could patronize me further. That night, sleep never came. My mind spun with questions—unanswered, unwelcomed, unavoidable. At last, I crept downstairs, the house still and dark. I sat at the computer and pressed the power button. The screen blinked to life, flooding the room with a pale light. And then—there it was. The breath caught in my chest. Sixteen deaths are linked to the reintroduction of the chokehold. Sixteen. Public outcry had forced a restriction to life-or-death situations. But the department hadn't stopped there. They'd acquired a 14-ton armored breaching vehicle—designed to smash through walls, terrify families, and instill submission—a weapon of war, deployed in neighborhoods.

The California Appellate Court had ruled it unconstitutional. It was too late for the families it devastated. The screen glowed with brutal clarity, and the pieces began to fall into place. The violence wasn't random—it was sanctioned, systemic—an undercurrent running straight from the top. And Daniel…he'd stood against it. Spoke out and refused to comply. He met gang members not with force but with empathy. He believed in justice, not domination—and I was beginning to understand what that had cost him. He helped gang members find jobs, and some of them, the courage to return to school. A few even returned as mentors, proving that change was indeed possible. Slowly, cautiously, the streets began calming. Then came Operation Hammer. Under orders to "hit hard" and "level the apartments," officers stormed buildings without warning. Walls crumbled. Belongings shattered. Residents—mostly Black and Latino families—were dragged into the streets. Thirty-seven people were detained. Seven were arrested. The haul? Six ounces of marijuana. A dusting of cocaine.

The aftermath was worse. Detainees were beaten, then hauled to the station and mocked—forced to whistle the Andy

Griffith Show theme. Those who refused were hit again. No officers were charged. The city paid four million dollars in lawsuits. But no apology. No justice. Just silence. The words blurred. I froze. Horror crashed down like a wave. My God. This is what Daniel had fought. This was the madness he stood against—armed only with empathy, integrity, and a badge that too many others had weaponized. I couldn't breathe. My throat closed, my chest ached, and my hands trembled as I shut the laptop. How had he borne it? I barely reached my room before collapsing on the bed. The tears came in violent sobs, shaking the silence of Moore Cottage. I clutched a pillow, but it couldn't muffle the truth. Daniel had stood against monsters. And now, I would, too.

4

Where the Heart Goes

I woke with a jolt, Hamish's sharp crow piercing the fragile quiet outside my window. Morning air spilled in as I pushed the pane open—cold, crisp, and laced with dew and earth. For a breath, the stillness held me—a whisper of comfort, a veil before the storm. But the weight of last night refused to lift. As I dressed, the call with Detective Johnson echoed in my mind. His clipped tone. The disturbing details. The pieces didn't align—something felt off in the light of day. Edges sharper. Questions louder. I shoved the unease aside, for now. There were chores to do. That, at least, I could control. I grabbed a basket and headed out for eggs, the cold boards of the porch creaking beneath my feet. A hawk circled above the barn. Hamish strutted through the yard like a general. Life moved on, indifferent. But I wasn't the same.

"Good morning, Steven," I called. "Such lovely sounds to wake up to."

"Morning, cousin. Need help?"

"No, just after a dozen eggs. I'll gather them—the girls are getting used to me."

"Better make it eighteen. David's stopping by."

"Ah… right. Eighteen it is."

Inside the coop, I greeted the hens, their soft clucks— dependable, comforting. I let my mind settle in the comfort of routine—warm straw, rhythmic pecking, the scent of earth. After collecting the eggs, I moved to the garden, where I gathered onions, potatoes, spinach, and blackberries. The morning sun wrapped everything in gold. Hidden among the tall stalks and berry vines, I whispered a quiet prayer for wisdom. The leaves stirred, as if in reply. A fragrant breeze brushed against my skin like a tender hand. I closed my eyes and smiled. One breath at a time. One truth at a time. With a full basket on my arm, I turned toward the cottage. The smell

of bacon, brewing coffee, and warm biscuits pulled Steven to the back door.

"Molly, your cooking is a magnet. How much longer? I'm starving!"

"Ten minutes."

Claire came downstairs, voice bright.

"Mmm, what are you making? It smells divine."

"Irish frittata and biscuits," I said, then added, with carefully measured cheer, "David just arrived."

Claire glanced at the table and smirked.

"I see someone's expecting him—you've already set his place."

"Oh no," I laughed, lightly deflecting. "But sit between David and me, would you?"

"Gladly," she said, sliding chairs and plates with a mischievous grin. "Let's keep things… balanced."

She called the men in. Steven and David entered, David's voice booming with its usual bravado.
"Molly!" he bellowed. "That smell could near wake the dead."

I summoned my best Zen smile.

"Then it's working."

He dropped into his seat like he owned it. Steven and I brought the food over. Steven paused, eyes glancing at the new seating arrangement, a crease of curiosity forming between his brows.

"You and I will sit at the ends," Claire said smoothly, "Molly and David across from each other."

Steven nodded, then took his place, but suddenly lit up.

"I've got fresh honey!" He dashed outside and returned with a gleaming jar.

"This'll go perfectly with those biscuits, Molly!" he said, grinning.

Everyone agreed wholeheartedly. I watched them dive into breakfast, conversation replaced by hums of approval and clinks of silverware. Compliments flew between bites.

"This is the most delicious omelet I've ever had," Claire said. Steven nodded in agreement, and David let out a low, satisfied hum—oddly reminiscent of one of the sheep. As we sipped our coffee, Claire gave a casual smile and turned to him.

"David," she asked lightly, "have you ever looked into your ancestry?"

For a beat, he froze—just long enough for me to notice. He glanced at me, then shrugged.

"Not really. I doubt there's anything worth finding."

That wasn't true. He *had* looked. He'd mentioned it once, years ago, to Clair, in passing. Why lie now? The moment passed, the conversation shifting until Steven turned to me.

"Any updates on Daniel?"

David's brow tensed.

"I've uncovered some troubling things," I said. "I'm not sure where they lead yet. Too many gaps. Too much evasion. It feels... like something is pressing in, just out of reach."

David leaned forward, his tone different now.

"What exactly are you working on?"

I hesitated, then spoke the truth.

"I think Daniel's death wasn't random. The deeper I go, the more resistance I meet. The truth feels deliberately buried."

David grew quiet. Then, almost unexpectedly, he spoke, but strangely without his accent.

"When I was a boy in Ireland, we worked the barley fields," he said slowly. "After the winter yield, we were allowed to burn the muck. I loved that time. The air was damp, and the cleanup was easier. But one year, I stood too close. The fire's fumes choked me. I couldn't breathe. I was rushed to the hospital." He paused, glancing toward the window. "Later, when I started digging into my past, the information they'd kept from me came together like thick, poisonous fumes. Designed to smother. To silence."

His voice lingered in the air like a cloud of smoke. The room fell into stillness. Claire, Steven, and I sat quietly, the weight of his words settling over us. They struck a nerve with me—his story shaped the unease I couldn't name.

"That's it," I said quietly. "That fear—that instinct to run. But I know I have to stay. To face the fire."

David nodded once, solemn. Then, just as suddenly, he clapped his hands. The sound smashed through the stillness like thunder.

"Well! Let's get cracking!" he shouted, rising so fast his chair toppled. He caught it, righted it, and strode out, the door slamming behind him. The spell broke. We blinked, startled back to earth. Still flustered, I turned to my chores, quietly fuming. Claire went to her computer, while Steven touched my shoulder with a quiet smile and helped with the dishes before heading out to help David. *What a morning,* I thought, glancing back at Claire, who was doing a poor job of hiding her laughter.

"Alright, Claire." I sighed. Maybe you're right— David *does* have hidden depths. But must he crash through them like a marching band?"

Claire laughed.

"Perhaps there's a volume dial buried somewhere in his DNA. But that moment this morning? That was new. Maybe we're finally getting past the bluster."

A Place to Land

The month swept by in a whirlwind of half-finished thoughts and restless nights, ending with the joyful arrival of Claire and Steven's first child—a beautiful baby boy named Jacob. Caring for him over the first two days was both blissful and bittersweet. My heart swelled with love for this new life, even as an ache stirred for the child Daniel and I would never have. Guilt crept in, shame laced through every sharp glint of

envy I tried to suppress. Claire, ever perceptive, took my hand, her voice soft and steady.

"Molly... having a child is one of life's greatest wonders and trials. But raising one alone, after the kind of love you and Daniel shared..." She hesitated. "It may sound harsh, but maybe it's for the best. When I look at Jacob, I see Steven."

Her words hit with quiet force. I paused, absorbing the truth she'd spoken aloud.

"I think I understand," I said quietly. "Your words resonate—it's just so hard to accept something I never truly had."

Claire was strong enough to care for Jacob by the third day. I was exhausted but grateful. Those sleepless nights had shown me something I hadn't expected—how much patience, love, and surrender a newborn demanded. Claire's words had rooted themselves deeper with each hour I held Jacob. As the weeks passed, life at *Moore Cottage* shifted. Brimming with pride, Steven welcomed nearly everyone in Rose Haven to meet his son. Claire gradually returned to her routines, and I busied myself preparing for the stream of visitors. I set the family's heirloom cradle, Steven's as a baby, in a cozy corner of the living room, where Jacob slept as loved ones gathered. With more time on my hands, I returned to Daniel's case, spending quiet hours at the desk in my room, piecing together threads. Then, one afternoon, a realization settled over me like the changing light through the curtains—I was beginning to feel at home in Rose Haven. Even Hamish's morning crow had become a soft nudge, a part of the rhythm. Laughter echoed through the house, and I found myself smiling without thinking. Was I putting down roots? And if I were... could I ever return to the life I left behind in Los Angeles? The thought struck me with an uncomfortable pang of recognition.

Yet, amid this revelation, an instinctual warning whispered: *A murder had taken place.* The thought weighed on me with an urgency I couldn't shake. Detective Johnson's cold responses and evasive updates weren't helping; I felt as if I

were up against a wall, alone, with a truth buried just beyond my reach. I needed a plan. The next day, I confided in Claire. She listened closely, understanding the importance of my search without needing an explanation. Within the week, I'd packed my bags, walked the gardens, said goodbye to each animal, and lingered in the fields to capture one last glimpse of the rolling hills and vast skies of Rose Haven. Parting from them, from Claire and Steven, felt like a slow unraveling of my very being.

The train ride back to Los Angeles was filled with a dread I couldn't ignore. Questions churned in my mind, layered with a bone-deep anxiety I hadn't known before. I wasn't just anxious about what I might find—I was distressed returning to our empty home. The place that once felt like a sanctuary now loomed in my mind as an echo of a life severed too soon. I tried to calm myself, resting my head against the cool pillow as the steady rhythm of the train lulled me. As my eyes drifted shut, the anxiety persisted, threading itself through the strange comfort of sleep like an unanswered question haunting me just beneath the surface.

"Ma'am, ma'am," the porter said, gently nudging my shoulder. "This is our last stop."

"Oh, thank you for waking me."

Struggling to emerge from a fitful sleep, I reached for my suitcase and slowly made my way to the train's exit. I stepped onto the landing amid people passing me in a frantic whirlwind with their trailing suitcases on wheels flying behind them. The air was electric with the grating sounds of car horns honking from the far street. My entire life had slowed to the pace of Rose Haven. I'd have to move faster or get run over. When I reached the station's front entrance, I was somewhat back in the L.A. pace and grabbed a cab for home.

Driving along the familiar streets seemed subtly different. The beauty and history remained, but I'd never noticed the emptiness of this crowded city until that day. Then we stopped in front of our home. It was like dropping to the

bottom of a roller coaster ride. Breathless, rooted to the spot, I looked around and thought about how surreal life felt. The cabby was staring at me through his rearview mirror.

"Are you alright, lady?"

"Oh, yes."

I paid him, took a firm hold of my suitcase, and slowly exited the cab. Entering our home wasn't as frightening as I'd imagined. Maybe it was because the musty smell of a closed house greeted me. I dropped my bag in the entry and forced myself to forge through those numbing thoughts trying to overtake me. I opened the shutters and windows and then put on a pot of coffee. The fresh air and aroma of coffee felt somewhat comforting as I climbed the stairs and unpacked my bags. Though I hesitated to look, I glanced now and then toward the closet. Behind those closed doors were Daniel's clothes. A strong desire to be close to him overtook me. I slowly opened the doors and stared steadfastly at every thought-provoking piece, then ran my hands across them until the pain was unbearable. Wrapping myself in his favorite coat, I cried until I had no more tears. Holding the collar of his coat close around my face, I whispered an agonizing goodbye. I must, again, face this harsh reality and continue to create a new life or perish. I removed the lingering comfort from around me, placed his coat on the bed, and went downstairs. I returned minutes later with coffee and boxes, then packed all of Daniel's clothes. I would decide what to do with them later, but this was my necessary and painful beginning.

Heartbroken, I ordered dinner to be delivered, then attempted to recreate the comfort I'd experienced in Claire's home. It would take time, but I had a Rose Haven advantage. I learned from Claire and Steven, and reluctantly, to some extent from David, that tragedy never leaves you the same, but affords you a choice to be better or bitter. The rhyme made me laugh until I realized that the choice was like a sentinel standing before me, waiting for a significant choice I must make. Unsure and frightened, I breathlessly chose to honor Daniel by

contributing to life as he would, even if a cloud of loneliness persisted. Each decision helped me inch forward. The following day, I bought food for the house, prepared to return to work, and aimed to discover the truth about the night Daniel died. It was my original purpose, and it helped me get out of bed, get dressed, and go to work.

Within a week, a friend told me that the police commissioner was arranging a party for his staff and officers. Sensing an opportunity, I approached my department head, Jason, hoping to snag an assignment covering the evening's fashion scene at the gala. He gave a dismissive chuckle and shook his head.

"Don't bother," he said, smirking. "Not much of a story for you there."

As I walked out of the office that night, frustration burned within me. Then, late Friday evening—the night before the gala—my phone rang. It was Shehanne. She sounded hesitant, almost apologetic. Her husband, a police officer, was down with the flu.

"Molly, I was wondering if you…Would you like to come to the gala with me?" she asked.

I just stared at the phone for a moment, my heart pounding as the pieces suddenly fell into place.

"Molly, I know it's last-minute, and believe me, I don't mind going alone. It's being held at the Dolby Theater! "Can you believe it? But would it be something you'd enjoy—or make you uncomfortable?"

I was stunned—not just by the invitation, but by the venue. The *Dolby Theater*? A police gala held in the same venue as the Oscars? This wasn't just a party—it was an opportunity. I jumped at it.

"Shey, I'd love to go. Listen, why don't I drive?"

"Are you sure, Molly?"

"Absolutely. I'll fill you in when I see you."

"Great! I'm thrilled. And not having to drive? Even better."

"What time should I pick you up?"

"Cocktails start at six."

"Perfect. I'll be in front of your house by five-thirty."

It felt strange attending a police function without Daniel, but I needed to go. The moment we arrived at the Dolby in Hollywood, the tone was set—valet service, red-carpet lighting—firsts all around. Cocktails were held on the lavish pool deck. It was the perfect place to blend in, observe, and slip into my Miss Marple mindset. My hand instinctively reached for a gold-rimmed champagne flute on a glistening silver tray—but I stopped short, choosing sparkling water with lime instead. I needed a clear mind.

Jason had been wrong—there *was* a story here. I mingled, listened, and made mental notes. Shey and I moved into the grand ballroom, where a panoramic view of Los Angeles glowed behind crystal-glass walls. A famed chef catered dinner. I couldn't help but wonder: how could the department afford such luxury? I turned toward the glittering skyline to conceal my rising unease.

Our table seated ten, directly across from Chief Bates and his wife, Sharon. Draped in an elegant couture gown, she radiated quiet poise. The Chief, however, seemed strangely subdued—eyes fixed on his plate, a calm too calculated. I waited for the coffee course, biding my time. The food was extraordinary, every course more indulgent than the last. When the chocolate soufflé arrived, I caught a fleeting glance between the Chief and his wife—a subtle smile, shared satisfaction. It unsettled me. I seized the moment. Slipping into an empty chair beside them, I offered polite conversation before leaning in, letting a gentle Marple smile mask my edge.

"Chief, forgive me for bringing this up at such a lovely evening," I said, voice devoted, "but I understand there's still an open investigation into Daniel's hit-and-run?"

A long silence followed. The Chief slowly set down his spoon, snapped for the waiter, and only then looked up.

"Molly," he said, smooth but dismissive, "we're doing everything possible."

He returned to his soufflé as though the conversation were closed. Sharon placed a delicate hand on my arm.

"How are you, dear?"

I returned her concern with a polite smile.

"Surprisingly well, thank you. The support from our wonderful department has made it easier."

I turned back to the Chief. "Would you mind if I stopped by the station now and then for updates? It would ease my mind."

"Of course not, Molly," he replied, all civility. "We all need something to do. And if it helps, by all means, you have my blessing. But I thought you were back at the paper?"

"I am. Just a simple fashion reporter."

He studied me, a hint of superiority curling in his smile. I held his gaze, smiling back. I'd seen that look before—underestimation always came before surprise. I returned to my table with a quiet thrill. I'd cracked the door open. Miss Marple would approve. Then something unexpected caught my eye. The flower centerpieces—simple, elegant—stirred something in me. A fleeting glance of memory, elusive but persistent. What was it? A detail I'd seen before? A connection not yet made? But the hour was late. Shey and I said our goodbyes, offering warm thanks for the elegant evening. I was grateful for the opportunity and for Shehanne. Back home, I scribbled every detail into my notebook—suspicions, clues, fragments of conversation. Something about that evening pulsed with a sense of purpose. The Dolby had given me more than an evening out. It had given me a lead.

Tailored Instincts

The morning after the gala, my mind still reeled from the conversation with Chief Bates. His dismissiveness hadn't silenced my questions—it had sharpened them. Sharon's carefully measured compassion. The centerpiece that roused a memory just out of reach. Something was amiss, and I intended to determine what was wrong. But before I could chase that thread, Monday at the newspaper descended like a whirlwind.

Jason, our editor-in-chief, was off in the Santa Monica Mountains interviewing a former U.S. president while both were on horseback—ah, the perks of an editor-in-chief. Meanwhile, the newsroom was buzzing. The iconic Italian fashion designer, Giovanni Lagana, was scheduled to arrive at the Beverly Wilshire Hotel that afternoon. I had the honor of interviewing him the next day. Between fielding calls and dodging panicked assistants, I managed to reach Jason.

"It might be smart to wear a Lagana piece for the interview," I said casually.

To my surprise, he didn't argue. "Go shopping, Molly! But remember—*understated elegance!*"

"Don't worry, Jason. It'll be perfect," I assured him, already grabbing my purse. He was still shouting after me as I ducked out the door.

"I want to *see* it when you're back!"

A boutique display stopped me cold just a few blocks from the office. A black jacket trimmed with Mulberry silk—it was timeless, tailored, and unmistakably Lagana. Understated elegance, embodied. The price was steep, but missing this opportunity would have been costlier still. Back in the newsroom, Jason looked ready to faint when he heard the price.

"Molly! Why didn't you check the discount racks?"

"By the time I searched through the garment district, any savings would've been lost in billable hours," I reasoned.

His face turned crimson. "You have an infuriatingly logical mind! And excellent instincts. Just get the article done."

"It's already on your desk."

He exhaled, exasperated. "Fine. Enjoy your jacket."

As I left his office, I felt a rise of confidence return. This Miss Marple mindset was starting to serve me well. The interview with Lagana is scheduled for tomorrow. But tonight, I had a different kind of wardrobe to review—files, memories, and questions that refused to fade. The real story was still out there.

Conviction

The afternoon of my much-anticipated interview with Mr. Lagana finally arrived, and for once, the morning lacked the usual office frenzy, granting me a rare moment of calm— or perhaps a deceptive lull before the storm. Dressed in understated elegance, I prepared to meet the beloved yet enigmatic designer. Despite his acclaim, rumors of mafia connections clung to him like smoke, leaving a quiet sense of unease.

Turning onto the elegant expanse of Rodeo Drive, I was greeted by a visual feast: towering palms, pristine white roses, exotic cars like ornaments parked outside opulent boutiques. But the beauty felt like a veneer, concealing something more. Then I saw it—the new Lagana flagship store, gleaming with chrome and glass. Sunlight bounced off its surface, blinding me for a moment. The grand opening was timed to coincide with Oscar week—a perfect publicity ploy or a carefully orchestrated distraction?

The Beverly Wilshire loomed ahead, timeless and grand. Valet relieved me of the usual L.A. parking headache. Climbing the steps, I couldn't help but think of the secrets these walls must hold: glamour and ghosts. Inside, the lobby was breathtaking, featuring Art Deco sconces, Carrara marble, and chandeliers that cast a celestial glow. But beneath the dazzle, a ripple of nerves stirred in my chest. I entered the

Boulevard Lounge and was guided to a window booth with a view of Rodeo. And there he was.

"Ms. Cleary?"

"Yes, I'm Molly Cleary. Wonderful to meet you."

Giovanni Lagana was striking, magnetic.

"I love what you're wearing," he said with a smile. One of my favorite jackets."

"A classic Lagana." I couldn't resist.

He laughed, gesturing to the seat. "Please, call me Giovanni."

I struggled to stay present—the luxury, the man, the setting—but my mind was cluttered with darker thoughts: Daniel, the investigation, the lingering weight of everything. Giovanni's charm was effortless. Over champagne and lunch, he asked about my background. It felt like he was conducting an interview with me. I managed to steer things back.

"I researched your background—Malta, your early days in fashion. Quite the journey."

His smile held a hint of something unreadable.

"Sound research, Ms. Cleary. I'm here to announce my winter collection. I want your paper to unveil it.'

"I'd be honored. Shall we continue the interview at your store?'

"No. On the red carpet. Oscar night."

I blinked. "That's... incredible. Slightly terrifying. But appealing?"

He smiled. "Good, I hoped you'd approve."

He reached across the table, his hand warm over mine.

"Let me dress you for the event. A gift."

My pulse quickened. "Giovanni, I'm overwhelmed. Thank you."

Beneath the excitement, a whisper of caution curled inside me. His charm was potent, but charm could be a mask. And I'd learned—masks hide more than just a smile.

The next morning, I arrived for the fitting. The storefront sparkled under the California sun. Giovanni's tailor greeted me.

"Mrs. Cleary?" I nodded. "I'm Anya. I'll be assisting you?"

Then, she escorted me to a dressing room bearing my name. Inside: a chandelier, a three-way mirror, and the most breathtaking emerald gown I'd ever seen. Anya guided me into the dress, smoothing every fold. It fit perfectly—no alterations needed.

"The color is stunning with your hair," she said, then added shoes, jewelry, and a delicate purse. I stared into the mirror, barely recognizing myself—when a knock broke my reverie.

"Come in," I said softly.

Giovanni entered, eyes lit with satisfaction.

"Perfect. Do you like it, Molly?"

"It's the most beautiful gown I've ever seen."

"Good. Meet me upstairs for your itinerary."

Anya quickly dismantled my Cinderella illusion and directed me to Giovanni's office. He handed me a two-page guide that contained arrival times, backstage access, interview details, and gown care instructions. It was flawless, and so was he—efficient, magnetic, and unnerving.

"I'll see you Oscar night," he said, juggling phone calls.

I floated out of the shop, my mind racing—every detail, every moment, perfectly orchestrated—too perfect. Like someone had planned every step I'd take, I felt like I was already in a story not my own. At the Times, Jason surprised me with a card for spa treatments the next morning—a peace offering, which I accepted readily.

On Oscar day, I stepped out of the salon feeling like a star—hair glossy, makeup flawless, nails gleaming. Jason had tried to rent a limo, but struck out. So, a yellow cab rolled up instead, its engine sputtering like it knew it wasn't part of the fantasy. Dressed in comfy jeans and sandals, I wrestled my

oversized bag—packed to the brim with interview essentials—into the back seat, doing my best not to break a nail.

"Where to, ma'am?"

"The Oscars. Back entrance."

He blinked. "You serious?"

"Very. And if you can, pick me up at midnight."

He laughed. "Okay, I'll be back. If your prince should arrive and take you home, call us. Don't leave me hangin', Cindy."

Backstage was organized chaos. Stars were everywhere, including lights, cables, and designers fluttering like butterflies. I changed into the gown with Anya's help, and every detail was handled with reverence. Giovanni guided me with a conductor's grace when I stepped into the backstage corridor. I slipped into the interviews, took notes, and absorbed every moment. At midnight, Anya led me back to the dressing room.

"Time to return the magic," she said with a tired smile.

The gown came off, and the spell broke. I was back in jeans, flats, and reality. I checked outside before entering the alley, and there he was, my night-in-shining-armor cab driver. With the red studio light above the door, his yellow cab looked like pumpkin orange. He popped his head out the window and said,

"Hey, Cindy! So, did ya enjoy the Oscars?"

What a fun character. I stepped dreamily into my orange coach, and we talked and laughed the entire ride home. The following morning came too fast. I slipped into work clothes that suddenly felt uninspired, still half-haunted by the emerald gown folded carefully back in its garment bag. The glamour of the night before already felt distant, like something I'd dreamed. But the flashbulbs, the velvet ropes, Giovanni's intensity… they lingered. At the Times, the usual hum of keyboards and coffee machines filled the air—business as usual. Thankfully, my desk was still clear. I pulled out stationery and wrote a note of thanks to Giovanni for the invaluable opportunity to work with, be dressed by, and learn

from him. I tucked it into an envelope, a symbolic closing of the night before. Mission completed. Then, just as I sat back in my chair, our newest intern, whom we secretly called Atilla the Hun, charged at me with a clipboard and no mercy in his voice.

"Jason wants to see you. Immediately. Chop, chop!"

No, I thought, ironically laughing as I went to Jason's office, *that intern is not Atilla the Hun. He's Lady Tremaine in drag, Cinderella's mean, wicked stepmother.* Without a word about my Lagana assignment, Jason told me to cover the wardrobe used on a critically acclaimed TV series at Twentieth Century Fox. I stood by his desk in silence. All passion for my work was gone. Could this be a nudge to make a change?

"Jason, I need time off."

He sighed. "Again? Molly, if you walk now, I can't guarantee your job will be here when you return."

"I know. But I have to do this."

"Is this about Daniel?"

"It's about me. About who I've become."

He frowned. "Go to therapy. Don't throw away a career for a ghost."

"I'm not throwing it away. I'm following something real."

Jason gave a bitter laugh. "Bliss? That's what this is?"

"Conviction," I said, quietly.

He threw up his hands. "Fine. But don't come back asking for a desk."

I packed my things slowly. Colleagues came to say goodbye. We hugged and shared soft words. I slid Daniel's photo into the box last. As I left the newsroom, a calming peace settled over me. I had no idea what lay ahead of me. But finally, I wasn't just grieving. I was done waiting. Whatever lay ahead—answers, danger, the truth—I would face it. And I wasn't afraid anymore.

5

What He Left Behind
The Peaceful Battle

War and Peace by Tolstoy drifted into my thoughts on the drive home, its weighty themes unexpectedly filling my mind. I couldn't help but laugh at the absurdity—why, of all things, that? And then it struck me—the reason *War and Peace* had taken root in my mind. I was in the midst of a battle. I had followed peace, but surrounding this unseen path, a war was raging—a war over the decision to uncover a relenting darkness. I knew peace was the sure path to follow, so I had to think past the fear and dare to stay the course.

Finding the truth about Daniel was solidified as my priority—I had to trust the process. I looked at the battered box I'd packed in a frenzy and carried it to Daniel's desk, his sacred space. Setting it down, I felt a weight settle in my chest. This—whatever *this* became—was now my job. My calling. I didn't fully understand it, but I knew one thing: doing what I believed was right had to count for something. Good would come. It had to.

The battle inside me didn't ease. For days, I drifted in and out of sleep, haunted by dreams—visions of stepping out onto water, only to plunge beneath its surface and sink. I'd wake gasping, each time more worn than before. Desperate, I prayed. Then finally, clarity came—soft, steady, unmistakable. And in response came the quiet courage I hadn't known I'd lost. I had to move. I had to *act*.

At Daniel's farewell party, I remembered Detective Johnson grumbling about the precinct's abysmal coffee. Today, I knew he'd be at his desk until two. So I stopped at the corner coffee shop, asked for their best roast, and walked out with a to-go cup that smelled like hope. I drove to the precinct. I trusted the coffee might smooth the path because I wasn't

exactly his favorite person, and his reluctance to share anything with me was well established. Stepping into the precinct, I paused just inside the doorway, trying to shake off the rising anxiety. I could already feel the weight of Johnson's inevitable glare. At the reception desk, I gathered myself. Then I looked up—and paused in surprise.

"Molly Cleary," the officer said with a grin. "What can I do for you today?"

It was an old friend I hadn't seen in years, but whose friendly face instantly put me at ease.

"I'm here to see Detective Johnson," I said.

He gave a low, sinister-sounding chuckle and leaned forward.

"Oh, you're a brave soul, Molly Cleary. He's at his desk. Did you bring him coffee?"

I held up the cup, smiling in response. With a mischievous glint in his eye, he nodded toward the back.

"Go on back. I'm sure he'll be thrilled to see... the coffee."

I clutched the cup more tightly and walked down the familiar hallway. Johnson's door was open. I paused just outside, inhaled, and channeled my inner Miss Marple. A gentle knock on the doorframe. He looked up. And there it was— that *Oh no, not you,* expression. Still, I smiled and stepped inside, polite and composed.

"Hi, Detective Johnson. I know you're busy, and I won't keep you."

Without waiting for an invitation, I crossed to his desk and placed the coffee squarely in front of him. He eyed it. Then eyed me.

"This is a bribe, Mrs. Cleary!"

"No," I said, matching his gaze. "It's recognition—for your valuable time... and your coffee complaints at the staff party."

His brow knitted into a hard line. "Hmm. Still smells like a bribe."

"I'm just concerned about your progress," I replied calmly. "And I hope you'll accept this as an apology for our last conversation."

Looking mildly disgusted, he reached for the coffee and took a tentative sip. There was a long, uncomfortable silence as he swallowed, then set the cup down without a hint of emotion.

Not bad," he said flatly. "Which brew is it?"

I told him, adding, "I can bring the beans tomorrow if you'd like."

His scowl softened into something closer to mild irritation. He took a deep breath.

"Beans... I may need a grinder. Yes, alright—beans will be good."

"I'll have the shop grind them for you," I offered quickly. "You'll be all set."

He didn't respond immediately, but I caught it—the faintest twitch of a smile tugging at the corner of his mouth. Wary. Very wary. Finally, with a dramatic sigh, he gestured to the chair across from him.

"Sit down. Against my better judgment, I'll bring you up to date."

What he offered was sparse. Measured. A senior investigator's version of crumbs. Every word was carefully selected. As he spoke, my gut twisted—I still felt something was off. Either he was deliberately concealing key details... or worse, he wasn't actively working the case. But I didn't push. When he finished, I thanked him and asked if he'd be in tomorrow morning. He exhaled with theatrical fatigue, rose slowly from his desk, and ushered me to the door with practiced politeness.

"I will," he said, gently but firmly.

I smiled as I stepped out.

"I'll bring the coffee beans at nine."

On the drive home, I stopped again at the coffee shop and placed an order: beans, ground; three syrups; and a tray of freshly baked pastries. The barista told me the muffins and tarts would be hot from the oven if I arrived by 8:45. Perfect. I'd walk into that musty office trailing the fragrance of cinnamon, espresso, and warm butter. And to complete the performance, I'd bring napkins and paper plates from home. He'd be dazzled.

The next morning, I left early for the café. The air still clung to dawn's chill. After adding an extra bag of freshly ground coffee beans to my order, I drove to the precinct. I parked in the officer's lot, where memories clung to every parking stripe. But as I stepped out, the past was quickly swept aside by the arrival of the morning shift. Familiar voices, warm greetings, and heartfelt hugs surrounded me like a wave. Coming back felt like opening a door I hadn't dared touch. When I pulled the pastries from the car, their eyes lit up even more. We walked in together, and Ciara slipped an arm around my shoulders.

"So, Molly," she teased, "who are these pastries for? They smell outrageously delicious."

A spark of an idea came to me.

"Ciara, how about I brew everyone the best cup of coffee to go with them? I brought an extra bag of coffee."

Inside the precinct's break room—the haven of the weary—I tossed the stale coffee, scrubbed the pot, and brewed the fresh roast. The smell enveloped the room like a warm scarf. Heads turned. Conversations paused.

"Hey, Molly, what are you making over there?" one officer called out.

"Just a little thank you," I said lightly, pouring the first cup.

"Coffee? No, that's paradise," another joked.

"Even the walls are looking better with that delicious scent. Mind if we grab a cup to go?" A young officer asked.

"Please do," I said, handing him a clean mug. "Pastry, too—don't make me take these home."

Laughter echoed through the room. It felt like I had brought something back for a fleeting second—something Daniel would've loved. I maneuvered through the room, offering refills and catching up in snippets. My role here was no longer official, but the familiar rhythm filled a hollow space I hadn't acknowledged. Then Johnson appeared in the doorway, coffee already in hand. He surveyed the scene with that familiar mix of irritation and reluctant approval.

"I see we've got a hospitality consultant on staff now," he muttered.

"Just doing my part for morale," I said.

"You might regret that," he replied. "Word gets out, they'll expect this every Friday."

Ciara stepped beside me. "We'll take our chances. It's been too long since this place housed quality coffee."

Johnson made a face but didn't argue. He turned and walked away. I followed, not pressing, just walking beside him. Inside his office, he sat, sipped his coffee, and opened a folder.

"We found something odd on one of the phone logs," he said, like we were already in the middle of a conversation. I waited—he continued.

"Encrypted outgoing call, right before Daniel's accident. The timestamps are off. We're verifying the tower pings, but... doesn't make sense."

My breath caught. "From Daniel's phone?"

"No." He hesitated. "I didn't say that."

"But you meant to." I kept my voice calm. "You're cross-referencing Daniel's case against that log, right?"

He didn't answer right away. Then, with a sigh, he looked at me.

"You're not stupid, Cleary. But don't start jumping to conclusions. We're in the middle of this. Things shift. I'm just trying to understand what he was up against."

He gave nothing more. Just a blink. A wave of dismissal. When I reached home, I made a cup of tea and sat quietly, letting the morning replay in my mind. Johnson's words echoed—too filtered, too careful. I moved to Daniel's desk and spread out my notes. Piece by piece, the wilderness puzzle was forming a trail. And it smelled of political smoke. An encrypted call. A manipulated timestamp. A connection they weren't ready to admit. Or, something more profound that they didn't want me to see. And I wasn't prepared to let it go. The comfort of home was a welcome relief. I kicked off my shoes, sank into the couch, and let out a long breath. Wrapping my favorite blanket around me, I tried to untangle the knots in my mind when the phone rang.

"Hello?"

"Molly, it's Jason. Listen, I need to talk to you. Can you come to the office?"

I closed my eyes. "No, I'm exhausted. But I can talk now."

There was a long pause. I rose and slowly walked to the kitchen, tightening the blanket around my shoulders and putting on the kettle.

"Jason? You still there?"

"Yeah… yeah, I'm here. Molly, your last assignment with Lagana? Huge. You've got thousands of emails. And your replacement, which we brought in, is lost. No one can fill your shoes. I know you're not coming back full-time, but... would you consider working from home a couple of days a week?"

I exhaled, loosened my grip on the blanket, and poured the boiling water into my cup. The warmth of the mug seeped into my cold hands.

"Molly?"

"I heard you," I said softly. "Can I call you back?"

"When?"

"Let me sleep on it. I'll call you tomorrow—late morning."

"Alright. But seriously, think about it. Just the exclusives. No one covers fashion like you."

"I'll call you tomorrow, Jason."

After ending the call, I stood in the kitchen, letting the steam and the fragrance of tea rise around my face. Then I wandered into our cozy office and glanced at the desk. Could I do it? Could I work from home, still keep one foot in that world while the other chased the truth about Daniel? Perhaps this was part of the process—a new kind of balance. I'd decide in the morning.

By mid-morning the next day, I called Jason back and asked for a raise. To my surprise, he didn't even hesitate.

"Done," he said. "I'll set everything up."

Though my heart raced, peace remained. I calmly accepted. I'd now earn more working two days a week than I did full-time. A steady, persistent pressure lifted. Jason asked me to stop by the office to sign paperwork, sync up the fashion system with my home setup, and arrange for direct deposits. He had everything ready when I arrived—plus an assignment for a high-profile studio event the next morning. All the formalities were handled quickly, and as I prepared to leave, I felt something I hadn't in weeks: light. On my way out, I glanced back at my old desk. A woman sat there now, hunched, eyes downcast. She looked miserable. My heart stirred. I couldn't leave without saying something. I walked over and smiled.

"Hi. I'm Molly. I used to sit here. Just wanted to say welcome."

She looked up, surprised.

"Thank you," she said. "That's the first kind word I've heard since I started."

Before I could ask her name, Jason's voice rang out from his office.

"Marcy!"

She stood slowly, spine stiffening, and marched toward him like a storm on legs—fire in her eyes. She slammed the

door behind her with the force of a woman who'd had enough. I lingered, watching Jason through the glass. He sat there, speechless. I smiled to myself. *Something tells me Marcy won't put up with Jason's nonsense. How refreshing.* Celebrating my good fortune, I stepped out of the office and into the sunlight, leaving the gloom and confinement behind. I drove straight to my favorite garden shop and purchased every plant Claire had suggested: rosemary, lavender, gardenia, and a gloriously fragrant Austin English rose bush. With time finally on my side that afternoon, I immersed myself in the garden. Birds chirped from nearby trees, a curious hummingbird hovered near the lavender, and butterflies drifted lazily between blossoms. It was glorious. I planted thoughtfully, arranging each herb and bloom to catch the light and breeze, especially from the view of my home office window. When spring arrives, the open window will usher in a symphony of fragrances—each one carrying a breath of Rose Haven, softening the city's sharp edges outside. It felt like a job well done—a quiet triumph.

Uncostumed Truth

Daily life improved, and this sunny, fragrant morning marked my first high-profile assignment in my new role. I had that old familiar flutter—nervous energy bubbling like champagne—as I drove through the studio gates. This was no ordinary assignment. The production was an eighteenth-century epic with a multi-hundred-million-dollar budget, filmed on location at Warner Brothers Studios. And at the center of it all was the legendary designer Evelyn Hart—a modern-day Edith Head with a sharper tongue and a more secretive entourage. Hart had won every major award in the business, and her reputation for precision and control was unparalleled. She was the gatekeeper of aesthetic perfection, the visual architect of some of cinema's greatest stories.

I parked and checked my notes, nerves pricking. According to my research, she'd once been a university linguist

before abandoning academia for couture, breaking into a design world still thick with cigar smoke and dismissive men. That kind of audacity resonated with me. A red light above the steel stage door pulsed, signaling that filming was underway. I waited, taking in the industrial hush of the lot. When the light dimmed, I stepped inside—and into a pressure cooker.

The atmosphere hit me like a wave: velvet-costumed actors pacing between takes, assistants racing clipboard-first across the floor, and designers threading needles mid-sprint. This wasn't just another set—this was elite territory. The Oscars paled in comparison. Every face carried pressure. And then she arrived. Hart swept in from behind a massive set wall, a five-foot-one whirlwind in a razor-sharp tailored suit. Even in her later years, she radiated force. Her silk blouse was crisp, the bow at her neck knotted with architectural precision. Her jet-black hair was cut into a severe bob, her rimmed glasses resting low but watchful on her nose. Even her perfume—an unmistakable swirl of Cartier and something older—seemed to part the air for her passage. She glanced at me as she passed and offered a magnetic, fleeting smile.

"I'll be with you in a moment, dahling," she said, her voice low and luxuriously amused. I could only nod as she disappeared behind another partition, leaving the faintest suggestion of power and curated chaos in her wake. While waiting, I moved toward the coffee station near the wardrobe to review my notes again and caught the tail end of a quiet conversation between two stylists.

"Did you see who was in Hart's trailer last night?" A pause. "She told security to scrub the log. Said it was a personal visit. That's the second time this week."

They fell silent when I stepped closer. I pretended not to notice, flipping through my planner as my mind raced. Why would a costume designer, no matter how powerful, need to erase a guest log? And why did the name *Hart* feel familiar? I'd seen it somewhere. Was it buried in one of Daniel's handwritten notes? I couldn't be sure, but the chill it left was

real. Minutes later, Hart returned. Her smile was polite but thin, watchful.

"So, Molly Cleary," she said, assessing me with quiet curiosity. "You've come to see the wardrobe that will win us gold."

"Something tells me you've already got that covered," I replied.

She held my gaze, then smiled again, sharper this time.

"Fashion tells the truth no one dares speak," she said. "It reveals exactly what you want to hide."

And with that, she turned and walked toward the dressing room wing, gesturing for me to follow. As the premier designer at Paramount Studios, Hart was on loan to Warner's, overseeing the entire costume department for the production. My job was simple: listen, observe, and report what she had to say. Unfortunately, there was no time for small talk. Her harried assistant—thin, breathless, and juggling three phones—whisked me through the backstage maze and into Ms. Hart's private dressing room. She offered me a beverage with a tight smile, muttered something about a wardrobe crisis, and disappeared in a blur.

Moments later, Hart entered—precisely on time, effortlessly composed. She conducted a polished and insightful interview, offering sharp observations, historical references, and an unexpected warmth. Then, just as quickly as she'd arrived, she thanked me graciously, gathered her clipboard, and disappeared to make her lunch appointment. I barely had time to collect my things before her assistant reappeared to escort me out. We moved silently through the now-empty, soundproof soundstage—a massive airplane hangar of a space, utterly transformed from the bustle I'd walked into just hours before. It was... eerily quiet. Not peaceful. *Vacant.* The kind of silence that hums in your ears and makes you question if anyone else is left in the world.

At the exit, the assistant gave a quick wave, already answering a call, and darted back inside. I stood alone, staring

at the enormous steel structure behind me. It looked less like a film set now and more like a secret warehouse. There is no place like Hollywood, I thought. A city built into a master illusion. A world within a world, where stories hide in plain sight—and truth rarely comes uncostumed. With one deep breath, I pushed open the heavy door, stepped into the bright Los Angeles sun, and squinted toward the horizon. Something had shifted. I couldn't name it yet—but it was coming. And I wondered, not for the first time: *What's next for me?*

As I pulled onto Sunset Blvd, Marcy came to mind. The new reporter, who was sitting at my old desk, had angry eyes and a tense posture. It was noon, and I'd be passing the Times building anyway. Why not stop in, update Jason on the interview, and see if Marcy is free for lunch? To my surprise, she said yes without hesitation. That impromptu meal turned into something unexpected—a spark of friendship that felt easy and overdue. Marcy, it turned out, had moved here reluctantly from New York, where she'd made her name as a tenacious crime reporter. The fashion column had been a last-minute placement, not her passion.

"I'm dying to hand it back," she laughed over grilled sandwiches.

Her husband, Dominic Renaldi, was a real estate broker who had just opened a boutique office in Beverly Hills. Marcy described him with affection and mild exasperation.

"Brooklyn born and bred, and now he's dodging palm trees like they're gunfire. The culture shock is real."

She asked for advice on helping him adjust, and I surprisingly invited them for dinner that weekend. The moment the words left my mouth, a quiet ache crept in. I'm hosting without Daniel. Marcy must've noticed.

"Everything okay, Molly?"

"Yes," I said quickly. "Just remembered something. Do you and Dominic like pork spareribs?"

"Are you kidding? We *love* ribs."

"I have a Louisiana family recipe I think you'll enjoy. Six o'clock work for you?"

"Perfect. We'll bring the wine."

By the weekend, I was genuinely looking forward to their visit. Marcy and Dominic brought a lively warmth to the house—hearty laughter, fast-talking charm, and just the kind of chaos that made life seem normal. Over dinner, Dominic paused, his gaze lingering on a framed photo of Daniel and me at a police banquet. He set his glass down.

"You were married to Lieutenant Cleary?"

"Yes," I said, surprised at the formality in his tone.

He nodded slowly. "I heard about the accident. I'm sorry."

His voice was gentle, but something unreadable passed across his face. Then he looked at Marcy, who gave a slight nod.

"You know," he continued, "a friend of mine—James Klein—is a lawyer. Very discreet. He's helped people access files they weren't technically supposed to see. If you're trying to get more clarity on... what happened, he might be able to help."

My pulse ticked up. *He said, 'the accident,' then offered discreet legal assistance. Why?*

"I'll think about it," I said, my voice steady.

Later that evening, we discussed hosting a party so they could meet more people. Dominic offered their home, saying it could fit a hundred guests, and offered to arrange staff and catering. As we finalized the details, something about him lingered in my thoughts. Charming, brilliant, but there was an edge beneath the polish. And then, as I cleaned up after they left, I remembered a name I'd come across in Daniel's research—*Renaldi*. Could it be a coincidence? Or had Dominic Renaldi once been more than a real estate broker? The thought surfaced, uninvited. *Whispers link the Renaldi family to the mob, back to the days of Eliot Ness and Al Capone.* Of course, they were

just rumors. At least, that's what anyone brave enough to ask had always been told.

Dominic's journey from Brooklyn to Beverly Hills hadn't been seamless. With a rugged presence that cut against the grain of Los Angeles glamour, Dominic Renaldi rarely blended with the city's polished elite. His boutique agency, *Beverly Hills Estates*, seemed to echo that defiance—scrappy, determined, and still struggling for a foothold. Dominic hadn't yet mastered the performance in a place where success required credentials and charisma. What struck me most, though, was the way he looked at me. His eyes never quite met mine. They hovered just above and beyond as if dodging some unspoken truth. It could have been nothing. Or perhaps it was that familiar whisper of instinct: *There's something he's not saying.*

Marcy was no less captivating. Strong, lean, and fearless, she held a black belt in karate and, before marriage, had served as a White House security guard. According to rumor, her ties to Dominic had cost her that post. At twenty-two, she returned to school and emerged as a relentless, brilliant journalist. Fiercely loyal, she stood by Dominic through the roughest years. They were magnetic. And unsettling. I was finalizing details for the party when Marcy called to cancel.

"Dominic's been called to Brooklyn on business," she said. "We'll have to postpone."

"No problem," I said, shelving the guest list. But something about her tone—tight, apologetic—stuck with me.

Back at my computer, I found an email with a few thinly veiled demands from Jason—assignments far below the exclusives I'd agreed to. With new clarity, I replied: *Per our contract, I'm declining these.* He reassigned them with a nervous laugh icon. And just like that, a calm washed over me. I was free to focus on what mattered. Still, Dominic's offer lingered. Attorney Klein. Discreet access to Daniel's files. I wasn't ready to act.

I reached for the Agatha Christie novel I'd picked up in Rose Haven. But after only a few pages, my thoughts were elsewhere, circling back to the Renaldis and their carefully constructed mystery. Then, like a thread snapping into place, an idea struck. I closed the book and picked up the phone. I invited Marcy, Ciara, and Linda to a casual Sunday lunch in the park. Bring friends, bring family. Keep it informal. I hoped to meet Attorney Klein in a setting less rigid than an office— something neutral, open, and observant. With the plan in motion, I turned to preparations—shopping, baking, packing the baskets and coolers with quiet purpose. As I worked, anticipation grew. This gathering could be more than just a friendly get-together. It might be the key. To Daniel. To Dominic. To Klein. To Renaldi.

A Glimpse of Hell

At the last minute, Marcy called with exactly the question I'd hoped for:

"Would it be okay if I bring James Klein with me?" Her tone was easy, almost careless, yet something in me stirred, a quickening I couldn't ignore.

"Of course," I said, too quickly. "We'd love to meet him."

I packed the car with coolers and baskets and plunged into the chaos of Los Angeles traffic. But as I turned toward the Santa Monica Mountains, the city's din faded, replaced by open sky and winding canyons. Griffith Park rose like a natural cathedral—quiet, expansive, fragrant with pine and eucalyptus. The hum of waterfalls and the song of birds filled the air. It felt like another world, a world where truths might quietly surface. Ciara, Joel, Linda, and Kyle had arrived ahead of me and found the perfect spot—shaded, peaceful, with benches enough for all. Joel's two portable grills sent tendrils of fragrant smoke curling into the breeze, and the scent of sizzling meat laid the foundation for a perfect picnic. One by one, families

arrived, laughter and casual chatter blending with the rustle of trees and the shrieks of delighted children chasing one another toward the swings and slides. Kyle worked the grill like a pro, calling out,

"A feast is on the way!" as he flipped burgers, hot dogs, and salmon.

The breeze caught the scent and carried it to the playground. Within moments, wide-eyed children wandered back, drawn by that universal promise of good food and good company. And then Marcy arrived, with Attorney James Klein at her side. They exchanged warm introductions with the group. He was polite and composed. Unassuming. A faint accent hinted at East Coast roots. But as he settled in, I noticed something immediately unsettling: he didn't quite meet anyone's eyes. The banter around the table was light—food, weather, weekend plans—until someone, half-joking, asked,

"So, James, are you a cop too?"

He gave a short laugh. "No, I'm not. Far too independent for that."

His tone was calm. Measured. But beneath the civility was an unmistakable edge of cynicism. The officers at the table stiffened almost imperceptibly. A quiet insult had landed. No one replied. My instincts whispered: *Not the man for the job. Miss Marple would've agreed.* Lunch rolled on. Plates emptied. Conversations turned to work. Kyle turned to me. "

Molly—any news on Daniel's case?"

I noticed James glance at me then, quickly and sharply, assessing. I deliberately slowed my response, enjoying another bite of grilled salmon, keeping my tone even.

"I've met with Detective Johnson several times," I said. "He's... focused. Methodical. But I don't think there's been much progress."

Marcy and James listened closely. Too closely. Kyle threw his hands up.

"Every lead vanishes into thin air. Our few suspects were cleared, and Johnson won't approve any advanced techniques."

James leaned in slightly, smiling.

"I've worked on dozens of criminal cases. Would it help if I took a look?"

The offer was generous, but something about how he said it felt too rehearsed. I gave him a warm smile, but my reply was gently edged.

"Oh, James, that's kind. But aren't you based on Fifth Avenue in New York? I imagine your fees are... considerable."

His gaze hovered uncomfortably above my eyes.

"Well," he said smoothly, "I do have a large staff to pay. But for you, I can make an exception. How does four hundred an hour sound?"

It wasn't the number that unnerved me. It was that same *eerie disconnect*—like something essential was missing behind his eyes.

"Thank you, James, but that's a bit steep for me," I said, with polite finality. "Still, I appreciate the offer."

He gave a tight smile.

"Maybe we can work something out."

Before I had time to respond, Ciara jumped in, rescuing me.

"I saw Detective Johnson last week," she said. "Asked him for an update. He was more agitated than usual. When I offered help, he snapped. Then caught himself, and—very carefully—said nothing at all."

We all fell silent for a moment. The park felt quieter now, despite the distant laughter of children and the rustle of leaves. Something about this lunch—about the presence of Klein—had stifled the air. The food had been good. The setting is beautiful. But now I was certain: This picnic wasn't just a social call. It was a scrutiny. And something about James Klein didn't belong.

Everyone appeared to be pondering Ciara's comment, which gave me a moment to notice Joel. He looked unusually uncomfortable today—more so than usual. His eyes darted from face to face, never settling, as if scanning for something... or someone. A strange silence hung around him like a shroud. When he caught me watching him, he abruptly stood, muttering something about grilling second helpings, as though trying to escape my scrutiny. There was something off in his movements—too brisk, too eager, as if fleeing from a question no one had asked.

Joel, a titan in his field, led the engineering department at a major Silicon Valley firm. He and Ciara had first crossed paths at a Mensa International meeting, where their connection was instant—an unspoken bond of intellect and mutual respect. She had always understood the covert confines of Joel's genius, knowing how easily others misread his aloofness. While Ciara had a gift for mathematical equations, Joel's mind outpaced even the most brilliant mathematicians in the country, perhaps the world.

When I first met him, he was a puzzle wrapped in discomfort. His thoughts outpaced his speech, leaving his words stilted, clipped, and often jarring in their bluntness. His tone lacked warmth, only raw intellect—unpolished and awkward. Over time, Joel confided that his parents had frequently told him he had an "off-putting personality." But Ciara adored him. And we loved Ciara. So we listened as she lovingly paved the social road for him with tales of his brilliance and accolades. She said he tried to practice social skills in private, but it was a monumental struggle. But today felt different.

Joel wasn't just his usual awkward self—he was distant. Withdrawn. His sudden enthusiasm to "man the grill" felt like an escape. As I watched him poke at the food, I saw his eyes flicker across the picnic, never landing, never connecting. Something was wrong. Questions bombarded my mind. What was bothering him? Did he know something we didn't?

Curiosity and doubt crept in—but I told myself this wasn't the time. I forced myself to breathe, relax, to be present with friends... and quietly collect clues.

The sun was warm, the breeze gentle, but a quiet storm pressed beneath the calm. Resting my clasped hands on the table, I couldn't help but wonder—did Miss Marple ever feel this uncertain? Did she ever wrestle with the urge to act before the time was right? I knew her creator, Agatha Christie, did. She often found solace in the sea—swimming, chatting with friends, or simply wiggling her toes in the sun-warmed sand. But there was no ocean here. No comforting grains beneath my feet. Just the hum of a park in motion and the quiet, unmistakable tug of suspicion.

I stood and joined the children, their joy infectious. I flew on the swings, letting the breeze scrub my thoughts clean. As I shot down the slide, laughter burst from me—genuine and effortless. It was the first time I'd honestly laughed that day. The sun slipped behind the trees, trailing golden ribbons across the grass—a quiet signal that it was time to go home. But I knew this tension—whatever it was—would not be left behind. Not tonight.

We packed up, clearing the tables and gathering our baskets. James and Marcy had joined in the fun and, at a glance, seemed to fit in beautifully. But I noticed James now wore dark sunglasses—and perhaps had one beer too many. He smiled often. Too often. As families began to leave, James and Marcy lingered to help with the last cleanup. James finished his final drink and slid his sunglasses to the top of his head. A bit off balance, he turned toward me to say goodbye. And then he looked at me. His pale blue eyes locked onto mine for a fraction of a second. I froze. There was something in them— something bottomless. Cold. Ancient. An eternity of something I couldn't name stared back at me. Something not quite human. Then, as if catching himself, James dropped the sunglasses back into place. His smile remained, but now it felt practiced—mechanical. It held no warmth—only calculation. I

stood rooted, lightheaded, unable to look away. Then Marcy's voice rang out—bright, unbothered.

"Come on, James, hustle yourself. I'm driving this time!"

The moment shattered. I broke free, stumbling toward my car. My hands trembled as I fumbled with my keys, heartbeat pounding in my ears. Behind me, James staggered to the Bentley and slumped into the passenger seat. Marcy honked, leaned out, and waved with that radiant, unshakable smile.

"Thanks again, Molly! That was wonderful!"

I waved back, but my smile was strained. Forced. As I pulled away, a cold horror settled over me. Had Marcy ever seen that look in her friend's eyes? I remembered officers, including Daniel, speaking about it. A stare they called *otherworldly*. Like something not entirely human was watching you. Until today, I hadn't understood. But now I did. And whatever it was, I wanted no part of it. James Klein was trouble. Every instinct I had screamed to stay far, far away. During one of Agatha Christie's archaeological digs in India, she once said, *"Follow your heart's direction; it's your best driver."* I wasn't about to argue with that logic.

That evening, Marcy called. Her voice was bright, animated, and overflowing with praise. She spoke for nearly an hour, listing the impressive credentials and success stories, James had garnered, and explaining why trusting him would be the smoothest and brightest path forward. It sounded flawless, logical, straightforward, and ever so easy. I murmured that I'd consider it, though unease stirred beneath the surface. I let her finish, offered my thanks, and hung up. As I drifted off to sleep, Agatha's words echoed. A whisper. A warning.

The following morning, I woke under the soft weight of my favorite comforter, sunlight dappling the walls. For a few brief minutes, Marcy's logic held. Handing the case to James would solve everything. No more digging. No more stress. It would be done. But as I sipped my coffee, the truth returned—

quiet and firm. *No.* A deep, resounding no that pulsed in my chest. I couldn't ignore that feeling. Not for ease. Not for convenience. I picked up the phone and called Marcy. My voice held firm, betraying none of the storm inside.

"I've decided not to go forward with James. But thank you for offering."

Our conversation was brief and pleasant. As I hung up, the tension drained like air from a balloon. What replaced it was quiet certainty—relief. I had listened to my instincts, and at that moment, I knew I'd made the right choice.

Later that week, I met Ciara for a quick lunch, trying to embrace the idea that life was beginning to shape a new normal. Over crisp salads and iced tea, we talked about simple things—Giovanni's upcoming seasonal sale, our next shopping date, and the latest gossip at the station. I was just about to tell her about my experience with James when her smile faltered. Her eyes clouded with worry.

"Joel's been acting strangely, she whispered. Not sleeping. Always agitated. I told him to see a counselor, but his reaction—" She stopped, her voice thinning. "He looked scared. Then silent. Like he'd shut a door."

My stomach tightened.

"His usual evasiveness has turned into something else," she continued. "I can't reach him, Molly. He's in his private world, and I don't know how to pull him out.

I reached for her hand but said nothing right away. I wanted to tell her it would all be okay, but the image of Joel at the picnic—jumpy, withdrawn, almost... haunted—came rushing back. It felt too close to the unease I'd seen in James.

"I did notice at the picnic he seemed more preoccupied than usual," I said gently. "Any trouble at work?"

"He says no. But he's been obsessed with a new computer security program lately. He spends hours in the home office. When I asked what it was, he said he was reconfiguring an existing program for the CIA."

I leaned in, the words demanding more space. "Wait—Joel works with the CIA?"

"You didn't know?"

I shook my head.

"He's creating something to defeat encryption, viruses, surveillance, firewalls—all of it. A way to access secure information normally locked behind layers of digital protection."

"That's impressive," I said, carefully. "And probably overwhelming."

"Yes... Yes, it is. But..." Ciara's voice drifted, her face full of doubt. "I shouldn't worry. If anyone can handle it, it's Joel."

Before I could respond, Kyle entered the restaurant—quick, breathless.

"Sorry to interrupt, but there's a domestic disturbance call. We've got to move."

Ciara stood, dropping money on the table.

"See you next week, Molly!"

"Be careful, you two!"

They rushed out, and I sat back, my appetite gone. On the way home, I drove past the precinct. In the parking lot, Police Chief Bates stood with his arms firmly planted on his hips, leaning toward a group of officers. Their wide-eyed expressions were unsettling—riveted and disturbed. Something about their body language made me slow down. What had he just said that made trained, composed men look like that?

Halfway home, a tug of instinct pulled me off course. I turned sharply into traffic and headed toward the place where Daniel had died. The closer I got, the harder my heart pounded. I parked across from the haunting stretch of pavement. The memory of that night still lingered here, like smoke that refused to lift. I sat for a moment, willing myself to breathe. And then a thought came: *What if I acted as an investigative journalist? Just for a day.* Ten businesses lined either

side of the street—twenty possible sets of eyes. I could visit each one, ask questions, gather details, and see what might've been overlooked. It was worth a try.

The most challenging step was the first—walking into the store directly in front of where Daniel's body was found. I introduced myself as a journalist with the *Times*, gathering follow-up information about the death of Officer Cleary. The owner, clearly busy, paused. His face softened as he remembered.

"Tragic," he murmured. "Still can't believe it."

He agreed to a brief interview and continued,

"My place was packed that night. I remember the car, though. A newer, dark sedan. Tinted windows. But I never saw the driver."

Then, as if a light flipped on, his brow furrowed.

"Wait—during the investigation, I saw another car. Same kind. Parked across the street. Headlights on. Just... sitting there, like it was watching."

He apologized for never mentioning it before.

"I guess I didn't think it mattered."

I thanked him and assured him I'd follow up. I continued down the block, visiting each store. Most had nothing new to offer, and the police had already collected surveillance footage. But that one comment—the waiting car with its headlights on—was new. It could mean nothing. Or it could mean everything. Either way, the emotional weight of the day began to settle in. I'd followed a hunch. I'd collected what I could. It was time to go home.

Soft shadows stretched across the room as evening deepened around me. Exhausted, I drifted into sleep, cradled by the familiar embrace of the couch, missing the end of a beautiful old movie. When I awoke the following morning, instinct took over—I reached for Daniel's warmth beside me. The movement was reflexive, unthinking. But then, like a bolt of lightning cleaving the quiet, it hit me: he wasn't there. The ache gripped me like a sudden plunge into ice water. I froze,

stunned by the weight of absence. It hovered above me, dark and heavy, like the first tremor of an approaching storm. For a moment, I couldn't breathe. I reached for the unfinished glass of wine on the table, hoping its bitter warmth would comfort me. But before the glass touched my lips, the phone rang— sharp, abrupt, slicing through the stillness like an alarm.

"Good morning, Molly! It's Marcy, were you sleeping?" Her voice burst through the receiver like a cannon shot. I flinched, the ceiling swimming above me, heart pounding.

"Hi, Marcy. Well, I'm awake... and seriously considering staying in bed."

"Molly, I'd like to meet with you."

There was something in her tone. Too cheerful. Too... intentional. I sat up, abandoning the wine.

"Okay—when and where?"

"There's a little café on the Santa Monica Pier. Can you meet me there in an hour for breakfast?"

"An hour?" I groaned. "I'm not fully human yet."

"Please, Molly. It's important."

I hesitated, then sighed. "Fine. But I have an assignment in Beverly Hills at noon."

"That's perfect. I need to be at the *Times* by eleven."

Her voice dropped suddenly, almost to a whisper.

"Is everything okay?" I asked.

"Yes," she said quickly. "But I can't talk now. I'll explain when we meet."

Click. She was gone. Curiosity mounting, I pulled myself up and set about restoring order to the chaos I'd created—throw pillows scattered, clothes draped over chairs, a half-finished note on Daniel's desk. I moved slowly at first, limbs heavy with the residue of sleep and sorrow. Then, without thinking, I began to prepare as if I were meeting Daniel—showered, dressed in my favorite navy blouse and tailored slacks, makeup minimal but presentable. I grabbed my briefcase, which held my camera, notebook, and a change of

clothes for the evening's event, and stepped out into the morning. It felt like climbing a steep hill with no clear summit—but with each step, the dark fog that had settled over me began to thin. Marcy was waiting. And something told me this wasn't just about breakfast.

What Daniel Knew

The Santa Monica morning was tranquil, the horizon filled with the first blush of sun. Along the pier, shopkeepers unlocked doors with slow, practiced hands, and the scent of salt and coffee beans rode the ocean air. The creak of boards beneath my shoes and the occasional clatter of bait buckets from nearby fishermen was mesmerizing as I walked the length of the wooden pier twice, searching—but no café. Confused, I returned to a bench at the entrance and sat, trying not to fidget. Gulls cried above, circling like sentinels. Children's laughter from the sand danced with the rhythm of crashing waves. For a fleeting moment, it grounded me. Then, I saw it—a gleaming white yacht with tan sails slicing through the water like a dream. I moved instinctively toward the railing, hypnotized by the sea, the wind, and the grandeur—until a hand touched my shoulder. Startled, I spun around.

"Marcy!"

"Sorry, Molly. Didn't mean to startle you."

"A bit of warning would've helped. And where's this café you mentioned?"

"There isn't one," she said with a glance over her shoulder. "A cab's waiting. We're going to Ivy at The Shore."

My brow furrowed. "You couldn't have said that before? This feels… secretive."

She smiled, but it didn't reach her eyes.

"It is."

The cab waited at the curb. As we slid inside,

Marcy's demeanor shifted—shoulders tight, jaw set—a mile passed in silence. Then, out of nowhere, she tapped the glass behind the driver.

"Pull over."

She thrust a bill into his hand, reached across me, and opened the door.

"We walk from here."

"Marcy, what is going on?"

She didn't answer. Just nodded toward the street. We walked a whole block in silence. The sparkle coming from the restaurant finally broke the tension.

"There's Ivy," she said flatly, voice low.

Inside, I scanned the familiar space—the ocean views, the crisp linens, the hushed elegance. It should've been calming. But the air around us buzzed with unspoken tension. Marcy's gaze wandered.

"Oh look—" she whispered, eyes widening at the sight of two A-list actors lunching nearby.

"Marcy," I said through clenched teeth. "Focus."

"I *am* focused. Just let me order something first."

She waved the waiter over. I debated between coffee and the Ivy Gimlet, finally opting for caffeine. Marcy chose the Upper Eastsider.

"It's got cucumber, mint, lime... a little gin. A green juice with perks."

I shot her a look. She leaned closer, her voice dropping.

"Okay. Joel was working on a classified program—data scraping through facial recognition software under the guise of national security. He noticed something was off. Misuse. Maybe even manipulation. Then—papers vanished."

"What does this have to do with me?"

She hesitated. "Daniel's precinct. It's tied in. Joel thinks Daniel flagged it for the chief. Quietly. But it went nowhere."

I froze. "You think this connects to Daniel's death?"

"I think it could. What I *do* know is this isn't just about your husband. It's bigger. A network, maybe. Conceivably even global."

My coffee trembled in my hands.

"Why tell me now?"

"Because I know you, Molly. You'll keep pushing and need to know what you're up against. I've dealt with this before. Lawsuits. Doxxing. Threats in the night. Surveillance that doesn't show up on records."

Her words landed hard, heavy, and real. I stared at the waves. The sun glinted off the water like shattered glass.

"You okay?" she asked.

"No," I said honestly. "This is more than I expected."

She nodded, understanding. "So, what do you think?"

"I think I need more coffee."

Marcy raised her hand and ordered two. I took a deep breath and leaned in. "Have you told anyone else?"

"No. Just you."

"Keep it that way. Until we know more, rumors will only bury the truth."

"Molly… this could get dangerous."

"I know," I said, eyes narrowing. "But if Daniel saw this coming, we owe him the rest of the story."

Outside, the cab idled at the curb. We climbed in without a word, the silence thick with everything we'd uncovered. Back at the Santa Monica Pier, Marcy gave me a quick, knowing glance before disappearing into the crowd, back to her world, her risks, her secrets. I stood there a beat too long, the ocean air pressing in around me, then turned and headed for my car—time to compartmentalize. Coco was next. The designer. The meeting. I navigated the freeway on autopilot, the city blurring past as my mind replayed Marcy's revelations on loop. But as I pulled up to the Beverly Wilshire's private entrance, the mood shifted. Two security guards stepped forward, crisp and alert, scanning my vehicle like I'd driven into a political summit. Then Coco appeared—gliding

out from behind a column in effortless elegance. Designer flats. Oversized sunglasses. That studied Parisian dishevelment looked anything but accidental. She slid into the passenger seat with the cool of someone used to red carpets and whispered deals. The game had changed. Again.

"Where to?" I asked, forcing a smile.

"You promised to show me the real Los Angeles," she said, her voice playful but edged with exhaustion. "Surprise me."

"I thought we'd start with the Garment District. Not glamorous—but it's where the magic starts."

She nodded, intrigued. "Perfect."

We drove south, trading small talk as we passed the glossy mirage of Beverly Hills and merged into the raw, beating heart of the fashion trade. The Garment District pulsed with movement—delivery trucks, racks of fabric, steam from press machines rising into the air. Coco's eyes lit up as we walked the narrow alleys between showrooms and factories.

"It smells like sweat and dreams," she said with an approving grin.

She charmed a patternmaker into giving her a tour of his studio. I watched from the doorway, amused by how effortlessly she moved through the chaos. Even here, she glowed. But I didn't miss the discreet security trailing us, keeping their distance but never losing sight of her. By five, Coco looked refreshed rather than fatigued.

"Dinner?" she asked, her eyes twinkling. "Someplace beautiful."

"Ivy at The Shore," I said. "You'll love the view."
As we pulled up to the restaurant, my phone buzzed—a text from Marcy: **We need to talk. URGENT.**

I locked the screen and forced a smile. I saw camera flashes down the block at the entrance—paparazzi again. Coco saw them too, her posture stiffening.

"Private entrance?" I asked.

She nodded, switching to French. "Oui, s'il te plaît."

I took the back route, and within seconds, we were through the discreet side door of Ivy's, greeted by staff who knew how to handle high-profile guests without fanfare. Inside, the view of the Pacific was breathtaking. The clink of glasses, soft jazz, and the subtle scent of citrus candles enveloped us like a well-tailored coat. But even amid the luxury, a thin thread of unease tugged at me—Marcy's text, Daniel's memory, Coco's ever-present security. It all hinted at something unsettling.

"You seem somewhere else, Molly," Coco said gently, sipping her cocktail.

I smiled, grateful she noticed. "It's just been a long day."

And it wasn't over yet. Dinner was a blur of candlelight, impeccable service, and the hush only wealth and power could afford. Coco ordered effortlessly in French, smiling at the waiter as if he were an old friend. I kept my phone face down beside my plate, resisting the urge to recheck Marcy's message.

"You've been quiet," Coco said, delicately slicing into her grilled branzino. "Not your usual sparkle."

"I've had... a morning," I said with a faint smile. "The kind that rearranges your thinking."

She nodded, her eyes scanning me carefully. "You're not just a journalist. You listen like someone who's lost something."

The words hit me squarely. I hesitated. "Yes," I admitted. "Someone I loved."

She set her fork down and leaned in, her voice soft.

"Then you understand why I have shadows that follow me."

Her eyes shot toward the corner of the room where her security team had blended seamlessly into the scenery.

"Coco, you said something earlier," I continued, pivoting carefully, "about fame drawing hostility. Have there been real threats?"

She nodded slowly. "Anonymous packages. Messages. Photos taken of my family in France. They think I don't know, but I do. I've learned how to smile through surveillance."

Her hand brushed her wine glass, but didn't lift it.

"Do you think it's business-related?" I asked.

"I don't know. I design clothes, not weapons. But I've stepped on toes. I backed out of a private contract last year—one with government ties. They wanted exclusive access to my biometric textile tech for uniforms. I declined. Too invasive."

Biometric textiles? I thought. I leaned in. "You mean fabrics that read movement or—?"

"More than that," she said, almost wistfully. "Heart rate, voice stress, even subtle thermal changes. Smart fashion. Wearable data."

"And someone powerful didn't like you pulling out."

She shrugged, but the elegant shrug said everything. That's when my phone vibrated again—Marcy. Another message: **They know you're asking questions. Be careful.** I glanced toward the window. A black SUV was idling across the street. Coco followed my gaze, then she said lightly,

"Would you mind if we cut dessert?"

"Not at all."

We left through the kitchen—her security's idea. She was gone in seconds, swept into a separate car before I reached mine. As I gripped the steering wheel, heart pounding, a chilling realization settled in: Coco's story wasn't just parallel to mine. It might be intersecting. And if her biometric fabric tech was connected to the surveillance systems Daniel had flagged… I didn't finish the thought. I drove off into the dark, headlights slicing through the thickening fog. I had work to do—and a husband's secrets to uncover.

The following day brought a strange stillness—an overdue chance to breathe. The heaviness of Marcy's warning and the surreal glamour of Coco's world clashed in my mind like warring symphonies. But now, I finally have space. Space to look deeper. I unlocked the bottom drawer of Daniel's

desk—his private archive. Inside was the usual chaos: notebooks crammed with scribbled thoughts, printouts with yellowed edges, a few photos, some too painful to look at for long. But then, tucked inside a file marked *GRB*—unrelated at first glance—I found it: a thin folder, sealed with a simple paperclip. My heart picked up speed.

The file's contents were clinical, but Daniel's handwritten annotations gave them heat. He had been tracking dozens of lawsuits against companies accused of abusing biometric technology, facial recognition software, predictive policing, and behavior-monitoring clothing. My breath caught. Coco's words from the night before came rushing back. *Biometric textiles. Fabrics that read vital signs, voice patterns, thermal cues...* Was that what Daniel had been sniffing around? And if so, why hadn't he told me outright?

I shuffled through the pages, overwhelmed. Many of the companies were household names—tech giants, private security firms, even medical conglomerates. But buried among the legal jargon and redacted lines was something more chilling: the implication that data was being sold—sold to law enforcement, to governments, possibly without consent. Sleep-deprived and growing increasingly unsettled, I tried to piece together the fragments of my memory. Marcy's cryptic warning about predictive policing. The locket—still unexplained. And then another memory: the flower centerpieces from the Policeman's Ball. They'd felt eerily familiar, like déjà vu laced with dread. A chill ran up my spine. The pages slipped from my hand and fanned across the hardwood floor. As I bent down to gather them, a single name leapt out at me: **Hampton Fife.** The name rang louder this time.

I rushed to my computer, searching. Within minutes, I found him. Chief Hampton Fife—one of L.A.'s longest-serving police chiefs. His story read like an old noir script gone sour. Midwestern-born and law-trained, he became the enforcer of a deeply fractured system. L.A. in the early 1900s

had been promoted as the "white spot of America," and Fife had played his role with brutal dedication. Worse still, I uncovered historical records linking him to sweeping policies of racial profiling, sanctioned brutality, and internal coverups. Controversy hounded his tenure, but he'd never been held accountable. Beneath his polished public image lurked a man fueled by resentment—born into poverty, a Protestant in a Catholic stronghold, an outsider who rose through the force not by honor, but by fear, manipulation, and ruthless ambition.

One document led to another. An archived interview with former Police Chief Gerald Bates revealed an unexpected link—Bates had once been Fife's driver. The job had forged a bond between them, two men hardened by bitterness, shaped by exclusion. That's when something Daniel once said echoed in my memory. He'd been investigating Bates, wondering how he'd climbed the ranks so fast despite weaker credentials. Daniel had suspected Fife's influence extended beyond the grave, propping up allies in powerful places—including Bates. He'd ranted about it over dinner one night, angry and sharp-tongued. Then he dropped it—and never brought it up again.

Now, it was all resurfacing: the surveillance, the misuse of biometric data, the cozy ties between old institutions and new technology. The deeper I looked, the darker the picture became. I sat back, shaken. The city I loved had secrets—ugly, generational ones—and Daniel had been dangerously close to exposing them. I wished I could ask him now, wished I'd pried deeper before he was gone. But possibly it was better that I hadn't. We'd preserved the sweetness of our last days— something untouched by suspicion or danger. Clues were stacking like storm clouds, heavy and relentless. With a long weekend ahead, I had the rare gift of time—to dive headlong into the research, strip away the disguises, and start forcing the fragments into a picture that made sense. I reached for my planner, already clearing my schedule when the phone rang, sharp, sudden, cutting through the stillness like a match strike. It was half-buried beneath Daniel's scattered notes, as if he had

dialed from some shadowed place. I froze. And then I answered.

Claire's voice reached me like a lighthouse beam through the dark.

"Molly, you've been on my mind. How are you? You sound out of breath."

I laughed—an honest, unexpected laugh—and felt a wave of comfort rush over me. I hadn't realized how tightly I'd been holding everything in. I told her what I could, careful not to unravel too much over the phone, but enough to feel the knot in my chest begin to loosen.

"Well, that settles it," Claire said with her signature warmth. "Come to Rose Haven. We're celebrating baby Jacob's first birthday this weekend. We all want you here."

For a moment, I hesitated. Even briefly, the thought of stepping away from the investigation felt impossible. But something about her invitation—its simplicity, its promise of joy—made me pause. Maybe it wasn't just a break. Perhaps it was necessary. As we spoke, my hands moved independently, gently returning Daniel's files to the secured cabinet. The locket still lay on my desk, its secrets pressing on me like a whisper I could almost hear. Could I balance both? Search for truth without unraveling myself in the process? I questioned if the answer wasn't in isolation but in connection. In the safety of family and friends. In baby laughter and birthday cake—in Rose Haven. And maybe—just maybe—it was time to unveil the locket.

6

Before the Storm

Catching the first flight out of Los Angeles, I arrived at Claire and Steven's just as the morning sun crested the horizon, painting the fields in hues of gold and peach. A year had slipped by since my last visit, yet the farm greeted me like an old friend—warm, worn, and full of whispered stories. Little Jacob, no longer a baby, toddled across the wooden floors on unsteady legs, his delighted squeals punctuating the morning stillness. Claire and Steven's once-fragile dream of selling goat cheese had flourished into a thriving endeavor—evidence of resilience etched in every rustic detail of their expanded kitchen and the hand-labeled jars stacked proudly on the shelves.

But not everything had changed. Hamish, the rooster, still held court on the fence post, his proud crowing cutting through the dawn air like a herald of continuity. The familiar scent of earth and straw, tinged with sweet hay and morning dew, wrapped around me like a memory. Oddly, I felt more at home gazing through Claire's window, where the mist curled off the fields and the goat pen lay in peaceful disarray, than among the glass towers and sirens of Los Angeles.

The reluctant handoff from spring to summer was stitched into the landscape: the tender greening of leaves, the wild roses spilling over the garden gate, the distant bleat of goats calling each other in the cool morning air. Inside, the scent of cinnamon and fresh bread clung to the walls, and for one rare, suspended moment, time felt beautifully irrelevant. Claire moved about the kitchen, recounting tales of spilled milk and stubborn goats. Her laughter was a ribbon of light that warmed the room. I moved beside her, setting the table, catching bits of her story, and basking in the domestic ease I could never reasonably claim for myself. Then the door flew open. David Donegal swept in like a gust of wind, boots thudding, eyes sharp, grin cocky. He took his usual seat as if

he'd never left. And oddly, I didn't mind. His presence, once irritating, now struck a strange chord—familiar, even welcome. Steven, ever steady, moved with quiet purpose. I watched him lift Jacob with gentle assurance, cradle him into the high chair, and begin feeding him a warm spoonful of mashed banana and oats—each one met with a soft coo and a sticky smile. There was something profoundly moving in the simplicity of it—a quiet symphony of love, effort, and rhythm—a life not without chaos, but rich in devotion. Something caught within me. A bittersweet ache. The kind that rises when you see what you'll never have, but still cherish witnessing.

"Molly, is everything alright? You've hardly touched your plate," Claire said, her voice edged with concern.

I blinked, pulled from my reverie.

"Yes, sorry. It's delicious. I'm just letting it sink in… every bit of it."

Across the table, David watched me closely, his expression unreadable. I considered asking him what was on his mind—but decided against it. Not yet. Later in town, amid the rose-scented breezes, my story of the locket faded behind Claire's whirlwind mission to prepare for Jacob's party. She moved purposefully, selecting a handcrafted birthday banner from a local artist—a keepsake stitched with meaning. On the back, she could jot a memory each year, and it came wrapped in an elegant, custom bag, ready to carry his milestones into the future. As we stepped onto the sidewalk, Claire lit up.

"Let's stop by Jenn's bookstore—she's saved a Miss Marple novel for tonight's reading!"

Jenn greeted us like old friends, waving us inside. The book, tucked behind the counter, felt like a personal invitation to mystery. I bought it without hesitation. Next, we ducked into Monique's Le Bon Boutique, where silk and sunlight mingled. Monique emerged with a blouse—deep sapphire, feather-light, and impossibly soft. I slipped into the dressing room and caught my reflection. In that quiet space, something cracked open. The silk whispered across my skin, a haunting

echo of being cherished—and without warning, my vision blurred with tears. Monique knocked softly.

"Molly, is everything okay?"

I cleared my throat, letting a smile rise—shaky, but serviceable.

"Hopelessly in love with this blouse. Can I wear it out?"

"Of course," she said, her voice kind. "Just give me the tags."

I handed them over with my credit card, quietly grateful for her grace. With my new blouse, Miss Marple tucked under one arm, and bags in hand, Claire and I hugged her goodbye.

"Au revoir, mes amis! See you tonight!" Monique called out as we walked into the light.

Halfway to Hanna's Café, I casually mentioned the locket. Claire froze mid-step.

"You found it?" she asked, eyes wide. I nodded, hesitating.

"What do you think it means, Molly?"

I didn't answer right away. Over lunch, the words finally came—my fears, suspicions, the shadows forming at the edges of what I knew. Claire listened in silence, her calm presence a steadying force. Her reassurance gave me something I didn't expect: clarity. I'd been circling the truth, but now I had to face it. Back at the farm, mystery night at Jenn's gave us a welcome distraction. But the following day belonged entirely to Jacob.

His birthday celebration unfolded like a storybook come to life. The banner hung in the kitchen, its colors catching the sunlight. Children darted between tables, with cake pressed on their little lips. The expression of discovery on Jacob's adorable face was priceless. He thrived in the symphony of joyful shrieks and the warmth of love that seemed to radiate from every corner of their home. Clear, vibrant helium balloons floated against the ceiling, each

concealing a secret treasure—a tiny toy or a ticket to an amusement park. Their ribbons dangled low, brushing against the wide-eyed, grinning children who reached for them as if reaching for the sky. A rubber swimming pool filled with plastic balls took center stage, drawing squeals of laughter that echoed through the house like music. Steven and David worked the room like agents on a mission, snapping photos and recording videos. Every moment was captured. David promised to compile them into a keepsake film. His gift? A college fund in Jacob's name. I was touched—but it was only the beginning.

That evening, David transformed the kitchen into a five-star dining experience. The aroma of lamb stew—shipped in from County Kerry—filled the air with savory promise. The first bite melted all doubt: it was divine. How could someone so infuriating also be so gifted, so quietly generous? Before I could unravel the mystery of David Donegal, reality called. Marcy. Her voice, tense and low, cut through the evening warmth.

"The court date for Joel and Chief Bates is next week. I think you should be here, Molly. Things are unraveling."

Chief Bates? I thought as my stomach tightened.

"I'll be there," I said, heart pounding.

But I didn't tell Claire. Not yet. I couldn't spoil the magic of the evening. Instead, I accepted a generous pour of Irish whiskey and let its warmth calm the edge of my nerves. Then came David's final act. He emerged from the kitchen, sleeves rolled, his six-foot-three frame commanding the room.

"Time for dessert," he said, with a grin that dared us to doubt him.

First, he served Irish coffee—robust and rich. We sipped. We swooned. Then came the finale: Guinness chocolate mousse, crowned with freshly whipped Irish cream, chocolate curls, and a daring splash of Bailey's. Gasps of delight were heard from all.

"David, this looks shockingly decadent," I said, genuinely stunned.

He shrugged, amused.

"What can I say? I have layers."

Laughter erupted around the table. And for a moment, despite the storm gathering in Los Angeles, I let myself stay in the glow, wrapped in silk, coffee, and fleeting peace. Claire and Steven clapped with delight, echoing my praise. Then silence fell, each of us caught in that glorious first bite. The mousse was decadent—rich, silky, with the perfect balance of bitter stout and velvety sweetness. David watched us with a knowing smile, arms crossed, his pride barely concealed. I looked up at him and asked,

"Where did you learn to cook like this?"

He shrugged modestly.

"Well, meh darlin' mother made each of us take a turn—one evenin' or mornin' a week—helpin' in the kitchen."

"She sounds like a wise woman."

"Aye," he nodded, eyes softening. "That she was."

I exhaled dreamily.

"I've always loved Ireland—but now I'm a massive fan of their food and drink. I'd better slow down, though. With all this alcohol, I hope I can make it to the airport tomorrow."

All heads turned. The sudden shift in tone caught them off guard.

"I had a call from Marcy," I said, their curiosity charged into concern. "She says the court date for Joel and Chief Bates is next week. I need to be back in L.A."

David set his hand gently on my shoulder.

"Don't worry, Molly lass. I'll be drivin' ya there myself. Gotta pick up my usual order anyhow."

Claire gave a small, unreadable smile. Steven said nothing.

"Thanks, David," I said carefully. "That's kind of you, but I already scheduled a cab."

"It's no trouble, truly, Molly. Cancel the taxi," he said firmly. "Besides, I'd be glad tae speak more about Daniel's case."

A flicker of irritation rose in me—gentle, but insistent. I didn't answer, just dipped my spoon into the mousse and nodded, my smile practiced. Whatever comfort he meant to offer missed its mark.

The following morning, Hamish's rooster-reveille pierced the stillness and, oddly, steadied me. I opened my window, inhaling the cool, earthy air. The agitation from last night hadn't vanished, but it had softened. I reached for my phone and canceled the cab. I finished packing after a hearty breakfast—eggs fresh from the coop, toast, and Claire's spiced apple preserves. David waited by the car, his usual confidence softened by something quieter, almost reverent.

On the way to the airport, he spoke of his years tracing his ancestry. The road had been long—brambled with red tape, obscured records, false leads—but he'd made progress. Significant progress. He'd discovered barriers in place that didn't want to be breached. He offered his help, though with a cautionary note.

"Whatever ye're lookin' into, Molly, it's wise tae keep yer digital footprint small. Safer that way."

He installed a discreet privacy app on my phone and warned me against sending casual emails or participating in online meetings.

"Face-tae-face, or not at all."

"I appreciate it," I said, though I wasn't sure how far to trust him. Then he added something unexpected.

"I've a meetin' next Friday at the UK Consulate in Los Angeles. If ye want tae talk more—about anythin'—I'll be there."

I thanked him but gave no clear answer. At the gate, we exchanged a brief goodbye. I boarded with my mind a whirlwind, every word David had said echoing in my head. Back in L.A., the city felt louder, closer, more volatile than I

remembered. That evening, my phone wouldn't stop ringing. Ciara. Marcy. And then a cryptic voice from my past. Jason. From the *Times*. His tone was clipped and urgent.

"How much do you know about Marcy's work on the FBI case? Can you come in first thing tomorrow?"

I stared at the phone. Any remaining calm from the farm was gone, and the next storm was already rumbling in.

I only know what I read in the paper, Jason."

Technically true. But far from the whole story. I couldn't exactly disclose my off-the-record meeting with Marcy. I ended the call, silenced my phone, and brewed chamomile tea, willing it to quiet my body, which was still dancing the jig from the Irish stew, whiskey, and Guinness mousse marathon. I curled up on the couch and let an old Agatha Christie film play across the screen. Jane Marple always knew what to do.

The following morning, my body felt like the Riverdance had trampled it. I chugged water, downed a protein smoothie, and dressed slowly, every motion a negotiation. Armed with coffee and resolve, I walked into Jason's office prepared for anything—except the hurricane waiting. He didn't even greet me.

"There's a pending takeover of the paper," he barked. "And a possible collusion lawsuit."

What?

I froze mid-sip. The lid popped off my coffee, flinging hot liquid across the floor like shrapnel. My intimidation dissolved into full-blown anxiety. Jason didn't slow down.

"There may be ties between *The Times* and the FBI— some kind of backdoor intel-sharing deal."

My head throbbed as I dabbed at the mess with tissues, my mind spinning. I tried to track what he was saying, but pain and disbelief dulled the edges. He slammed both hands on his desk, eyes wild.

"Do you know anything about this?"

I stared at him, vision swimming, and my fingers fumbled for aspirin. I popped two and swallowed hard.

"No," I whispered.

He stared a moment longer, then abruptly extended a manila folder.

"Your next assignment. You've got an hour to meet the head of Wardrobe at Paramount Studios. They want coverage for a new movie—a big campaign. Go."

He waved me away with the weary authority of a man unraveling at the seams. I left, too stunned to argue. Outside his office, I spotted Marcy. She was typing quickly, focused, but when she looked up and saw me, her eyes widened. She shook her head in a sharp and deliberate, do not engage manner. Gasping, I veered toward the exit and didn't look back. I hadn't even shut the car door when my phone rang—it was Ciara.

"Molly," she said, voice flat. "Detective Johnson's closing Daniel's case."

My heart stuttered.

"What?" I asked, already bracing.

"Officially ruled an unsolved hit-and-run. No witnesses. The car's owner is a U.S. senator. He was at a conference. His family, too. Fingerprints match them—nothing suspicious. No usable evidence."

It landed like a stomach punch. The world spun.

"A senator," I said, more to myself than to her. "Of course."

"I'm sorry," Ciara said. "I thought you should hear it from me."

"Thanks," I whispered, the ache in my head now matched by one in my stomach. I ended the call, hands trembling. The case was being buried. And someone powerful wanted it that way. Mechanically, I drove to Paramount Studios. I photographed the lavish period costumes, gathered a few sound bites from the press team, and left—the whole exchange felt hollow. I should have been intrigued—but my

mind was trapped elsewhere, circling the inevitable: Daniel's case was slipping through my fingers. When I got home, exhaustion pressed down on me like wet concrete. I sat in the car, unmoving, until the weight became unbearable. I gripped the door for balance, forcing myself upright. The walk to the door felt endless. Inside, I collapsed on the couch. Sleep pulled me under like a tide. In my dream, the dove returned. He perched on the roof's edge, his white feathers radiant against a storm-dark sky—a silent sentinel. A presence reminding me I wasn't alone—that this fight wasn't over.

When I woke, groggy but lighter, the heaviness had lifted. My breath came easier. I moved slowly, making myself a simple lunch. Each bite grounded me. When I finally sat at my desk, I wasn't just rested but clear. Chief Bates. Something about his meteoric rise never sat right. Daniel had questioned it, quietly, in the margins of his notes. Now I understand why. Curiosity turned sharp. I pulled up my laptop and reached out to Marcy for guidance. She answered, keeping her voice low.

"I can't talk long. I'll stop by after work."

Less than an hour later, there was a knock. Marcy stepped inside, eyes wide, breathing hard.

"Molly," she whispered, "don't go on those sites right now. They're being monitored—everything is. And with the investigation live, your searches could draw attention. They can trace it all back to you."

I flinched, pulse thudding in my ears. "I don't have anything to hide, Marcy. I'm not publishing—just checking facts."

"They don't know that," she hissed. "I'm telling you— Jason warned me not to dig. He doesn't want *anyone* poking into Bates or that case."

"What about freedom of the press?" I asked. "And it's still a free country, right?"

She looked over her shoulder.

"Just lay low. Please. Don't talk about this on the phone, either. Let's keep things... analog."

114

"Okay, Marcy," I said, though my heart beat faster. "Thanks for stopping by."

But she didn't leave. Instead, she stood frozen in the doorway, gaze distant, face pale.

"Marcy, are you alright?"

"I thought I was just doing my job," she said, her voice cracking. "But Jason was furious. No explanation. Then somehow, before it went to print, my story—*my story*—leaked. Got scooped by the competition."

"What are you talking about?"

"It'll be everywhere tomorrow," she muttered, then added softly, "See ya, Molly."

She turned, slammed the door, and ran for her car.
I stood there, stunned, my heart pounding. *What story? What had she uncovered?*

The following morning, I poured coffee with trembling hands and opened my laptop. And there it was. Marcy's article splashed across rival platforms. The headlines were divisive. Explosive. Dangerous.

Columnist Marcy Renaldi Exposes Joel Conway's Role in Alleged FBI Cover-Up

By *Marcy Renaldi, Senior Political Columnist*

Sources close to the National Intelligence Committee now suggest that Joel Conway, former adviser to an undisclosed member of a former president's cabinet, may be an active participant in a growing FBI cover-up.

Conway, who holds unique knowledge of internal intelligence briefings and inter-agency communications, has issued what some are calling a brazen demand: In a formal letter to the committee, he requested a complete list of topics to be discussed, copies of all documents to be referenced, and the constitutional and legal rationale behind each line of inquiry *before* he would agree to testify.

These preconditions are not those of a cooperative witness. Conway appears to be seeking information, not offering it. His maneuvering suggests an intent to obstruct, not assist, the committee's urgent investigation into potential abuses of power within federal agencies.

More concerning is Conway's refusal to comply with a legally issued subpoena. His silence is not only alarming—it may signal a broader refusal to testify among other insiders who could offer crucial testimony about the scope and sequence of decisions at the heart of this unfolding scandal.

Conway is one of the few civilians with direct access to key players and internal processes. His insight could prove pivotal, yet he remains unwilling to share it. The American public deserves transparency. If key figures like Joel Conway continue to dodge accountability, then the truth behind this alleged FBI cover-up may never come to light. And in that silence, the story dies.

Leaning back in my chair, I closed my laptop with a quiet click that sounded louder than it should have. The numb disbelief settled in like fog. I wanted answers—why Jason had been furious, what Marcy wasn't telling me. And what Joel and Ciara must be feeling... They were my friends. To see them dragged into this web of innuendos—exposed, implicated—must have been horrifying.

I turned toward the garden outside my window—my Rose Haven sanctuary. Sunlight filtered through the leaves, painting dappled shadows across the stone path. A soft breeze rustled the trees. The stillness of it all offered a fleeting moment of calm, as if the garden itself whispered, *hold steady*. I drew in a slow breath and dialed Ciara. She answered almost immediately, her voice steady—but fragile. A quiet strength barely hiding the fatigue underneath.

"Hi, Ciara. I just wanted to check in. Are you holding up okay?"

"Thanks, Molly," she said, exhaling softly. "I assume you saw Marcy's column."

"I did," I murmured, my heart tight. "I can't imagine what you and Jason are going through."

A pause. Then, the crackle of a police radio flared in the background. Her voice shifted—sharpened by resolve.

"I have to go. Kyle and I are heading out on a call. Don't worry, Molly. The truth will come out. We'll be okay."

"I'll hold that thought," I said quietly.

But the line had already gone dead. I sat in silence a moment longer, trying to anchor myself before I drifted too far into fear. There was work to do. Jason had a new assignment waiting. And if the newsroom were shifting as fast as I suspected, I'd need to meet him armored in clarity—and calm. I arrived at *The Times* with my head held high, but as I stepped inside, I froze. A newly installed metal detector stood between me and the front desk, flanked by two guards who didn't smile, didn't blink. Their eyes followed every movement, assessing a threat where none existed.

"Why the sudden security?" I asked, trying to sound casual.

There was no answer. They barely acknowledged my presence as I handed over my ID and stepped through the detector. The process was slow—intentionally slow. A thin sheen of sweat began forming at my neck's base.

"New protocols," one guard said flatly, waving me through.

I moved past them, unsettled. The newsroom, usually a bustle of greetings and caffeine chatter, felt tense and strained. No one looked up. No one smiled. Everyone was buried in their screens, fingers flying, eyes wide—an unsettling sight. I turned toward Jason's office and stopped cold. I saw him hunched at his desk through the window, his back stiff. In one hand, a bottle of Scotch—his favorite. In his other hand, a double shot glass was already half gone. He tossed it back with the practiced ease of someone who'd done it before. Jason

didn't drink before noon. Not once in all the years I'd known him. When he saw me, he jolted upright, shoved the bottle and glass into a drawer like a guilty teenager. I pretended not to notice. He looked pale. Edges frayed, as if something vital inside him had begun to splinter, quietly but irreversibly. I knocked softly and opened the door.

"Morning, Jason."

No response. He didn't look at me.

"I noticed the metal detectors. What's going on?"

Still nothing.

"Jason?" I said again, stepping closer. "Something's changed. Is this about Marcy's article? About Joel?"

Slowly, he raised his eyes to meet mine. What I saw in them sent a chill down my spine. Jason remained silent and expressionless as he handed me a manila envelope. Peering up at me over the rim of his glasses, he slurred,

"Molly, your ticket to New York is in there. I arranged first-class this time."

"Thanks, Jason. But... what's happening to everyone?"

He didn't answer—just waved me off. Saddened, I turned to leave. I heard the drawer slide open again behind me as I reached the door. Without turning back, I asked softly,

"Jason, are you alright?"

"Hurry, Molly," he mumbled. "Don't be late for your flight."

I closed the door gently behind me. Without glancing left or right, I walked straight out of that now-oppressive building, across the sidewalk, and into the sanctuary of my car. I drove toward Los Angeles Airport with silence curling around me like mist I couldn't outrun. At the gate, I boarded and was shown to my seat—a proper lie-flat pod with space to exhale and just enough elegance to pretend the world wasn't falling apart. My window seat had no neighbor. Champagne arrived with a five-star menu. I leaned back, watching the door close as if sealing off the weight of the city behind me. For a few hours, the darkness couldn't touch me.

We landed at JFK, and I caught a cab to Damrosch Park at Lincoln Center—home to the Metropolitan Opera and the American Ballet Theatre, its grandeur unmatched. That day, it belonged to fashion. The biggest names were there— Versace, Chanel, Louis Vuitton, Valentino—and dozens more lit the runway with brilliance. Covering Fashion Week was a rare joy in my job, and the view was flawless from my seat in the press section—I captured every shimmering moment. Even though the dream of owning one of those designs faded quickly, the beauty lingered long after the last model stepped offstage.

That night, I caught the final flight back to LAX. It was another first-class experience—another fleeting return to calm. The in-flight dinner was exquisite, and the film was one I'd long meant to see. For once, the rhythm of travel felt like luxury, not survival. When the movie ended, I sighed, reluctant to let go of the reverie. I reviewed and submitted my fashion column for tomorrow's edition, triple-checking every name, quote, and impression.

The pilot's voice came over the intercom: *"We'll be landing in Los Angeles in twenty minutes."* I knew what waited for me: the stories, the secrets, the storm. But for now, I closed my eyes, savored the last sip of champagne, and let the glow of fashion's magic shield me just a little longer. Because the intrigue—still tangled and unfinished—was waiting just beyond the runway.

No Promises

Getting a late start the following morning, I grabbed the scatter of mail off the entryway floor, dropped it on the side table without a glance, and bolted for the precinct. As I entered Detective Johnson's office, my mind was already replaying what I expected to hear. It was official, Detective Johnson had closed Daniel's case. His voice, void of emotion, carried the usual bureaucratic caveat. *"With time, the offender may*

still be brought to justice." It felt like a death knell to hope. I pressed for a copy of the transcripts. He refused.

"Sorry, Mrs. Cleary," he said, reaching for the next file on his desk.

I was politely dismissed. Frustrated, I left the office— only to find Ciara, out of uniform, waiting in the parking lot. Her expression was tight, arms folded—until she saw me.

"They're calling it a 'mandatory vacation,'" she said, forcing a tired smile. "All because of Joel."

She hugged me quickly and leaned in.

"Can I stop by your place in thirty minutes?"

"Of course."

Before I could ask anything more, she was gone. Turning back toward my car, I spotted Detective Johnson near the rear entrance. He stood frightfully still, staring directly at me. I forced a smile and said,

"Did you change your mind about the transcripts?"

His glare didn't waver.

"Goodbye, Mrs. Cleary," he growled, then stood his ground as I pulled away. A chill ran down my spine. Nearing home, something else caught my attention—a grey sedan parked across from my house. The man inside wore dark glasses despite the overcast sky. Under normal circumstances, I wouldn't have given him a second thought. But after Johnson's hostility and Ciara's cryptic request, it felt... deliberate. I passed the car slowly, noting the license plate. Instead of stopping, I drove around the block to catch Ciara before she got home. Thankfully, we were neighbors by less than a block. I flagged her down, handed her the plate number, and we agreed to return to our homes and speak later. Minutes after the car drove off, she called.

"I ran the plate," Ciara said. "He's one of the detectives from the precinct." She sighed. "I should've known. They're watching me—probably watching you too. I don't know how deep this goes, Molly—but we need to be careful. About everything."

"You're right," I said. "But I'm not going to let intimidation run my life. I haven't done anything wrong. Starting now, I'm done living like a prisoner."

"I'm trying to do the same, Molly. But I can't shake this fear—if Joel goes down, I may never work again. Law enforcement is all I've ever wanted. And I'm good at it."

"You are," I said firmly. "One of the best. And if the worst happens…" I hesitated, then shared Claire's words, which she told me once. *If the worst happens, trust that God has something better. Everything will work out to improve your life.*

Ciara let out a quiet laugh.

"I'm not religious like you, Molly."

"I'm not religious, either," I said gently. "But I've learned—especially through Claire—that there's more to this life than we see. It's something you have to experience. It's lovely, you'll see."

She paused, then whispered,

"I'll think about it. I hope you're right. This past year's been the hardest of my life."

Then, realizing what she'd said, she gasped.

"Oh, Molly… I'm sorry. I can't believe I just said that, after all you've been through."

"It's okay," Ciara. "Truly. The beginning of a major change is often the most challenging part. You and Joel will get through this—keep your trust in the right place."

"Thanks, Molly," she said, her voice softening. "Talk later?"

"Talk later," I promised. "Bye, Ciara."

I grabbed the mail from the entry table just as the phone rang.

"Hello?" I answered, still sorting through envelopes.

"Molly, it's David Donegal," came the smooth voice, urgent but composed. "Forgive the interruption. I was concerned you hadn't answered my letter."

I forced a neutral tone. "I've just returned and only now picked up the mail."

At the bottom of the stack, there it was—his letter.

"Well," he continued, "can I take you to lunch? You can fill me in on Daniel's case. The Polo Lounge, perhaps? I remember you liked it. I could pick you up in an hour."

I hesitated, annoyed by the ambush, and he sounded different. "I'll meet you there," I said, cutting the call with clipped courtesy.

Driving through Laurel Canyon, I wondered why I continued to entertain David Donegal. Loyalty to Claire and Steven? Or something more challenging to name? I told myself it was just lunch, the sunshine, and the Polo Lounge. But something tugged at me—his accent. Once unmistakably Scottish, or a mixture, now oddly softened. Almost polished. When I stepped into the Polo Lounge's cool air and lush decor cocoon, I instantly spotted him—tall, immaculately dressed, deep in effortless conversation with the waiter. He looked like he belonged in every room he entered. He turned, saw me, and his face lit up. Arms outstretched for a hug. I extended my hand instead.

"Hello, David. Welcome to my neighborhood. How was your flight?"

He momentarily paused, caught off guard, but recovered graciously as he pulled out my chair. The scent of his cologne was subtle, expensive, and familiar.

"Uneventful," he said. "I'm here on business with the British Consulate—but I hoped I might be of help in Daniel's case while I'm in town."

We ordered. The chatter drifted easily between Rose Haven and L.A., goats and traffic, until I finally said what had been bothering me.

"Your accent. It's changed. I remember it being... stronger."

His eyes met mine with surprising vulnerability.

"I'm trying to uncover the truth about my past, Molly—my lineage. There's a possibility I'm British—at least

partially. Speaking more refined English, I've found, makes it easier to get answers. People take me more seriously."

His voice had softened. The sharp edges dulled. And I saw a gentleness in him for the first time. Claire's words floated back to me, an echo of something long buried: *Don't let his gruff mannerisms fool you. He has a good heart, although it has been badly damaged. And he's brilliant—more than he lets on.*

I leaned forward. "So, you're not Irish?"

"I am that and Scottish. But there's more. I've traced threads that might connect me to Britain. Hence the Consulate meetings."

Then, pivoting seamlessly, he asked. "How's Daniel's case progressing?"

I'd planned a polite escape after dessert. Instead, I found myself lingering, sharing everything with him. The lack of progress. The closed files. And finally, the locket. David didn't interrupt. He didn't offer hollow encouragement or sweeping theories. He listened—really listened. And when he spoke, it was only to ask thoughtful, relevant questions.

"I have a few contacts here," he said carefully. "Would you mind if I asked around?"

I nodded. "Just be discreet."

When we stood to leave, he extended his hand. I took it. His grip was warm, steady—his hand large enough to eclipse mine completely. For a beat too long, we held on. My heart gave an involuntary thump. I eased my hand away, smiled, and thanked him. We parted without a promise. And yet, an unseen current lingered.

A Light in the Orchard

As I left the Polo Lounge, sunlight danced through the palms, but my thoughts clung to shadows. Something about David lingered, the quiet strength in his questions, the way he listened without trying to fix or twist. I had barely turned onto

Sunset Boulevard when my phone rang with a call from Ciara. Her voice was tight, controlled, but I knew that tone.

"They've scheduled the trial," she said. "Opening arguments start tomorrow."

And just like that, the momentary calm shattered. I paused to catch my breath, then answered,

"I'll be there, Ciara."

The following day, fear and determination etched deep lines into Joel and Ciara's faces as they entered the courtroom. They walked like people holding back a tide, aware that everything—reputation, livelihood, even freedom—was on the line. The charges against Joel were no longer whispers. They stood fully exposed in the stark light of the courtroom, and every day, the prosecution built its case like a fortress of steel, stacking damning evidence piece by piece, blow by blow. Joel's suspension-with-pay was a footnote now; the media had sunk their teeth into the story, and they weren't letting go.

Yet Ciara never faltered. She sat beside her husband, spine straight, expression unreadable. But I knew her. I saw the strain in her jaw, the sleeplessness in her eyes. She believed in Joel—still. And I believed in her. But I couldn't silence the plaguing doubt. What if Daniel had been caught in the same net of corruption now threatening to devour Joel? Seven days in, the media circus swelled into a national spectacle. Headlines screamed about corruption in the LAPD, and whispers turned into accusations. Friends—trusted ones—warned me to walk away.

"Cut ties. It's the smart thing," they urged.

But abandoning Ciara? That wasn't smart. That was betrayal. I met her in secret. We talked in hushed tones over coffee and met in the upper levels of empty parking garages, our voices swallowed by the open night air and the echo of our footsteps. Each time, our bond deepened—two women clinging to truth in a world spinning off its axis. Then the jury returned. The courtroom held its breath. The word fell like a hammer.

"Guilty."

But only on two counts of perjury. Relief flooded Ciara's face, tears spilling freely. Yet a nagging question prevailed. What about the espionage charges? Joel's lawyer explained it quickly: the lies stuck, but the government hadn't met the burden of proof for espionage. A fine was issued. Prison was off the table, for now. After the verdict, Ciara disappeared. No one knew where she'd gone. Still, the reprieve was fleeting. Days later, Jason was summoned to testify before the Senate Select Committee on Intelligence. A retired CIA operative, Janet Lane, had come forward with explosive claims implicating Joel and others in a tangled web of espionage. Jason denied everything. But the FBI didn't stop. They dug deeper into Joel, Jason, the department, and Chief Harold Bates. That's when things twisted further.

While picking up a new assignment at *The Times*, I stumbled into a maze of classified threads. First, I learned that Jason's trusted source had been retroactively reclassified as an espionage conduit. Second, an overlooked legacy emerged: Bates' grandfather, a well-known communist sympathizer, had a profound influence on Harold in his youth. Though never a card-carrying member, Bates had publicly praised what he called "societal duty," quoting—unknowingly or not—phrases pulled straight from the "Twelve Rules of the Builder of Communism." Most heard civic encouragement. But hidden within Daniel's notes were warning bells. Especially the phrase: "Those who don't work, don't eat." Bates had said it once in a televised interview. Few noticed. But someone at the FBI had.

The deeper I looked, the more it seemed Bates wasn't just powerful—he was quietly omniscient. He possessed cutting-edge tech, embedded in the early stages of the National Crime Information Center (NCIC). Not merely accessing data, but weaving it together with uncanny precision. Every phone call, every license plate, every thread of digital noise—he filtered it, rearranged it, built dossiers others couldn't imagine. And in that quiet mastery, he ruled. I was assured the evidence

would reach the judge, so the next morning, I made my way to Jason's office. It looked like a paper storm had hit. But Jason was nowhere. His assistant met me in the hallway, breathless, eyes wide.

"Jason collapsed. Chest pains. He's at Cedars Hospital."

I stood frozen. The timing was too perfect. Too clean.

Weeks passed. Jason survived, but barely. When he returned, the FBI pounced again, spurred by Janet Lane's persistence and the growing political firestorm. At first, Jason deflected. But under mounting pressure, he cracked. Piece by piece, he began to reveal more of himself. A microfilm. A package. Hidden on his farm. Documents with Joel's handwriting. State Department material. Espionage. Confirmed. The fallout was seismic. Joel and Ciara's world imploded. She left, retreating to her parents' home in the Midwest. Joel, ever the optimist, still chased job leads—naively thinking he could rebuild.

The committee remained divided. Accusations circled. Truth blurred. Jason retired quietly, his health deteriorating. Chief Bates? Untouched. Untouchable. As the headlines faded and the chaos quieted, I stood among the wreckage. Relationships shattered. Reputations scorched. And in the silence, one question echoed louder than ever: *What truly happened to Daniel?* Was his death part of this web of deceit? The locket. The secrecy. The surveillance. I didn't have answers. I wondered if it's time to go back to the one place untouched by the lies—Rose Haven.

The chaos at *The Times* didn't end with the scandal—it deepened. As readership plummeted and credibility eroded, the newspaper packed up its battered legacy and relocated its headquarters to El Segundo, near the Los Angeles International Airport. The move wasn't just geographic. Ownership changed hands, too. The new figure at the helm was a man like no other—Mr. Akihito Takahashi. Renowned American transplant surgeon, billionaire bioscientist, media

mogul, and creator of a revolutionary cancer drug that has saved countless lives. His achievements stretched beyond imagination, and standing in the shadow of his legacy, I felt a strange mix of awe and apprehension.

With my latest assignment filed, I requested a meeting. Part of me hoped he might offer insights into Daniel's death, and another part needed to know where I stood. Despite the hammering of construction outside, Takahashi's makeshift office radiated calm. He greeted me with a serene smile and poured tea with ritualistic grace. At first, the conversation was gentle—he praised my contributions to the fashion section, his voice smooth and measured. But when I carefully broached Daniel's death, his expression remained unchanged—his smile locked in place—but his eyes grew remote, unreachable. And then, almost casually, he delivered the real blow: sweeping changes were coming. My future at *The Times* was... uncertain. The words hit like a sudden pressure drop. I set my teacup down, willing my voice to stay steady.

"Should I be looking for another job?"

Takahashi's response was maddeningly diplomatic: the decision, he said, was mine. I left his office with the distinct feeling I'd been politely dismissed. As I glanced back through the glass wall, he sat motionless behind his desk, still smiling— but there was something deeply unsettling about it—an unspoken menace that hung in the air. Power. Threat. Both.

Outside, the late afternoon heat pressed down as I fumbled for my keys, my mind racing with questions and worst-case scenarios. Everything familiar was slipping away— *The Times*, Daniel's legacy, even my sense of safety. The phone rang, dragging me out of my spiral. David's name flashed.

"Lunch?" His brogue wrapped around the word, as familiar as it was reassuring.

"Yes." The answer tumbled out before I could second-guess.

"Aye! I dinnae expect such a quick answer," he said with a low laugh.

Lunch in the sunshine sounded like an escape hatch I couldn't refuse. When I arrived, I found David already waiting inside the restaurant, tucked behind a lush hedge of flowering plants where the soft rush of a fountain muted the world beyond. The setting was pure tranquility—so opposite the storm raging inside me that I almost believed, for a heartbeat, that I could breathe again. Over chilled champagne, we traded stories—mine cautious, his laced with sharper edges.

"Ya could be under investigation, Molly girl. Guilt by association, aye? Joel and Ciara's mess is not as far from ya as ya'd like to think."

The words landed like cold water on my skin. Maybe that was why Takahashi had been so vague. Perhaps my name was already tainted by whispers. David leaned in, trying to lighten the mood.

"I'll be leavin' in a couple of days. But before I go, I'd like a wee bit o' history. Will ya be meh tour guide, lass? Lost in thought, it took me a second to register the question.

Molly, are ya dreamin', girl?" he teased, laughing.

"Oh—sorry, David. What did you ask?"

He smiled broadly. "Will ya show me 'round a bit before I go?"

A small smile tugged at the corners of my mouth. "It seems I have the time," I said dryly.

"Where would you like to go?"

He brightened. "The Port o' Los Angeles! Aye, I hear it's the number one container port in a' the States."

I shook my head, smiling. "It's true. I've lived next to the busiest port in the country—and never really seen it."

The irony made me laugh. Like the native New Yorkers I once met who had never set foot inside the Empire State Building—so close to something remarkable, yet blind to it. Yet here I was—living beside the busiest seaport in the Western Hemisphere—having never thought about it. For the next two days, I saw Los Angeles through the eyes of a man fascinated by everything. David's wonder was infectious. His

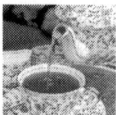

bold curiosity turned everyday places into adventures, and for the first time in what felt like forever, I caught glimpses of the city's magic again.

Two fun-filled days passed in a blink, leaving me refreshed—and unexpectedly sad to see them end. I drove David to the airport, said goodbye with a lingering wave, and promised myself I would return to Rose Haven soon. On the drive home, loneliness crept in like a slow tide. Daniel had always been my home. How could any relationship, any future, ever measure against that? But then, unbidden, one of Daniel's favorite phrases surfaced, *"One step at a time, sweetheart."*

The next morning, without an assignment to distract me, I faced a new and deeply personal challenge: To say goodbye to my dearest friend and husband—and to take one more step toward the truth about his death. I stood before Daniel's closet, its door half-open like an old wound. His neatly packed boxes of clothes and shoes waited silently, untouched memorials of a life that now felt impossibly far away. My breath caught. The urge to slam the door shut and flee almost overtook me. I gripped the doorframe, my fingers digging into the wood.

"God," I whispered, my voice raw and shaking, "help me to keep going. Show me the way."

A soft wave of courage—warm, almost tangible—settled over me. With trembling hands, I reached for a small wooden box tucked on the top shelf. Daniel had built it as a Boy Scout, carefully crafting each joint and sanding each corner smooth with his young hands. Cradling it against my chest, I opened the lid. Inside lay his wedding ring and his police commendations—quiet testaments to the man I had loved so fiercely. Later, I would carefully place them on the desk in his office—a shrine not of grief but of honor.

With a heavy heart, I cleared the closet, carrying the remaining boxes to my car. I drove to a local mission, where I knew Daniel's belongings would be put to good use. As I handed them over, I felt the sting of finality—and a fragile

sense of peace. I was still standing. And somehow, I knew—
this was only the beginning.

Intriguing Interruptions

Pleased with my small victories, I celebrated with a
special dinner and a cozy movie night on the couch. It wasn't
my favorite kind of celebration, but for now, it was enough.
Halfway through my meal, my phone rang.

"Hi, Molly, it's Marcy. Can you talk?" Her voice was
muffled, tense. I muted the TV instantly.

"Sure, Marcy. Are you okay? Still at the Times?"

"I'm stressed—and yes, still there!" She took a shaky
breath. "Molly, I need to see you. In person. Are you busy?"

"No… not really."

"I'm sorry for dropping this on you, but it's
important."

"Of course. Come over."

"I'll be there in twenty minutes."

I tried to resume the movie, but unease crept in,
making the room feel smaller. When the knock finally came, I
peeked through the window. Marcy stood on the porch,
clutching a bottle of wine, her nerves practically visible. She
rushed inside the moment I opened the door. We poured two
glasses of wine and settled on the couch. I tried to keep my
voice casual.

"So, Marcy—what's going on?"

There was a long, unsettling pause. Then, without a
word, she drained her entire glass in one gulp, refilled it, and
leaned back, breathing heavily.

"Molly, something's wrong. I've been hitting walls for
months. Every time I think I'm close to the truth, it vanishes.
Like quicksilver—you think you've caught it, but it slips away."

She glanced at me, searching, and asked, "Have you
had any new assignments?"

I hesitated. Then I told her about my meeting with Takahashi and how I felt that my job was hanging by a thread. Her expression darkened.

"Yes, Mr. Takahashi is all smiles on the surface. But underneath? He's controlling everything."

I leaned forward. "What do you mean?"

"He edits my crime pieces. Just enough to sound like me—but critical pieces always disappear."

Her voice dropped lower. "And I've been warned: no interviews with Joel or Ciara. Not even off the record."

I sat back, stunned.

"And it's not just at work." Marcy continued, pacing the living room with her wineglass. "Dom's acting strange, too, staying out late. Moody. I thought—maybe an affair." She stopped, turned to me, eyes wide.

"I followed him, Molly. He was meeting with Police Chief Bates."

I sat bolt upright. "Bates? I didn't know they even knew each other."

"I didn't either," she said grimly. "When I confronted him, carefully, he claimed he was handling paperwork for the new Beverly Hills office."

"Beverly Hills has a separate police chief," I said quietly. Marcy froze, realization dawning.

"Oh my God. You're right."

"Let's not jump to conclusions," I said, though my stomach twisted. "But we shouldn't meet here anymore. There's a drive-through burger place on Venice Boulevard. Always packed. Noon meetings. Safe, public."

Marcy nodded, still visibly rattled.

"This feels bigger than Los Angeles," she whispered. "It feels like... Washington. Or London."

The thought jolted me, and an idea clicked into place.

"I just watched a movie about MI6 tradecraft," I said, half-laughing, half-serious. "There's a mailbox on Los Angeles Boulevard that we both pass. If you need to meet, pretend to

mail something, and mark a chalk line on the west side of the box. If I can meet, I'll erase your mark and leave one on the east side. We'll meet at the burger place. Noon."

Marcy's laugh was brittle but real. "It'd be funny if I weren't terrified. Okay. I'll buy chalk."

We shared a shaky laugh. I asked if she was okay to drive. When she hesitated, I brewed a strong double espresso. She downed it like medicine, then left, the night swallowing her up. For the next few days, I threw myself into the joys of gardening, trying to ground myself in something real—soil, air, sunlight. But even as I worked, my mind sifted through conversations, half-truths, and warnings. And Daniel's case loomed heavier than ever. When I couldn't take the uncertainty any longer, my next move was to confront Detective Johnson directly. Without an appointment, I drove to the precinct. This time, the familiar walls brought a strange comfort—until I heard the news. Detective Johnson was gone; he had been transferred to New York, where he now headed the NYPD's Special Operations. It felt like another deliberate wall sliding into place, blocking me. But then the desk sergeant—an old friend—appeared with a grin.

"Don't worry, Molly. We've got someone new handling Johnson's files—Detective Tulsi Blair."

He scheduled a meeting that afternoon, and with unexpected time to kill, I swung by *The Times* hoping for a new assignment. Mr. Takahashi wasn't there. Instead, a young woman, bright and professional, stepped forward.

"Hi, Mrs. Cleary. I'm Janet, Mr. Takahashi's assistant. I'm sure it was just an oversight, but there's a fashion show tonight at the Lighthouse Artspace. The main gallery."

Grateful for the normalcy, I smiled.

"Thank you, Janet. I'll cover it."

Armed with coffee and a new assignment, I crossed town for my meeting with Detective Blair. She was everything Johnson wasn't—sharp, dynamic, disarmingly real. As I explained Daniel's case, she listened intently, took careful

132

notes, and asked pointed questions. Her presence felt like the first breath of fresh air after months underground. She didn't promise miracles. But as we shook hands, she offered something rarer.

"I'll call if there's anything to report."

I walked away feeling a fragile flicker of hope. I had no idea I would be entering a dark valley.

Wine, Warning, and the Woman from Saks

Lines of keenly motivated guests, brimming with anticipation, stretched down the glitzy sidewalk of Sunset Boulevard outside the Lighthouse ArtSpace. I was back in my element—camera in hand, surrounded by lights, elegance, and purpose. The fashion show was dazzling, the most extravagant I'd seen in a while, and I was pleased to have captured it all. A familiar voice cut through the crowd as I gathered my things to leave.

"Molly!"

I turned—and there she was. Mrs. Bates. I crossed over quickly.

"Mrs. Bates—hello! I didn't expect to see you here."

She smiled warmly.

"Hi, Molly. Please—call me Sharon. A friend invited me. She's a buyer for Saks."

"It's good to see you," I said genuinely. "How are you?"

"Well enough. And you?"

"I'm doing surprisingly well. The Times just moved—new location, new ownership."

"Yes," she said lightly. "Harry mentioned it."

"Do you know Mr. Takahashi?" I asked.

"No, but from what I hear, he's brilliant."

"Exceedingly," I agreed. "I'm looking forward to working with him."

"Oh, you're still with the Times?" she asked, tilting her head.

"Yes. Covering this show is my assignment tonight. But... did you think I'd left?"

"Somehow, I had the impression there was a staff turnover," she said. She leaned in slightly, her voice warm. "But I'm glad you're still writing the column. Truly, Molly, your interviews and advice have kept me in fashion longer than I care to admit."

Before I could respond, a tall, impeccably dressed woman approached.

"Molly, meet Dina MacFarland," Sharon said brightly. "Dina's the buyer for Saks. Dina, this is Molly Cleary, fashion columnist for the Times."

Dina looked like she had just stepped off the runway herself—tall, striking, the effortless grace of someone born to the world of high fashion. Our conversation was light, easy—until an odd, weighted pause passed between Sharon and Dina. Sensing my cue to leave, I gathered my things. But unexpectedly, Sharon caught my arm.

"Would you join us for coffee?"

Surprised, but intrigued, I agreed.

Coffee became wine, and wine became dinner. The night unfolded with surprising intimacy. I learned Sharon and Dina had been childhood friends, raised in Denver, their family's inseparable. It sounded idyllic. However, as the evening wore on, the warmth began to fade. I watched Sharon silently down the last of her wine, her hands trembling slightly. Tears welled in her eyes.

"Are you, all right?" I asked gently.

"No," she whispered.

Dina, visibly uneasy, quickly leaned in.

"Molly—you're a reporter. But I hope... your friendship comes before the story."

My heart tightened.

"I'd like to think so. But what's this about?"

134

There was a heavy pause. Then Dina nodded at Sharon.

"It's time."

Sharon wiped at her eyes and said, almost inaudibly,

"I'm considering a divorce. Harry's... changed. For two years now, life's been dark. The house feels... wrong, as if someone else is there. I thought I was losing my mind. But I'm not. Something is strangely frightening."

Her words cut deep. Yet, I wasn't shocked. There had always been something unsettling about Chief Bates. But hearing it from his wife gave it chilling weight. I reached out, squeezing her hand.

"I'm so sorry, Sharon. Tell me how I can help."

But almost instantly, Sharon withdrew, retreating behind a wall I couldn't scale. Dina flashed a polite, brittle smile, trying to mask the fear swirling between them. The tension thickened. It was time to go. I reached for my wallet, but Dina waved me off.

"No. I've got this. Don't worry about Sharon—I'm taking her home with me. We'll figure it out."

Sharon's fog lifted for a moment.

"I'm sorry, Molly. For unloading."

"It's okay," I said softly. "Call me if you need anything."

I hugged her tightly and left.

Outside, the night air was cool against my face. But Sharon's words clung to me like bad perfume. The idea of Chief Bates—a man with that much power—being *off-center* was terrifying. I understood exactly what she meant by *something dark*. But I couldn't let myself spiral. I had work to do. I touched the potted bush at my doorstep—a silly ritual, a whispered prayer. *"I leave all my worries on you,"* I murmured. I laughed under my breath, stepped inside, and finished my column—filing it just in time for the morning edition. But even as I hit send, I knew one thing with aching certainty: Sharon's words weren't just about fear—they were about warning. And

then, with sickening awareness, I realized Chief Bates might only be the beginning.

7

Beneath the Surface

The danger wasn't coming. It was already here, hiding behind smiles, behind power, behind people I once trusted. I just hadn't seen its face yet. Beneath the surface, the fault lines had already begun to shift, and before I could catch my breath, the week slipped by in a strange blur. My fashion column's readership soared, yet no word came from Mr. Takahashi about future assignments. I worked harder, smiled wider—but unease clung to me like a second skin. Then, out of nowhere, a letter arrived from Ciara. She was holed up at a cabin in Big Bear with Joel. Her message was brief and unsettling. Could I meet her there? A specific time. No explanations.

With no pressing deadlines at the Times, I packed a bag and left. The drive up the mountain felt like stepping out of one life and into another. Crisp pine air flooded the car as I wound through dense forests, the world narrowing to a single, winding road. The clean scent of earth and wood chased the city from my mind. It was too beautiful to rush. I pulled over, letting the quiet seep into my bones. That's when I saw her— a deer stepping cautiously from the trees, a fawn pressed to her side. They crossed the road, disappearing into the forest like a whispered secret. Something about it—the fragility, the fleetingness—gripped my heart.

I sat for a moment longer, breathing in the moment. Then, refreshed but wary, I continued up the mountain. Soon, I found the private road leading to the hidden retreat. The A-frame cabin appeared like a dream, perched above the shimmering lake, dappled in late afternoon light. For a heartbeat, everything seemed peaceful. Then the garage door rattled open, and Joel frantically waved me in. A chill raced up my spine. Still, I obeyed, pulling into the garage as the door slammed shut behind me. Joel's face was pale, drawn tight with fear. He motioned me forward, his hands shaking.

"Molly—thank God. I'm at my wits' end. The media—they're relentless. They twist everything."

His voice broke into raw, stuttering bursts, the panic leaking out at the edges. He told me how he and Ciara asked his mother to move into the guesthouse, how even grocery runs had become risks. They were barely holding on. I placed a hand on his arm, steadying him—and myself.

"Joel, you don't have to explain. I'm here."

His gratitude was almost painful to watch.

"Just seeing you helps more than you know."

He pushed open the French doors, revealing a path winding through towering pines.

"Ciara's waiting for you. Down at the boathouse."

I followed the path, each step carrying me deeper into their hidden world. Inside the boathouse, the air was heavy with the scent of pine, lake water, and spearmint tea. Ciara handed me a steaming cup, her hands trembling slightly. I told her everything—about the fashion show, the unexpected meeting with Sharon and Dina, and Sharon's chilling confession. Ciara's eyes widened with every word. I leaned in, anxiety prickling.

"What are you going to do, Ciara?"

She set her cup down with a sharp clink.

"I'm going back," she said, her voice firm—but the slight tremor betrayed her fear.

"Joel thinks it's too dangerous, given his history with Bates. But I need to help. Especially for Daniel."

I gripped my teacup tightly as her following words cut the air.

"In case something happens to me, Molly, stay out of it. I need you to promise. Don't get involved!"

A familiar shiver ran through me—I couldn't respond. Shattered, I turned toward the window, and the lake shimmered under the setting sun, but the beauty suddenly felt like a mirage.

"Do you still think this goes all the way to Washington?" I asked, my voice raw.

"More than ever. Blair's risking her life to investigate Bates. She's not sure we can prove anything—but she's trying."

I couldn't speak. The pressure inside me tightened until my head throbbed. Wordless, staring at the tranquil water, pretending the world was still safe. Behind me, Ciara's voice broke softly.

"Molly, I'm only telling you this to protect you."

I nodded without turning.

"I understand."

Still facing the lake, I told her about Daniel's notes. The underlined names. The initials GRB. The locket I found in the garden—the feeling that someone had been watching us even then. When I finally turned to face her, Ciara's face was pale, her expression drawn.

"Did you ever report it to the police?" she asked quietly.

I shook my head. "Daniel was careful... cautious. He didn't trust anyone."

Ciara pressed her fingers to her temples, thinking fast.

"Let me tell Detective Blair. She needs to know about Hampton Fife—and GRB."

Reluctantly, I agreed. Relief mixed with fear inside me. At least now, the right people were involved. Ciara's brow furrowed deeper.

"Hampton Fife... the name sounds familiar."

She went still, the color draining from her face.

"Is it a person?" I asked sharply.

"I don't think so," she said, voice brittle. "But I need to be sure."

She hesitated, then added urgently,

"Molly—don't share this with anyone else."

I promised, though a knot formed in my chest even as I spoke. Ciara glanced toward the door.

"Come on. I want to check something."

We returned to the house, the light dimming fast. Joel was slumped asleep in front of the television, the glow flickering across his strained face. Ciara motioned me into the study, moving quickly but quietly. She tried to open Joel's computer, but the password had been changed. Her face crumpled.

"Oh no, Molly," she whispered. "I think Hampton Fife is the name of an aeronautics firm Joel was working with... and GRB is the man in charge."

We stared at each other, a silent exchange of heartbreak and fear. Ciara's voice dropped to a near whisper, thick with sorrow.

"Let me take this to Blair. She'll know how to proceed."

She caught my hand, her grip fierce.

"Molly—promise me. Stay out of it. At least until we know more."

I nodded, anxiety rising.

"I promise. But let me know what you need when the time comes."

Ciara gave a small, broken smile. And in that moment, the fragile thread between truth and danger stretched thinner than ever before.

"I can't promise anything," Ciara said, her voice urgent. "But you'll be putting people's lives in danger if you act like you're solving the puzzle. Pretend you know nothing— even with Joel. Please, Molly."

"I will," I said quietly, the weight of her words pressing deeper.

She closed Joel's laptop with a sharp, deliberate click, sealing away secrets neither of us could yet name. We moved silently through the dimly lit garage. The air felt heavier here, colder, like a vault locking behind us. When we hugged goodbye, her arms were rigid, trembling. Her wide, worried eyes locked on mine even as she reached for the garage button.

"Molly," she whispered over the low hum of the rising door, "I'll find a way to contact you if I get conclusive information."

I nodded, my throat tight, as I backed out slowly. The garage door slid shut behind me with a finality that made my stomach churn. It felt like I had just left two prisoners behind. Their uncertain fates clung to the air, heavy and desperate. I drove down the mountain in a strange, detached haze. The ghostly and thick fog unfurled through the trees, blurring the lines between road and wilderness—and reality itself. When I saw a turnout ahead, I pulled over instinctively, desperate for air.

I stepped from the car into the brisk night, locking the door behind me. The cold bit at my cheeks, sharp and sobering. The forest loomed, dark and still—but somehow inviting. I wandered a few steps in, the towering pines closing around me, their earthy scent grounding me against the storm inside. Leaning against a massive tree, I closed my eyes. Somewhere far off, a bird called once, then silence. The soft rustling of needles overhead sounded almost like a whispered prayer. Images of Miss Marple floated through my mind—her quiet strength, her painful choices. She had stood at a train station, watching the love of her life board a war train, never to return. She had made the better choice—choosing justice, choosing honor—despite the heartbreak it left behind. Maybe it wasn't so different, I thought. Whether by war or by murder, loss carved the same deep scars.

And with every piece of evidence, with every whispered warning, I was more certain than ever: Daniel hadn't died by accident. He had been murdered. The fog in my mind cleared. Ciara's warning sharpened to a single, burning point of truth. With a deep, steadying breath, I pushed away from the tree. The road ahead was still shadowed and treacherous—but I wasn't turning back.

Into the Silence, Something Stirred

The weekend arrived—and with it, an unsettling emptiness. No assignments. No leads. Just silence and waiting—the cruelest kind of test. I drifted through the hours, restless and edgy. I combed through Daniel's last notes, scrubbed the house until it gleamed, and even tended the garden. I thought of Miss Marple—her quiet patience, her refusal to rush the truth. But patience was harder to summon when real lives, not fictional ones, were at stake. Ciara's. Joel's. And maybe my own. I wanted to act. To force the hand of fate, like Jesse Stone charging into danger without a second thought. But I wasn't Jesse Stone. And this wasn't a novel. With a reluctant sigh, I sank into Daniel's old armchair, embracing Miss Marple's path instead: Patience. Observation. Waiting for the cracks to show. Still, the tension gnawed at me, relentless. Maybe a quick escape to Rose Haven would clear my head. I toyed with the idea, but even that felt like running.

Exhausted by my spinning thoughts, I headed out for a decaf cappuccino, craving the familiar comfort of my favorite coffee shop. The familiar routine helped steady my nerves. But when I returned home and slipped back into Daniel's study, the weight of it all came crashing down again. I lowered myself into his chair, the leather cool against my back, and closed my eyes. I could almost feel him for a moment—his steady presence, arms around me, the quiet strength that had always anchored me. A faint trace of his aftershave lingered in the air. Tears blurred my vision. It was impossible—but it was real. I stayed still, breathing it in, letting his visceral presence guide me. When I opened my eyes, an interesting clarity had settled over me. If I couldn't act yet, then I could dig.

My thoughts turned to Marcy and Dominic—their connection in Washington, their sudden silence. Marcy's White House credentials. Dominic's shadowy past. Whispers I had once dismissed now clawed at the edge of my mind. Driven by

instinct, I pulled Daniel's laptop closer and began to dig. Hours slipped away as I sifted through public records, news archives, and scattered reports. The deeper I searched, the heavier the unease grew. The Renaldi name wasn't clean. The stories were vague, buried under polite headlines and forgotten scandals. But when I finally unearthed a background check on Dominic, my heart skipped a beat. The rumors weren't just rumors. The Renaldi family had ties to the mafia. And suddenly, the danger surrounding us felt closer than ever.

As I leaned closer, absorbed in the implications, the screen suddenly blinked—and went black. I froze. The room around me seemed to contract, the silence loud in my ears. A cold prickle crept over me. Was someone watching? Was this a warning? Panic loomed, but it only fueled my determination. Marcy's role in White House security. Dominic's possible mafia connections. The threads were beginning to weave into something dark—and dangerously real. But fatigue was setting in, heavy and insistent, clouding my thoughts. Reluctantly, I shut everything down and locked the front door. But some doors, once opened, don't close again—and I feared I'd just stepped through one.

The Phone, the Poem, and the Princes

The following morning, a small and nondescript package waited outside, hidden behind the flower pot. I opened it carefully, finding a simple, generic mobile phone. And a note: *Call me on your gift phone only. Claire.* The air thickened, wrapping around me like a noose. Last night's strange computer blackout flashed back in vivid detail. Now, a burner phone sat in my palm, heavy with implications. The shadows in the room seemed darker, and the air grew thicker still. For a fleeting second, it felt like I had stumbled into the pages of an Agatha Christie novel—except this time, I wasn't a reader. I was living it. I punched in the number with trembling fingers.

"Hi, Claire. I received your package, and I'm calling as instructed," I said, forcing a light tone. Laughing nervously, I added, "What's this all about?"

Claire's voice was steady but low.

"Hi, Molly. David sent that phone—it can't be tapped or tracked. He stressed that what he's uncovered needs to stay confidential for now."

I straightened, my heart hammering against my ribs. Claire hesitated, then continued.

"He's found something. A possible political connection between England... and Daniel's death."

It confirmed that a door had indeed opened deep inside the world, and there was no closing it now. Any lingering trace of amusement vanished, replaced by a cold, bitter chill. I gripped the phone tightly, my voice dropping to a whisper, as if someone might be listening.

"I don't know what to say, Claire. Of course, I'll keep anything you tell me to myself, but... this seems particularly strange. I thought the phone was from you."

"Molly, this might seem frighteningly covert," Claire said carefully, "but David's uncovered something monumental. A King James poem. A letter. Other classified documents. It could change everything."

I froze, the room around me blurring again at the edges. David—the man I'd once brushed off as harmless noise—had stumbled onto something explosive. And somehow, I was now tangled in it. This wasn't just a warning. It was a summons. I wasn't standing in my house anymore. I was standing at the edge of a minefield—and every step forward could be my last. Claire solemnly began reading the poem:

Upon the passing of Edward the Fourth, whose life was measured from the year of grace 1442 to 1483. He left to this earth two sons: Edward, heir anointed, and Richard, his brother, young. In the year of our Lord 1483, Richard, Duke of Gloucester, did rise as Lord Protector of the realm. Yet ere the summer's end, the young princes were borne in secret to

the Tower, whence they were seen no more. Long hath the whisper endured that their deaths were by their uncle's command, and that their bones should be laid to rest within the hallowed stones of Westminster. Yet lo, through centuries veiled and voices silenced, new labors unearthed a hidden truth: The bones entombed were not of royal blood, nor the line of kings. And great tumult did stir the courts and corridors of power, for the shadows of treachery yet lingered, unbroken by time.

Claire finished reading the ancient poem, her voice trailing into a heavy, reverent silence. Then, after a breath, she continued, her tone whispered and grave.

"Hidden beneath that solemn stone," Claire said, "they found a sealed parchment, titled *All the King's Men*, and a letter—unsigned, but addressed to *'My Dearest Boudica.'*"

Her words seemed to echo in the stillness, weighted by centuries of secrecy. I sat frozen, each word sinking deeper, like stones dropped into dark water. Finally, I found my voice.

"Claire... It's almost too much to comprehend. What must David be feeling?"

Claire's reply was measured and steady, a lifeline in the rising tide of unease.

"Molly, I know it sounds impossible. But David is no ordinary investigator. He is precise, unyielding, and, above all else, true. This discovery—these words lost to time—they have shaken him to his very foundation. Yet he holds steady, like a surgeon wielding a blade. *All the King's Men*—and perhaps the letter—could tear down the accepted history of a crown."

As her words faded, a strange stillness encumbered me. The walls of my home office seemed to lean inward, the familiar comfort replaced by a shadow reaching back through the centuries. Claire spoke again, her voice soft but insistent.

"Molly, do you have time to hear the letter?"

The enormity of it all swam through my head. I clutched at the one small, familiar comfort I had left.

"Ah, yes, Claire," I said at last, forcing a wry smile into my voice.

"But I think I'll take a page from Miss Marple's book first — a hot cup of tea and a few slices of toast to fortify me."

Claire gave a soft chuckle—a brief island of warmth in the rising storm.

"Very wise," she said. "I'll begin when you're ready."

As I prepared myself. Claire's voice dipped lower, as if unveiling a relic too sacred for ordinary ears.

"This letter, Molly, was found tucked within the parchment. Written by a woman living in hiding, during a time of pestilence and famine."

She paused, and I heard the faint tremor in her breath.

"Let me summarize. David and Steven need my help. We'll read the rest when we're all together. It speaks of hope... and fear. Of a miraculous sign — a dove — and the arrival of a stranger bearing food. But more chilling than the story itself is what she reveals at the end: the princes were not slain. They were smuggled away, hidden under new identities. And one survived."

I clutched the phone ever-tightly, my pulse roaring in my ears. I hadn't told Claire about my encounter with a dove in the garden. And somehow, this wasn't the time.

"Claire," I said carefully, "do we know which brother survived?"

"No," she replied. "The letter doesn't name him. But David's uncovered more. He believes the boys were first sent to a builder in Colchester, then later separated. One was sent into Scotland."

The words hung heavy in the air between us. I sat motionless, the edges of my world tilting slightly. The information sounded more like a key than just history—a living entity stretching from a centuries-old betrayal straight into the heart of whatever David had uncovered—and whatever danger was rising now. My mind reeled, trying to stitch the pieces together, but the thread kept slipping from my grasp. This wasn't just about ancient kings anymore. This was about bloodlines. Secrets. Survival.

146

On the other end of the line, Claire hesitated, her breath audible through the crackling silence.

"David's still piecing things together. But someone—someone powerful doesn't want this truth to surface. And they'll do anything to keep it buried."

A shiver laced my spine. This wasn't just about the past—it was about the living, and what—or who—they would kill to protect.

"Claire," I said, pushing past the heaviness of the moment. "This is a once-in-a-lifetime finding! David must be thrilled. Do they know how old the writings from the woman are?"

"No, but they're looking into it. David's been unusually quiet—this discovery has shaken him more than we expected. And there's something else. He told Steven he mysteriously inherited a winery in southern France from someone he didn't know. He's gone for a week to learn more. What do you think, Molly?"

"It's incredible how life can change in an instant. One moment can ripple into a lifetime of consequences. Is there anything I can do?"

"Just keep his secret, Molly. Your friendship seems important to him. I'll let you know if I hear more. In the meantime, any updates on Daniel's case?"

"Only suspicions—still no evidence."

We said goodbye, promising to stay in touch. But as I hung up, a chill remained. The past wasn't finished with us yet. It was reaching out, pulling us deeper into its web of shadowy secrets.

Bloodlines and Backchannels

When Claire asked if I'd heard more about Daniel, that unsettling curiosity about Marcy and Dominic resurfaced—an alert flashed at my mind's edge. The investigation was calling again, an insistent whisper I couldn't ignore. Miss Marple knits when she needs to concentrate; I find clarity in a perfectly brewed cup of Darjeeling. As I inhaled the tea's warm, floral scent, the world outside fell away, leaving only the sharp focus of the moment.

Images flickered: my computer screen shutting down mid-investigation, Marcy's odd behavior over lunch at Ivy at the Shore. Her casual phone call afterward—barely noticeable then—now blazed in my memory like a beacon slicing through fog. She dialed a number and said, "Okay," and minutes later, our cab arrived as if summoned. At the time, I'd been too dazed to question it. Now, the synchronicity was suffocating. What had I revealed to Marcy without realizing it? Had she spun just enough truth to hide her involvement?

Pulse quickening, I reached for my burner phone and called Ciara. We arranged to meet at a secluded spot a mile from the base of Big Bear Mountain. In the crisp air, I laid out everything—the glitches, the doubts, the fears I couldn't shake. Ciara listened, her brow knitting tighter with each word.

"Much of Dominic's information has been scrubbed," she said, her voice low with frustration. "But old paper files might still exist," Ciara said. "I'll reach out to Detective Blair and get back to you."

Later that week, we met for lunch. Ciara's findings sounded straight out of a noir gangster film. She leaned closer, her voice low, urgent.

"Dominic's father—Dominic Castellano Senior—worked for Aniello Dellacroce, the Gambino underboss in Queens, New York," she said. "A young John Gotti entered the picture shortly after. Gotti rose fast, but paranoia rose faster. He believed Castellano Senior was a threat. So he

ordered his murder." Ciara's voice softened. "Eva Castellano was home that night, waiting to share joyous news: she was pregnant. Instead, she got a death notice. Terrified, she fled, carrying only a suitcase. She changed her identity and later married Joseph Renaldi, a respected accountant. Records show Dominic Renaldi was born soon after." Meeting my stunned gaze with a pause, she continued.

"Dominic Renaldi is the son of Dominic Castellano Sr. He grew up clean, with top grades and no criminal record. Moved to Brooklyn at twenty-one to work in real estate. Eva built a quiet life."

As she spoke, darker questions strained at my mind. Where had Dominic's rough edges come from? Did he know the truth about his bloodline? Had someone from the old world approached him? Or had Washington molded him into something else? When I first met Marcy and Dominic, they seemed warm and disarming. But now the cracks showed—and I wasn't sure if they had distanced themselves... or marked me. I shared my fears with Ciara, who nodded grimly, saying,

"I'll pass everything to Detective Blair. She has access to restricted files if organized crime is involved. But Molly..." she smiled wryly, "this case is like trying to catch a thousand cats. No promises."

We laughed, the tension breaking for a moment. Then, reality set back in—heavy, inescapable—as we parted ways.

8

Unimaginable Discovery

An empty month dragged by. The Times dangled assignments like bait, but nothing real materialized. With dread piercing my pride, I forced myself to resurrect an ancient resume, piecing it together like a stranger's obituary. Then Evie called. Detective Blair wanted to see me. Today. I was out the door in minutes.

The precinct walls were haunting, like a memory I wasn't sure I trusted anymore. Familiar faces lit up with recognition—smiles, greetings—but they only deepened the ache I couldn't name. When I reached Blair's office, she rose to greet me with professional warmth; the space behind her seemed somehow cleaner, sharper, and organized.

"Detective 'B' ordered a deep clean," Evie said with a little too much cheer.

Blair offered coffee—a porcelain cup, real cream, a substantial spoon—but her next moves spoke louder. The door clicked shut. The blinds snapped closed. The lock turned, sealing us inside. I gripped the cup automatically, the thin porcelain suddenly too fragile in my hands. Blair sat across from me, her expression carved from stone.

"There's something you need to hear," she said. She didn't sugarcoat it. She didn't blink.

"Twenty years ago, a body was found in a wooded lot near D.C., a Young male. No ID. No family. The trail went dead... until now." The air in the room shifted, heavy and electric. "We traced a connection to the Renaldi family. Eva and Joseph. Three kids are still at home. But Dominic—the eldest—vanished after college. Occasional postcards. Sporadic calls. Last message? Said he was moving to California." Blair leaned forward, lowering her voice to a knife-edge whisper. "The man they call their son—Dominic Renaldi—is an impostor."

My mind rejected it at first. A reflex. Mothers knew their children. Didn't they? But the harder I fought it, the faster the truth caved in around me. Whoever Dominic was, he had slipped into a life that wasn't his. And God only knew what he had done to keep it.

During Dominic's college years, his parents tried to visit, but Dominic's busy life always kept them away— emergencies, travel delays, half-hearted excuses that, looking back, felt almost orchestrated. They believed his calls, his promises, and his sudden marriage to Marcy, complete with carefully staged photos. Their joy in his every achievement became a veil, keeping them from seeing the shadow coiling just beneath the surface. Blair refilled our coffee cups slowly, the silence thickening until it was almost suffocating. Then she said it.

"Molly, I believe the body in that grave... is Dominic Renaldi."

The words hit like a fist to the chest. Somehow, I managed to croak out,

"So who's Marcy's husband?"

Blair's mouth was a thin, hard line.

"I have a theory," she said. "No proof yet. But I believe it's Stefan Gotti—the grandson of John Gotti. Same height. Similar bone structure. We've identified evidence of multiple cosmetic surgeries, including facial restructuring and hairline alteration. Enough to make the lie believable." She paused, voice tightening. "The surgeon who performed the procedures? Died of a heart attack within months. Circumstances suspicious enough to set off alarms." Her stare pinned me to my chair. "We have every reason to believe Stefan murdered Dominic, silenced the surgeon, and stole Dominic's life—part of a vendetta that's been years in the making. As for Marcy... there's no indication she knows the truth about the man she married."

"This is... astonishing," I stammered, my mind whirling. "But why tell me this?"

Blair leaned back, unreadable.

"For two reasons. First, to put you on your guard. Second, you're close to Marcy and Dominic—Stefan, possibly you might remember something we've missed."

I nodded, struggling to absorb it all. Then a light broke through the fog.

"Wait—there was something. Over lunch at Ivy at the Shore. Marcy seemed... different. Cautious. She talked about the dangers of investigative journalism—the surveillance, the threats. Almost like she was warning me." The memory sharpened, burning through the haze. "And the cab driver—it was all too perfectly timed. I didn't see it then, but that day marked my last real assignment at the Times. After that, just scraps."

Blair's gaze darkened.

"Molly, you need to keep your distance from the Renaldi family. We're getting close. If they feel cornered..." She let the warning hang heavy between us. "And about the locket—I have suspicions. But I need proof."

The cold finality in her voice was smothering.

"I understand," I whispered. "I'll stay clear."

Blair walked me to the door, her hand tightening briefly on the knob—a silent warning stronger than words. I nodded and stepped out, dazed, offering vacant greetings to familiar faces as I made my way home.

At home, everything looked the same. But it wasn't. The kettle rattled on the burner. A draft shifted the curtains. A shadow moved—no, not a shadow, just my imagination. Possibly. The sense of wrongness thickened, clinging to the walls, seeping into the air. Something was off. And I wasn't sure I was alone. Sitting on the couch with my tea, my gaze swept the room—and stopped abruptly. The small table in the corner was slightly askew. Barely noticeable. But wrong. Someone had been here. My heart pounded. Every instinct screamed to run, call the police—*but what would I say?* I had no proof, no safe way to explain any of it.

Gritting my teeth, the search began——each room, every drawer, every file rifled through. Nothing appeared missing, but everything felt violated. With hands trembling, the phone was in my grasp. Detective Blair had to be called. She answered on the second ring.

"What's wrong?" she asked, her voice sharp, already on high alert.

I forced the words out. "Someone's been inside my home. Nothing's missing, but... a table was moved. I know it sounds small, but it's not right."

Blair didn't dismiss it.

"You did the right thing calling me," she said, her voice low. "Stay calm. Stay alert. It could be a warning—or a test. Either way, don't engage. Keep everything locked. I'll have someone drive by tonight, but Molly..." She hesitated, just long enough to freeze the blood in my veins. "They know you are part of this now. You need to be ready."

The line went dead. My cozy retreat, once a sanctuary, now felt like a crime scene waiting to happen. I knew there was no undoing this, no returning to before. Los Angeles—where I was born and Daniel and I built our lives—feels foreign now. It hit me like a slap: *nothing was left for me here.*

I drifted into the garden, and the scent of jasmine and rosemary enveloped me. The late afternoon sun slipped low, casting long shadows across Daniel's favorite roses. The memory of the dove, with its calm, steady gaze, surfaced like a lifeline, steadying my breath. Somewhere between fear and longing, a wild idea took root. *Maybe it was time to leave.* Almost without thinking, I reached for a real estate flyer that came in the mail. The name at the top caught my eye—Mrs. Weaver. I called before I could talk myself out of it. She promised to come by the next day. I told myself it was just a visit. No commitment. Just curiosity.

But after she toured the house and gave me her estimate—far higher than I expected—I suddenly realized: *Home wasn't four walls. It was what I carried within me. It was Daniel,*

153

always. Tears stung my eyes as I watched the light spill across the floor—the last glow of a chapter ending. Before I could second-guess myself, I said.

"List it," while you're at it, check Rose Haven. Something small. Something safe."

A new chapter was beginning—frightening, exciting, and the slightest hint of joy. Mrs. Weaver promised to send me any listings that fit my description. For now, all I could do was wait—and stay invisible. Cautiously excited, I called Claire to share my decision. She was thrilled, promising to keep an eye out for the perfect place. The rest of the afternoon blurred into a flurry of job searches and real estate listings, each click pulling me closer to a fresh start. Strangely, a profound calm settled over me, replacing the weeks of fear I'd clung to like armor. It felt right. It felt hopeful.

But as twilight deepened and the house dimmed around me, a thin thread of unease stirred, quiet but persistent. As if the city itself was holding its breath. As if unseen eyes were waiting for my next move. Somehow, I knew...Leaving wouldn't be enough to outrun what had already found me, yet the calm assurance stirred beneath the stubborn, widening ripples.

The Edge of Paradise

That week, though I had no confirmation of a sale or a new home, I began dismantling the office. Each item I packed carried its particular weight—memories woven into paper, leather, and wood. Clearing the space felt like untangling the life Daniel and I had built, thread by aching thread. I packed our books last, dusting them carefully before placing them in the box. Each one felt like a fingerprint from the past. When I reached Daniel's favorite—its cracked spine and worn pages speaking volumes—I paused. Opening it, I could almost see him again: focused, intent, absorbing every line. It wasn't just a book to him. It was a guide. My fingers lingered over a

passage on negotiation and protecting law enforcement families—words Daniel had lived by. But when I closed the cover, something caught my eye for the first time. Author: FBI Special Agent (Ret.) Deidre Castellano.

A jolt ran through me. Castellano. The same name as Dominic Renaldi's biological father. Daniel's old words echoed: *"I don't believe in coincidence. Let's check it out."* Adrenaline tightening my breath, I dove into research. Hours stretched into days. And then, finally, I found it. Deidre Castellano, retired agent. Second cousin to Dominic Castellano, Sr. The revelation was breathtaking. Without hesitating, I contacted her publisher and left a message, my words careful but urgent. Two days later, my phone rang.

"Hello, this is Deidre Castellano," came a brisk, steady voice, calling from Guadeloupe Island. She and her husband lived in the Caribbean, working on their memoirs. Her voice was strong and confident—a woman who knew danger but didn't flinch. Delight flowed through my nerves—but so did a sliver of warning. Deidre Castellano had a lifetime of secrets. And now, for better or worse, she was about to share one with me. Without thinking, I blurted,

"I'd love to meet you."

A pause stretched long enough to question my impulse—until Deidre answered warmly,

"I'd enjoy that, Molly. Next week work for you?"

"Yes, it does! I'll send my flight details," I replied, surprised at my answer and how steady I sounded.

"I'll look forward to it," she said. "Jack and I will meet you at the airport. Stay as long as you'd like—we'll talk over lunch and more."

"Five days," I said, barely believing the words.

When we hung up, I sat motionless, heart racing. I was going to the Caribbean. An island. Deidre Forsythe. The clarity of turquoise waves flooded my imagination, washing away the cold shadows of Brentwood. I almost laughed aloud—who was this bold version of me, untethered from practicality? I

called Jason, who'd booked my travel for years. He found the fastest route to Guadeloupe and handled everything.

"I'll be carrying your book," I told Deidre when I called to confirm. That weekend, I boarded the plane. My fingers clenched her memoir as the aircraft lifted off, and I spent the long flight marking passages, crafting questions. The cabin passengers erupted in applause when the wheels touched down, but I barely noticed. Disembarking, I stepped into a substantial comfort—warm, fragrant, forgiving. The scent of orchids and sea salt laced the air. You're safe now, it seemed to say.

A voice called out from the crowd.

"Molly! Is that you?"

I turned and recognized her from the book jacket— Deidre Forsythe in the flesh, seated in a wheelchair—radiant, confident.

"Yes—hello!" I hurried toward her, heart fluttering.

She extended a graceful hand.

"It's grand to meet finally. This is my husband, Jack Forsythe."

Tall, silver-haired, with the effortless charisma of a born protector, Jack shook my hand. The adoration in his eyes when he looked at Deidre was unmistakable. They drove me to my hotel in a sleek, stunning Bentley, pointing out landmarks with affection and pride. Their connection to the island was palpable—it bloomed from them, as alive as the terrain around us. When I asked them to stay for dinner, they accepted without hesitation.

The hotel restaurant, suspended over the ocean, felt more like a dreamscape than a dining room. Water crashed beneath us. The horizon shimmered. Jack wheeled Deidre to our table, then pulled out my chair with gentlemanly flair. We sipped local beer from frosted glasses, the scent of sea and spice mingling in the air. Dinner consisted of Callaloo Soup, buttery lobster over rice, spiced pumpkin purée, and a crisp seaweed salad. Each bite was a revelation.

156

As we ate, their story unfolded like something out of a Cold War thriller: two undercover FBI agents posing as kitchen staff in the White House during a classified security breach. They uncovered the mole in just three months—but somewhere between midnight stakeouts and whispered code words over dishpans, they fell in love. Jack's smile found Deidre, soft with memory, and said.

"I knew I loved her before we cracked the case."

Years later, Deidre took a bullet to the spine. Forced into early retirement, she adapted with dignity. Jack stayed on until age seventy—his injuries "nothing more than an acceptable inconvenience," he joked. It was a dinner soaked in history, courage, and charm. As we parted, Deidre invited me to lunch the next day—to ask questions, to learn the truth. I walked them to their car, and Jack called over his shoulder,

"Molly, tell the cab to take you to *Forsythe à la Maison*. Everyone knows the way."

I stood waving as they drove off, completely captivated by this formidable couple. I should have been exhausted, but instead I was electric with energy. Slipping off my shoes, I wandered barefoot along the beach. The restaurant's golden lights twinkled over the warm sand, casting a glow on each foamy wave that swept over my feet. It felt surreal—like I had stepped into a dream stitched together by moonlight and salt air. This place, I thought, could be a sliver of heaven.

Back in my room, I flung open the windows, letting the rhythmic hush of the surf spill inside. The ocean's lullaby wrapped around me, and I drifted into the most restful sleep I'd had in months. By morning, anticipation had set my thoughts spinning. I dressed carefully, preparing to meet Deidre and Jack at their home. Though the island's primary languages were French and Antillean Creole, the thought of navigating in rusty French thrilled me. I rehearsed simple phrases under my breath, heart thudding. But it was hard to stay focused. The island's spell tugged at me with every scent of sugarcane and frangipani, every burst of color from the

tropical flowers. I jotted a few last-minute questions for Deidre and tucked her book under my arm before calling for a cab.

The driver was both cheerful and quiet, navigating narrow roads with effortless confidence. When we stopped, I blinked in confusion. A modest cable car station stood perched at the edge of the Porte de l'Enfer Cliffs.

"I think there's been a mistake," I said, peering out. "There's no home in sight."

He chuckled and gestured toward the waiting cable car.

"Forsythe à la Maison," he said. "It's waiting below."

I stepped out slowly, heart racing now for an entirely new reason. The cable car creaked as I boarded, the sea far below crashing the cliffs like a warning—or an invitation. The doors clanked shut behind me, and the car descended toward whatever answers awaited. I departed the cable car and entered a realm where past and present blurred. Below the cliffs, cradled by lush greenery, sat *Forsythe à la Maison*—a romantic echo of Provence nestled in tropical paradise. To the side, a teak platform held a small sailboat with a striking blue, orange, and white sail, angled toward the sea as if ready to take flight. A boardwalk stretched from the platform across pale sand, leading to the water's edge. I pictured Deidre—freed from burden and memory—gliding across the sea, wind in her hair, unbound by time and constraints. But suddenly breaking through my daydream, the intricately carved teak front door swung open before I could knock.

"There she is!" Deidre called out with a smile, Jack beside her.

Their welcome wasn't formal or performative—it was genuine, almost familial. Inside, the scent of fresh blueberry muffins mixed with the rich warmth of dark roast coffee. Jack poured as we settled around a circular glass table positioned before a panoramic view of the Caribbean. The ocean sparkled, throwing brilliant flecks of sunlight like confetti against the horizon.

"I never tire of that view," Deidre said softly, catching me staring in silent awe. "Every morning feels like a promise—new hope, new possibilities." She gave a small, wistful smile. "But let's not get lost in paradise. You came with questions."

I nodded, pausing only to gather my thoughts. Then, I began with a breath that felt like crossing a threshold. I asked about the Castellano family—what she remembered, what she knew. Her expression shifted, distant but clear, as if peeling back the layers of a forgotten life.

"When I was six," she began, "we visited my cousins Dominic and Eva Castellano at their estate in Virginia. It was... breathtaking. They had wealth, yes—but also elegance. Cars I'd never seen. Fabrics that shimmered when they moved. But more than all that, there were horses. Dozens. And one in particular—" Her voice faltered, her eyes now shining with memory. "A white Shetland pony," she said, almost in a whisper. "He wasn't just beautiful—he *knew* things. He'd look at you, right into your soul. I ran to Eva, asking whose he was, because there were no children to ride him. She smiled and said they hoped to have a child like me one day. Until then, he was mine." She paused, letting the memory linger in the sunlit silence. "It was the first time I remember feeling like I belonged somewhere. I went to that estate to be near him. Every day I could."

A subtle tension pulsed beneath her nostalgia—an ache too deep to name. I felt it too, as if that memory of innocence was haunted by a truth neither of us had yet named. But the story darkened. Deidre's voice dropped lower, carrying the weight of years.

"My parents discovered Dominic's ties to a criminal syndicate. They severed all contact without warning—no explanations, just... silence. Not knowing why made it unbearable—I was furious at my parents. I hated them for it." She looked away, staring out over the sunlit waves as if seeking answers she'd never received. "Then, a few weeks later, they

told me Dominic was dead. Eva had disappeared. It was like... like someone had erased them from existence."

The rawness of her grief pressed against the air between us. I could almost feel her six-year-old heartbreak, loss without explanation, love without closure. In time, her parents, seeing her despair, shared a gentler version of the truth: Dominic had been involved in something illegal, something that had cost him his life. They didn't vilify him, Deidre said, but guided her toward better choices—toward light instead of shadows.

She poured her pain into sports, excelling at tennis, surrounding herself with beauty, honor, and resilience. Yet the ghost of Dominic—and the questions he left behind—never entirely disappeared. As she matured, her parents revealed more: Dominic's wealth had been built on treachery, his death tangled in secrets too dangerous to speak aloud. Deidre leaned forward now, eyes sharp and searching.

"I was two years into my FBI career when I found Eva again," she said. "By then, she had three children and was pregnant with her fourth. I congratulated her and mentioned how lovely it was that her oldest son was named Dominic." She paused—and in that moment, something shifted. The air grew taut, electric. Deidre's voice dropped to a near-whisper. "She didn't smile. She didn't say thank you. She just... stared at me. And then she said—very softly—that she didn't choose the name. *It was chosen for her.*"

A chill shot through my spine.

"What did she mean?" I asked, my voice low.

Deidre shook her head slowly.

"I didn't know then. But I knew one thing with certainty: Eva was afraid."

She sat back, the sunlight briefly catching the silver in her hair, casting her face in a light that seemed almost spectral. Deidre recalled that tears welled in Eva's eyes, as she haltingly told of naming her son in memory of her late husband, who had longed for a son before his life was cut short. Then,

remembering how Deidre had loved the Shetland pony, she added that they had given him to a family with children. That was their last meeting. Deidre's voice cracked as she uttered each word to me, as though the past was a wound that never fully closed. The waves crashed outside, their endless rhythm the only sound between us. Catching her breath, she jumped years ahead to Washington. Deidre met *him,* Dominic Jr.

"The resemblance was haunting," she said. "He was in college, seeing a girl named Marcy. But that wasn't what struck me most." Her voice dropped to a whisper. "He called himself *Dom*—and the way he looked at me…" She trailed off. I watched her gather herself. Her face, usually so poised, momentarily froze. "It was as if I were staring into someone else's eyes. Someone darker. You only see that particular look in people who've learned to hide things. Dangerous things. I've seen it in those who cross the line, Molly—and it chilled me to my bones."

She leaned across the table, her hand finding mine. Her grip was firm, but not aggressive—it was a bridge. A plea. And a warning.

"If you've discovered anything about *Dom*, please tell me." I hesitated. The weight of what I knew pressed at the back of my throat: the meeting with Detective Blair, the documents, the photographs. But I couldn't reveal any of it until I understood more. I forced a small smile and nodded.

"I'm still gathering information," I said calmly, evenly. "But yes, if I learn anything... I'll let you know."

That was all she needed. No further explanation passed between us. We both understood the dance—how to ask without asking and answer without revealing too much. Still, something inevitable had happened. Jack stood, suddenly eager to offer a tour. Deidre mentioned I was welcome anytime and encouraged me to stop by again if I had any new questions. Their warmth was genuine, but something was just beneath it, something protective. Conceivably, even calculated. Their interrogation skills, honed over the course of decades, were

masterful. I felt like I'd been dancing through a net—never trapped, but never truly free either. As we hugged goodbye, I said,

"Thank you both again for your kindness and for welcoming me like an old friend. I'll spend the rest of my days here, swimming, lying in the sun, and sleeping. No more questions for now."

They smiled, visibly relieved. Jack pressed a hand to my shoulder.

"You know where to find us if that changes."

As I stepped back into the brilliant island sun, their door closed behind me with a gentle finality. But inside my tote, among sunscreen and sunglasses, were the notes. The real questions. The ones I hadn't asked yet. And I knew, without doubt, that *Dom*—whatever his truth was—had already begun to pull me deeper than I'd planned to go.

The island sun dazzled so brightly it felt almost surreal—too brilliant for the weight of what I now carried. I returned to the hotel, trading sandals for bare feet, and wandered the shoreline, letting the gentle waves kiss my toes. The late afternoon sun hung low, casting molten ribbons of gold across the water. It was breathtaking—and yet, beneath the beauty, tension hummed. I sat down on the warm sand, pulling my knees to my chest. For a long time, I watched the surf continue to roll and break, like the slow breathing of the earth itself. I entered the rhythm, casting within it the tangle of fraud, mystery, and betrayal. I imagined them gathered—the unanswered questions, the dark possibilities—and returning them to the hands of a God who already knew the truth—a quiet surrender. And strangely, it worked. Some confinement, of which I was unaware, departed, making room for peaceful laughter. I was free to soak in the paradise around me without second-guessing every joy. The next few days passed in a dream. I swam in crystal-clear waters, lounged beneath palm trees, and slept soundly, untroubled by nightmares. On my last morning, I wandered the island's charming streets, reveling in

its beauty. Then, a small flower shop caught my eye—I entered. The air was rich with the scent of fresh blooms, a living portrait of the island's vibrant soul.

Amidst a riot of color, it was the cluster of large white Lilies that drew me in—their stunning, fragrantly unblemished petals a perfect symbol of Deidre and Jack: their grace, strength, and complicated past stitched into beauty. The shopkeeper crafted an extraordinary bouquet with careful hands. As I paid, a tiny notecard captured my attention—a sketch of a whimsical, serene white pony. It felt like fate. I penned a brief but heartfelt message of thanks and asked the shopkeeper to deliver the bouquet and card to *Forsythe à la Maison*.

Walking away from the shop, I felt lighter, a sense of completion settling within me. At the airport, boarding pass in hand, I sat by a window overlooking the endless stretch of sea. The peace I had so carefully wrapped around myself slipped away like sand through fingers. I stared at the infinite, glittering blue—and knew that paradise was over. A formidable adversary was lurking just beyond a hidden veil.

When Silence Turns to Threat

The following morning, an urgency hovered above me. I returned to our home office, determined to finish what I had started. Once steeped in the warmth of shared memories, the house now echoed with silence. Before flying to Guadeloupe, I had packed nearly everything—only my laptop and a few investigative notes remained. Today's mission was simple: prepare the house for a buyer—staging, I believe it's called. But the reality of moving alone, with Daniel gone, a murder unresolved, and danger looming, made the task anything but simple.

To hold the shadows at bay, I turned on a home-decorating show—my favorite form of denial—and mimicked their cheerful, curated transformations as I moved from room

to room. It was a minor, welcome illusion of control, but nestled within the staging, I realized my home had morphed into merely a house. I imagined Miss Marple giving me a nod of approval. Daniel would've smiled too. After a mere two days of meticulous work, I called Mrs. Weaver. She was thrilled—three pre-screened couples were already interested, and she wasted no time setting the first viewing for the weekend.

With her at the helm, I allowed myself to turn to another obligation—the annual police family picnic. This year, I would arrive under a new, unwanted title: *widow of a fallen officer*. The word clung to me like an ill-fitting coat—too heavy, too soon, and all wrong. The weekend came. I handed over the keys to Mrs. Weaver and left behind the shell of my old life.

At the park, the familiar buzz of laughter and barbecue smoke swirled through the air. Friends and colleagues greeted me with warm hugs and soft-eyed sympathy. I smiled. I nodded. I played the part. But behind the polite exchanges, a gnawing ache settled deeper. Daniel's absence was everywhere. Feeling a panic to run, Detective Blair's warm smile caught my eye across the crowd, a quiet summons I couldn't ignore. For a moment, I hesitated—was I ready for more bad news? Before I could decide, my phone buzzed. A text from her: *We need to talk. Urgent.* Panic softened, I crossed the grass to meet her, and once we were alone, she leaned in, her voice low and measured.

"Can you meet me at the office early Monday morning?"

Something in her tone—an undercurrent of urgency—stirred a cautious spark of hope inside me. I nodded. We parted, her request looping through my mind like an unfinished promise. Before leaving, I sought out Sharon Bates to thank her for organizing the picnic. Her recent coldness lingered in my memory, but politeness won out. I kept my composure, offered sincere compliments, and moved on. Her response was clipped, almost mechanical—more like a duty than a kindness. A shiver brushed down my spine as I walked away.

When I arrived home, the house felt cavernous, its silence haunting. My phone pinged—Mrs. Weaver. Breathlessly, I read her message: two couples were already asking for second showings, and she'd found four listings in Rose Haven that fit my wish list. Her excitement leapt off the screen, and I felt a spark of anticipation, like the warmth of a new life. That night, her in listings arrived. I stared at the photos, my heart hammering. The fear was sudden and irrational—as if choosing a new home would somehow erase the life Daniel and I had built. I laughed nervously, willing the tension away, and made a cup of tea. Slowly, carefully, I reviewed each listing. One seemed to reach out to me.

A beautiful home, just minutes from Claire and Steven, with a sprawling garden that looked straight out of a dream. The thrill coiling in my stomach was wild, a dizzying mix of hope and terror, like standing on the edge of a roller coaster's first drop. Looking away from the possibilities to my present room, it looked polished, almost sterile. Every photograph, every trace of life had been stripped away, leaving only a glossy stage set for strangers. Claire's words whispered in my head: *Leave it in God's hands.* I forced a breath, ordered takeout I barely tasted, and queued up a movie. But I knew that food and distractions wouldn't fill the silence.

"I will get through this," I said into the empty room.

The following morning, I left my past—and my future—in Mrs. Weaver's capable hands and headed for the precinct. The station buzzed with the energy of a new week. Officers in crisp uniforms, fresh coffee brewing somewhere nearby, the low hum of radios—it all felt oddly reassuring. Detective Blair spotted me with a grin. I came prepared: her favorite Italian coffee, a cappuccino for me, and two warm croissants. When I set the treats on her desk, her face lit up like I'd handed her a winning lottery ticket.

"How did you know I needed this, Molly?"

"Good guess," I said with a wink.

Cradling her coffee like treasure, she took a long, luxurious sip, then closed her eyes in bliss as she bit into the croissant. I grabbed mine and joined her little moment of rebellion against the grimness of police life.

"You're easy to please, Detective Blair."

She laughed. "Oh, call me Tulsi. Please."

At last, she sobered, reaching for a thick file on her desk. Her eyes met mine, and the moment shifted.

"Alright," she said, flipping it open. "Here's why I asked you here." She slid a page toward me. "The surgeon who performed the facial reconstruction on Stefan—Dr. William Blakely died of what was initially ruled to be natural causes. He had a known mild heart condition from birth. His physician, Dr. George Michaels, supervised his care for years." She paused. "We recently obtained permission to exhume Blakely's body. Toxicology found faint traces of *Taxine,* a plant-based toxin known to cause sudden arrhythmia. In someone with a heart condition, it could easily be mistaken for natural death. No one looked closely at the time."

I leaned in, pulse quickening.

"Molly," her voice tightening. "Dr. Blakely's death certificate listed natural causes. But with the new evidence, it's clear now—he was murdered. And if someone was willing to eliminate him to cover Stefan's trail... they won't hesitate to silence anyone else who gets too close."

The weight of her words settled between us, heavier than anything the morning sun could burn away. The chilling details about Dr. Blakely were unsettling enough, but they still didn't explain how any of this was tied to Daniel. I leaned forward, my voice quiet.

"And Daniel? Where does this connect?"

Tulsi lowered her voice, glancing toward the hallway.

"We don't have a clean link yet. But if Stefan had ties to Bates—and Daniel was getting close to exposing something—it's possible his death wasn't random. We're

starting to think he was circling something bigger than even he realized."

My breath caught.

"What about Marcy?

She shook her head.

"No direct tie. Not yet. But Molly, don't share this. Not with anyone. The more you talk, the more risk you carry. And I don't want to lose another person to this."

I didn't realize how pale I'd gone until she reached across the desk and gently touched my arm.

"That look on your face—I know that look. You're starting to understand just how dangerous this is getting."

I nodded slowly, the fog lifting just enough for dread to settle in.

"There are no guarantees," she said, "but we're keeping a very close eye on you."

I forced a smile. "Thanks. I'm no longer sure what to think. Have you uncovered the identity of GRB or Hampton Fife?"

Tulsi pulled out another folder. "Ciara was right. Hampton Fife is the aerospace firm where Joel worked. GRB? That's *General Ridley Baffington*, the company's CEO."

Astonished, I said, "Seriously?"

"And there's more. The car that struck Daniel belongs to *Senator Randolph Warren,* a member of Congress who happened to be in town that night. He and Baffington were both attending a private meeting at a former U.S. president's ranch just a few miles from where the accident occurred."

My stomach dropped. "Are you saying they were both near the scene?"

"Yes," she said carefully, "but for now it's just theory. I don't have the evidence to make a move. Not yet."

The puzzle was vast. Faces and names blurred—Joel, Stefan, Baffington, Warren, Chief Bates, Sharon... each one a potential thread to unravel, or a trap.

"I've been thinking about relocating," I told her quietly.

Tulsi's eyes narrowed.

"Please don't. Not yet. Give me another month, maybe two. We're close, but I need you nearby. Things are still shifting."

A wave of vulnerability hit me like a cold current. I needed perspective—clarity that wouldn't come in a precinct office. For Miss Marple, that meant knitting. For me, it was strong tea and seafood.

"I understand," I said, rising. "But if this gets any darker, you'll need to tell me—everything."

She gave a solemn nod.

"You'll know when it's time."

I left the precinct and went to *Linden's Café*, a quiet haven with soft jazz, linen napkins, and the best seafood crêpe on the west side. I slipped into my usual corner booth and pulled out my notes. As I waited, I breathed in the calm. The scent of garlic and herbs mingled with espresso from the bar, calming me. When the steaming plate arrived, I took the first bite and let the flavor linger, hoping it would magically comfort me. Names circled in my mind like vultures—Joel, Dominic-slash-Stefan, Marcy, Sharon, Chief Bates. All tangled. All suspicious. And still, like a needle caught in old wool, one moment kept surfacing: my strange meeting with Sharon and Dina MacFarland. Something about that encounter still didn't sit right. That day had always felt... off.

It began with Sharon's unusual reaction when I met her at the fashion show. *"You're still with the Times?"* she'd asked, feigning surprise. At the time, I chalked it up to poor small talk. But now? It felt like a misstep—like someone trying too hard to sound casual, but slipping. And then, later that same afternoon, the out-of-the-blue coffee invitation. Sharon Bates didn't do casual meetups, not with me. Yet we were sipping lattes while she confided that she might leave her husband. Divorce. From Chief Bates. At first, I assumed she was just

emotionally drained, maybe reaching for a lifeline. But something didn't sit right. She had been *watching* me—carefully, cautiously, like a handler watching their mark. Was she testing my loyalty? Feeling me out to see how much I knew? Or worse... trying to shift my focus? The memory bristled. The more I replayed it, the more it felt rehearsed—like a scene written for misdirection. Distracting me with a personal confession while something bigger passes behind my back. But what?

Then came that persistent name. A name that refused to fade. *General Ridley Baffington.* His presence had loomed at the periphery for weeks, on Joel's records, tied to Hampton Fife, even whispered in connection with Daniel's last few weeks. I couldn't prove anything yet, but every instinct screamed: *he's more than a name on a file.* Was he pulling strings behind the scenes? Or was he just another piece placed to throw me off the real trail?

Miss Marple would know. She'd lean back in her chair, click her needles, and say nothing until she had everything. I smiled faintly at the thought, grateful for the clarity she offered—even in my imagination. Lunch was delicious, but I barely tasted the last few bites. Too many thoughts vied for space. As I paid the bill and stepped outside, the cool breeze against my face felt like a reset. I needed answers.

As I walked back to the car, pieces began to click: fleeting glances, off-script phrases, and the uneasy timing of specific meetings. The truth wasn't hiding—it was buried just beneath the surface, beneath layers of loyalty, politics, and fear. And I was closer than ever. Closer than anyone wanted me to be. The drive home was short, but my mind raced. I mentally lined up my next steps: finish sorting the house for Mrs. Weaver, dig deeper into Baffington's connections, and most of all—stay alert. I had a nagging feeling I wouldn't have long before someone else made a move. A flash of movement caught my eye when I pulled into the driveway. At first, everything looked normal. The late afternoon sun bathed the

porch in warm gold, and the neighborhood was quiet. Unusually quiet. My pulse ticked faster.

I parked and approached cautiously, keys tight in my fist. There it was—subtle but unmistakable. The front door. Slightly ajar. I knew I had locked it when I left. I *always* did. Every instinct screamed *Don't go inside,* but angry logic overruled fear. Whoever had been here could still be inside— or long gone. Either way, I needed to know what I was walking into. Carefully, I pushed the door open with my foot, standing to the side. Nothing leaped out. No sound. No immediate sign of movement.

I stepped into the entryway. The air inside was cool and wrong. A faint scent of something unfamiliar lingered, a chemical tang strong enough to notice. My shoes scuffed the floor as I moved deeper into the house, my senses stretching in every direction. Nothing seemed disturbed at first glance— no shattered glass, no overturned furniture. But when I entered the office, my heart jolted.

My laptop was open. I had shut it and locked it before leaving. I was certain. And across the screen, a message glowed, stark against the blank white background: *"Stop digging, Molly. Last warning."* A staggering violation—my stomach twisted. My mouth went dry. I backed away slowly, my mind already racing through possibilities. Was this just a warning—or the beginning of something worse? Miss Marple would have called the police and gathered the facts carefully. But this wasn't St. Mary Mead. This was my home, my life, and someone had just declared open war.

I took a breath, steadying my hands enough to grab my phone and snap a photo of the message before it disappeared or someone decided to send a more permanent warning. The game had changed. And ready or not, I was plunged into the mire. After the message disappeared, I stood there for a long time, staring at the empty laptop screen as if it might flicker back to life and reveal more. But it didn't. I forwarded my findings to Detective Blair.

No broken windows. Yet, signs of entry. A silent, chilling announcement that someone had been inside my home—and could be watching still. I locked the house down, double-checking every window, every door, but sleep was a lost cause. All night, I lay awake, heart pounding with every creak of the old walls, every distant rumble of a passing car. It wasn't just fear anymore—it was wariness, calculation. I was being warned. And warnings had a way of becoming threats if ignored. By the time the sky paled into morning, exhaustion clung, but so did a sharpened determination. I wouldn't run. I wouldn't be bullied into silence. I would move forward.

The House That Called Me

A sense of urgency shadowed me that following day. I called Tulsi, but she was out of the office. I left a message with her assistant, Evie, asking her to call me back. As I prepared for the day, Mrs. Weaver called, saying she had an enthusiastic buyer who would pay above my asking price. Would I like to see the Rose Haven home that caught my eye? I stared at my phone long after the call with Mrs. Weaver ended. A serious buyer. Above asking price. The words should have thrilled me, but they landed like a warning instead. Too fast. Too easy. And with Tulsi still unreachable, a chill crept beneath my excitement. Was I being pushed to move—or pulled? I was almost consumed with the feeling that someone might want me out of Los Angeles, away from the investigation and closer to silence. But Claire was in Rose Haven. The house she found sounded like a dream. If I delayed too long, the opportunity might vanish—and with it, the only clear next step I had. My gut whispered caution, but instinct demanded action. I booked the flight and called Claire. Whatever awaited me there, I needed to see it with my eyes.

Claire was waiting on the other end. I didn't overthink it. I didn't have time to. At the airport, I moved through security on autopilot, grateful for the crowds' anonymity and

the travel rhythm. My phone buzzed once, but there was no message from Tulsi. I boarded. As the plane ascended, I placed my headphones over my ears and let the music carry me above it all—above the case, the threats, the noise. Through the window, the mountains unfolded in quiet majesty, and my body gave in to rest. I slept. An hour felt like a moment when I heard,

"Ma'am, we're arriving in Rose Haven in five minutes. Please fasten your seat belt."

I stirred from sleep with a rare feeling of peace. For the first time in weeks, I'd slept deeply, as if my body finally believed I was heading somewhere safe. As the light pierced my sleep-heavy eyes, I straightened and fastened my belt, suppressing an unexpected giggle. Had I just laughed? The plane banked gently, and my breath caught as the landscape unfolded below. Rolling hills, patchwork fields, and a ribbon of coastline shimmered in the morning sun. I pressed my forehead to the cool window, captivated. Rose Haven from the air is like a painting—untouched, beckoning.

With a featherlight touch, the plane kissed the tarmac. A soft cheer rippled through the cabin, the kind reserved for landings that feel too smooth to be real. I couldn't help but smile again. We disembarked through a long, tunneled jetway into the small terminal, where the scent of fresh bread and wildflowers filtered in from somewhere. Then I saw Claire waving with both arms, calling my name as if she were calling me home. Emotion surged unexpectedly. I hadn't realized how much I missed her. I hurried toward her with my small carry-on, and we embraced without a word, but the kind of hug that said everything.

"I missed you," she whispered.

"I missed you, too."

Moments later, we were buckled into her car, winding away from the airport and heading toward a new possibility: the house. When Claire pulled up to the property, I was awestruck. Nestled at the edge of town and just a short walk

172

from Claire's, the location was ideal, but the house itself stole my breath.

"Molly, what do you think?" she asked.

"Oh, Claire," I whispered, stunned. "I'm speechless. It's even more beautiful than the photos. I can't wait to see inside."

Just then, a sleek SUV pulled up. The realtor stepped out, jangling the keys in one hand.

"Hello, ladies. Welcome. I'm Maggie Clarkson."

She was effortlessly elegant in jeans tucked into tan suede boots, a white silk blouse, and a tan suede jacket. Her long, dark ponytail gleamed in the sun. With high cheekbones and a serene composure, Maggie looked like she'd stepped out of a Parisian fashion spread. She unlocked the wrought iron gate, revealing a polished flagstone courtyard framed by sculpted planters brimming with lavender, lilac, and gardenias. As I stepped through, their fragrance enveloped me in a warm, inviting wave that stirred something deep within me. My breath caught. The French cottage before me was beyond charming—the word home seemed to echo in my mind.

Its vaulted, slate-shingled roof curved gently over a thick arched door of weathered teak. A graceful overhang created a sphere-like alcove above the entrance, where a wooden sign swayed lightly in the breeze. *Rose Cottage*, it read. I was spellbound. Tears welled up unexpectedly.

"Molly," Maggie said gently, her voice breaking the trance. "The carved teak café table and rattan chairs out front? They were purchased on the Champs-Élysées."

She gestured toward the intimate setup outside the four large French windows, their blue trim glowing in the sunlight. The table looked like a place where secrets could be shared over coffee, or dreams written in notebooks under the stars. I turned to Claire, whispering,

"The Champs-Élysées means Elysian Fields in Greek mythology... paradise. Claire, this place *feels* like paradise, doesn't it?"

She smiled through misty eyes.

The front door was flanked by two elegant pots overflowing with more fragrant blossoms and delicate trees. Maggie opened the door, and I stepped into a light-filled entry hall, its clean lines and gentle curves echoing the house's quiet elegance. But it was the living room that completely undid me. Vaulted ceilings stretched above a white marble fireplace. The same blue-trimmed windows that opened onto the courtyard perfectly framed the café table and garden. I moved toward them, drawn by the captivating beauty.

"Oh," Maggie said, "the table and chairs come with the house."

I turned, tears falling freely now. Claire handed me a tissue and kept one for herself, saying softly,

"Molly, this home is sheer perfection so far. Don't you think?"

Breathless, I nodded. "Yes. It's beyond my dreams. I read it was recently renovated with modern amenities—I can't wait to see the rest."

We toured the upstairs next. Each of the three en suite bedrooms was airy and full of light. The main suite was exquisite, offering dual views—one of the harbor, the other of the town. A cozy alcove beneath the window practically begged for a writing desk. It was as if the house had been waiting for me. Back downstairs, Maggie led us into a gleaming kitchen. Marble countertops stretched beneath elegant pendant lights, and sunlight bounced off pristine stainless steel appliances. Just off to the side was a formal dining room that could seat twenty, its long table set beneath a dramatic crystal chandelier, ready for dinners filled with laughter and wine.

But then… A faint, familiar scent caught in the air—feminine, floral, and utterly out of place. My heart gave a slight, sharp lurch. It wasn't the garden. It was perfume. A chill threaded through me. Trying to steady myself, I moved toward the large window over the kitchen sink and focused on the view. The harbor shimmered in the late afternoon light. Quaint

rooftops peeked through trees. The lighthouse stood in stoic watch over the town. It should have felt peaceful. But the scent clung to the air like a whisper I couldn't quite catch. Sensing the change in me, Maggie stepped closer and spoke gently.

"At night, the lights from the harbor and the lighthouse shimmer like stars on water," she said. "And when the fog rolls in, the horn sounds across the bay. It's comforting—like the town itself is watching over you."

I nodded, but the unease remained. The perfume still lingered, and my eyes scanned the kitchen for *anything* that would explain it. There was nothing. Only that scent, hauntingly familiar, refusing to be forgotten.

"Maggie, have you shown the house to someone recently?" I asked, careful to keep my voice even.

"Yes," she replied with a shrug. "Just a couple from Los Angeles."

A chill flooded beneath my skin. My smile faltered. *Los Angeles?* That perfume—the one I couldn't shake—suddenly took on more weight. I opened my mouth to ask their names, but stopped myself. Maggie, bound by confidentiality, wouldn't reveal them. Still, the knot in my stomach twisted tighter.

"I see," I murmured, then steadied my voice. "Let's continue."

I couldn't afford to fall into suspicion—not now, not when I was standing in what could be my new beginning. Possibly, Tulsi's caution about staying in Los Angeles until her investigation wrapped was more pervasive than I thought. But I was here now. And I needed to finish this. We followed Maggie through a charming mud room, its design both practical and elegant, with custom-built shelves, woven baskets, and antique iron hooks. She pushed open the door at the far end, and immediately, a warm breeze carried in the intoxicating scent of mimosa blossoms. The perfume from the kitchen vanished, overtaken by nature's heady breath.

I stepped out and froze. We had entered an English garden in full bloom, like something out of a dream. Flowering vines climbed trellises, lavender buzzed with bees, and peonies the size of teacups swayed in the breeze. Butterflies fluttered through the air like confetti. Then, a pale yellow flagstone path meandering through the garden captivated my imagination. Bordered by glinting copper lights, their tiny glass bulbs catching the sun like fireflies trapped in crystal.

Maggie laughed, light and melodic. "The owner is a novelist. One of her favorite films is *The Wizard of Oz*. She had the path installed as her version of the Yellow Brick Road— her tribute to wonder and imagination."

Claire gave me a playful nudge. "Sound like anyone we know?"

I smiled, but my thoughts spun. A novelist. Los Angeles visitors. A garden designed for magic. Why did it all feel too perfect? Or maybe too intentional? I took a slow step onto the path. The smooth stones radiated gentle heat beneath my shoes, as though the house itself were alive, humming with stories yet untold. Just ahead, the path curved toward a tall green hedge, behind which a hint of glass shimmered— possibly a greenhouse or a hidden sitting area.

Every part of me longed to believe this was fate. I'd found a safe place to land. But something inside me whispered otherwise. Not yet. Not until I found out who else had stood in this kitchen. Who had left behind that scent? Still, I followed the yellow brick path. Because some truths, no matter how dangerous, must be walked toward.

Claire and I exchanged amused glances, my earlier unease momentarily forgotten. Laughing, we became like two wide-eyed children, eager to follow the winding path to its secret destinations. The first stop revealed a storybook bench beside a life-sized statue of a woman cloaked in ivy, her stone features softened by time. Gardenias bloomed in a halo around her, their heady fragrance weaving with the mimosa in the air.

Further along, we passed an Acacia and Plumeria tree, their branches intertwined as though breathing secrets to each other. The garden teemed with magic—every bend revealing another quiet marvel. Yet, as we wandered deeper, a subtle tension returned. Something still clung to the edges of the day. It wasn't fear exactly—more like awareness. The hush between wind gusts. A breath held too long. I slowed as we neared a cobbled staircase to the water's edge. Below, a rustic wooden dock jutted into the glistening cove, the light flickering off gentle ripples like scattered diamonds. We turned a final corner and stepped into a courtyard straight out of a painter's dream—alive with birdsong, Plumeria blooms, and charming clay animals tucked among the flowerbeds. Claire and I couldn't help ourselves. We clicked our heels together with a laugh, channeling Dorothy.

"There's no place like home," I whispered. And then we saw it.

Nestled in the ivy-draped hedges at the end of the path stood a secluded outbuilding—an enchanting, self-contained office that could double as a guesthouse. It was the final jewel in the crown. Water features trickled nearby, and cleverly camouflaged speakers played birdsong so naturally, it took a moment to realize it wasn't real.

"Claire," I breathed, afraid that the illusion might shatter if I spoke too loudly. "This entire property... It's beyond my dream home. It's like it was made for me."

She grabbed my hand. "Then don't let it go."

Heart pounding, I turned and hurried back up the path with her, our minds made up. Maggie sat on the front step in a patch of sun, scribbling notes in a leather-bound planner. I took a steadying breath, still giddy but resolute.

"Maggie," I said, my voice calm, certain, "I'd like to place an offer on the house."

Her face lit with satisfaction. "Wonderful. I'll contact the owners immediately."

177

I felt weightless, thrilled as though the house had chosen me, asking me to stay and care for it while it wrapped me in its healing beauty—an uncanny and magnetic gift. As Claire and I lingered for one final walk-through, I ran my fingers along the cool stone walls, memorizing their textures. The house had lovingly reached out for me, and I could already see myself here, writing by the window, cooking in the light-soaked kitchen, finding peace I never thought I'd know again.

We passed through the front entry one last time. The late-afternoon sun, slanting through the French windows, cast long, golden beams across the floor. Something caught the light as I reached for my bag on the slender console table by the wall. I froze. A small gold charm was nestled inside a shallow ceramic dish filled with polished stones and lavender buds. Oval. Elegant. *Purposefully placed.* I picked it up slowly. It was warm—almost hot—and etchings I recognized instantly—t*he same markings as the one engraved on the locket* I had found in my garden. The lines were sharp. Clean. Intentional. A message. I brought it closer. The faintest trace of perfume clung to it—that same ghostly floral scent from the kitchen, not gardenia, not mimosa. Something else. Something… familiar. Wrong. Claire leaned over my shoulder.

"What is it?"

My voice barely rose above a whisper. "A charm. I think… someone left it for me."

Her brow furrowed. "Here?"

I nodded slowly. "Not dropped. Planted."

The air changed. The warmth of the house dimmed as suspicion threaded through my ribs like ice. I suddenly felt watched. Chosen. Hunted. The house hadn't just welcomed me. It had *called* me. And someone—someone who had touched Daniel's life, maybe even ended it—was still playing a game, and I was swept, hopelessly on board.

The charm loomed in my coat pocket as Claire and I returned to the car, the sun dipping lower in the sky. The house, for all its magic and wonder, now felt like a stage—

perfectly set, but watched from the wings. We drove in silence, the buzz of our earlier excitement fading under the strain of what I hadn't said. I hadn't told Claire everything—not about the perfume, symbol, or how the charm matched the locket buried in my garden. I needed time. A clear head. And answers.

Struggling to recapture the beauty of the morning wonder, we pulled up to Hanna's Café. Inside, the chatter of locals hummed around us. Hanna waved from behind the counter, her wide smile and flour-dusted apron as comforting as ever.

"This place never changes," Claire said, settling into our usual corner booth.

It didn't. The honey-hued walls, hand-lettered chalkboard menu, and antique teacup collection lining the shelves were all just as I remembered. For a fleeting moment, I believed everything could still be simple. Then my phone rang. The ringtone sliced through the café like a warning bell. I glanced down, and my stomach clenched—*the precinct.*

"Excuse me," I said, already on my feet. I stepped outside, the door chime tinkling behind me as cool air met my face and pulled me sharply back to L. A. reality. I answered.

"Hello?"

"Molly, it's Evie. I'm with Tulsi—she's in the hospital."

The world dropped out from under me.

"What? What happened?"

"She had heart palpitations while driving. She managed to pull over, but she passed out. Her car rolled into a parked vehicle. Minor injuries, but the doctors are worried. She's been in and out of consciousness. I thought you should know."

A chill coursed through me. "Evie… does she have a history of heart trouble?"

"No. None. Her last physical was clean. The doctors are confused."

I took a breath, thinking fast. My pulse quickened.

"Evie, listen carefully. Tell them to check for *Taxine.*"

"Taxine?"

"It's a toxin from the yew tree. Tulsi was researching it recently—it could be relevant. And Evie—don't leave her alone. Not for a second. Insist on a guard at her door. Quietly. Don't use the word 'Taxine' around anyone else. Just the doctor. Understood?"

A pause. "Okay. I will. You're scaring me, Molly."

"Good. Stay scared—but smart. I'll be on the evening flight."

I ended the call and stood frozen on the sidewalk, the sound of laughter from inside the café now distant and unreal. I pressed my palm to my chest, grounding myself, trying to still the tremor running through me. Claire spotted me through the window and met me at the door.

"That look on your face," she said gently. "What happened?"

"The dark cloud's back," I said softly. "Tulsi's in the hospital. Possible poisoning."

Claire's lips parted in shock. "Molly..."

I didn't wait for the next question. "She was investigating Daniel's death. She was getting close. Now she's unconscious in a hospital bed. And I just found a charm in Rose Cottage with the same crest as the locket from my garden."

Claire blinked. "You didn't tell me that part."

"I couldn't, not yet. I wasn't sure what it meant. But now... someone wants me to know they're still watching. Still close."

"Molly," she said quietly, "I hope you're not buying that house just to run from this."

"I thought I was running toward peace," I replied. "But maybe I was just stepping onto the next battlefield."

We sat in silence, sipping our now-cool coffee, as shadows crept across the floor. The illusion of safety had shattered, and something more sinister had taken its place. The last flight to Los Angeles was about to leave; it was time to go.

Claire drove me to the airport curb, hugged me, holding on just a moment longer than usual.

"Promise me you'll be careful," she whispered.

"I'm too careful," I said. I'm going back to finish what Daniel started."

Claire left as I waited to board the plane. My dearest cousin's words echoed through my mind. Was I moving to Rose Cottage to escape the chaos my life had spiraled into? Maybe. With work no longer a refuge and danger circling closer by the day, starting over in a quiet village felt like salvation; perhaps I had misplaced expectations. Doubt crept in, covertly and relentlessly, winding its way around my earlier certainty like ivy choking a tree.

I paced the sterile airport floor, clutching my bag tightly, my thoughts spinning. Fear, hope, longing—they all clashed beneath my ribs. But then came something else: memory. I had faced storms before. I had stood my ground when everything fell apart. And suddenly, I could see it. Not the whole future. Just the next step—stretching out like a narrow path into the unknown. Clinging to what I'd learned, I resolved that I didn't need all the answers right now. I only needed to take the next step. With a slow breath, I released my grip on the illusion of control. And with that surrender came something unexpected: Peace. Clarity. Quiet, steady, earned. Rose Cottage wasn't just an escape. It symbolized the sanctuary I was beginning to build inside myself. As I boarded the plane, I held onto that truth. It grounded me like a sip of fine wine—smooth, calming, quietly bold—a reminder that I wasn't alone in my grief or this fight. I buckled in, closed my eyes, and drifted into a much-needed sleep, letting the quiet carry me back to Los Angeles, where the answers—and dangers—waited.

9

The Poisoned Silence

Arriving in bustling Los Angeles, I barely had time to catch my breath. I called Evie the moment we landed.

"The news isn't good," she said, her voice tight. "Tulsi's still unconscious. The doctors are running more tests."

I headed straight to the hospital, heart pounding, hoping the toxicology report would confirm what I feared— and explain what I couldn't yet understand. Inside, the chaos was immediate. Nurses dashed through corridors. Doctors barked instructions to clusters of wide-eyed interns. The fluorescent lights buzzed faintly overhead, the antiseptic air sharp and sterile. Every step forward was a battle—against the panic in the hall, and the dread rising inside me.

Evie was waiting for me near the ICU, pale and wringing her hands. Tulsi's room was down the hall, guarded by a uniformed officer posted outside her door. The sight of the armed presence brought a moment of relief. Someone, at least, was listening. A sterile waiting room across from her door became our vigil. Evie and I tried to pass the time, introducing ourselves to the guard in a futile attempt at conversation. His answer was clipped and clear: no one enters without written clearance. We had just returned to our stiff plastic chairs when a middle-aged man in a white coat approached. His face was drawn, and his fatigued posture spoke volumes.

"Dr. Horowitz," he said, offering his hand. Evie stood quickly and introduced me, explaining I was the one who suggested screening for Taxine—and insisted on a guard. His demeanor shifted subtly.

"Thank you," he said, his voice quiet, respectful. Then he got to the point. "A trace amount of Taxine was detected in her toxicology screen. There's no antidote. We're managing symptoms—keeping her heart rate and blood pressure stable is our top priority. She's on Atropine to counteract the

bradycardia and arrhythmias. So far, she's holding on." He paused, his eyes steady. "Whoever gave her this knew what they were doing. Even with the right treatment, the effects of Taxine are unpredictable. We've consulted a top toxicology specialist with experience in plant-derived poisons. We should know more soon."

I felt my breath hitch. Even a trace confirmed everything. He extended a hand, offering a kind but cautious smile. Evie's fingers closed around his, the pause betraying her unease.

"Doctor... is there any way we can see her?"
He paused. "I can't allow anyone inside. But follow me—you can at least take a look."

We trailed him across the corridor. He opened Tulsi's door just a few inches, enough for us to glimpse inside. My breath caught in my throat. Tulsi lay motionless, her skin pale, lips tinged slightly blue. Monitors beeped steadily, and a tangle of wires encircled her now fragile frame—machines pulsed beside her—silent sentinels in a sterile, too-quiet room.

Dr. Horowitz murmured something about her vitals, about the Atropine and oxygen levels, but his voice receded into the background. All I could see was Tulsi—fierce, brilliant Tulsi—reduced to this stillness. My stomach clenched. He closed the door gently.

"We're required to report her condition to Internal Affairs daily," he said to Evie, "but I'll ask the nurse to contact you with any updates—immediately."

We both nodded, murmured our thanks, and turned to leave. As we stepped out into the cool night, the devastation of it all settled across our shoulders like a weighted yoke. The mystery had just taken another turn. And whoever had tried to silence Tulsi had nearly succeeded.

The Oath Fractured

With the dawning of a new day, I refused to dwell on that all-too-familiar sense of being unmoored. I opened the bedroom window, allowing the soft warmth of the California air to enter. Outside, the Los Angeles mountains stood in quiet defiance of chaos, stoic and sun-drenched. Their presence, ageless and unwavering, calmed the restlessness inside me. For a moment, the day felt possible. One step at a time, I told myself. After a quiet, satisfying breakfast, I brought my coffee into the office and called Evie. She sounded tired but steady.

"She's hanging on," she said. "Still drifting in and out, but the doctors think she's stabilizing. I'm meeting with her temporary replacement later this morning."

Relief threaded cautiously through me.

"Thank you for staying by her side," I said, ending our call.

Before I could gather my following thoughts, my phone lit up—*Mrs. Weaver.* Her voice bubbled with cheer.

"Hello, Molly! I have wonderful news. The buyer agreed to the sixty-day escrow. I can start the paperwork today. What do you say?"

I smiled, though the joy felt distant, like it belonged to another version of me. Still, I welcomed the moment.

"Let's begin," I said, matching her tone.

"Fantastic! And how did things go in Rose Haven?"

"I put in an offer on a place that feels... right. It might even be *the* place."

"Well then," she said warmly, "I think this is all coming together better than you imagined. I'll be in touch soon. Congratulations, Molly."

As I ended the call, a glimmer of something stirred—hope, maybe. The kind that dares to return when you're not looking. I let it dance for a beat, picturing Rose Cottage bathed in late afternoon light. But as I sipped the last of my coffee, reality came creeping back in. Tulsi. The Taxine. The fact that

someone had meant to silence her. The warmth of the moment cooled. Questions I couldn't shake settled in again. Who would poison Tulsi? She'd hinted at someone—someone who feared she was getting too close. But was that someone tied to Daniel? Or was this an entirely new thread in the same dangerous tapestry?

The rest of the day blurred into a feverish attempt to piece the puzzle together—leafing through Daniel's notes, cross-referencing them with Tulsi's findings, chasing strands that refused to tie into anything solid. The deeper I dug, the more a gnawing unease took hold of me. The answers were close—I could feel them—but still cloaked in shadow, waiting for the right moment to emerge.

I thought of Agatha Christie, her genius for hiding clues in plain sight. Subtle breadcrumbs woven into every line. She didn't just write mysteries—she disguised truth as fiction and left the reader to unravel both. I couldn't help but wonder... had I missed something like that in real life? My thoughts circled back to Chief Bates. The man sworn to protect and serve. The man whose oath echoed in my mind as I reread it, this time with growing dread: *'On my honor, I will never betray my integrity, character, or the public trust...'*

His actions didn't mesh with his words. His shady associations and whispered comments, his thinly veiled disdain for those unlike himself, his quiet tolerance—if not outright acceptance—of extremist ideologies, his refusal to address police misconduct, and his calculated manipulation of public anger weren't just arrogance or ignorance. It was rot, and it ran deep. And then there was that strange evening with his wife, Sharon Bates, and her gentle friend, Dina. What was Sharon trying to communicate beneath her surface calm? Had she already filed for divorce—or was she being coerced into silence? Was there something she knew... but couldn't say?

The questions piled up like kindling. Something darker was unfolding—something far worse than corruption or infidelity. The puzzle was shifting beneath my hands, the pieces

no longer fitting the picture I thought I was assembling. Ciara was right. Getting to the truth wasn't a clean pursuit. It was like trying to catch a thousand cats—chaotic, elusive, and liable to scratch you the moment you got too close. But I wasn't backing down. Not now.

The Weight of Truth

News arrived that Detective Blair had regained stable consciousness, though she remained under critical watch. Her voice was weak, her vitals still fragile, but she was awake and aware. It was the sliver of hope the department needed. Her temporary replacement, Detective Karen Blanding, and Commander John Graves from Internal Affairs were granted a brief window to speak with her. If Tulsi had anything to say, now was the moment to capture it.

The nurse adjusted Tulsi's bed with practiced care, raising the head slightly and propping her with fresh pillows. The room held a stillness laced with tension. Machines beeped steadily. IV bags swayed slightly from their hooks. Tulsi's face was pale, her eyes hollowed by fatigue but sharp with urgency. She removed her oxygen mask with trembling fingers. Her voice came out raspy, fragile.

"Did you find my notes on the case?"

Blanding and Graves exchanged a tense glance. The question wasn't a surprise. The pressure to locate those notes had been mounting.

"We haven't found them yet," Blanding began gently, but before she could continue, the attending physician entered, his authority commanding the room.

"She needs rest," he said firmly, moving to replace the mask and lower the bed again.

But Tulsi wasn't done. She reached out, a hand curling in the air like a lifeline. Her eyes pleaded. The doctor hesitated, watching the monitor spike, then relented with a sigh and a

nod. Blanding leaned in, careful and steady. Tulsi's breath was shallow, but her words came out with piercing clarity.

"The man calling himself Dominic Renaldi..." She paused, gathering what little strength she had. "He has no fingerprints. I'm certain he's Stefan Gotti. And he has a contact inside the precinct."

The impact hit Blanding like a sucker punch—silent, sharp, and meant to drop her without leaving a mark. She held her expression still, but her heart thundered. She gave a slight, knowing nod. Before Tulsi could say more, the doctor stepped in sharply.

"That's enough! Everyone out."

There was no room for argument. As Blanding and Graves exited into the hallway, the tension between them was palpable. Graves didn't wait. Without a word, he pulled out his phone and issued quiet, urgent instructions—officers were to follow up on Tulsi's intel immediately, with absolute discretion. They were now dealing with a ghost, a man without an identity—and possibly a traitor within their walls.

The stakes had never been higher. Within hours, the investigation reignited. Select officers retraced every thread Detective Blair had been pulling before her collapse. No detail was too small. And then came the break. Lab confirmation arrived: the remains in the grave belonged to *the real* Dominic Renaldi. The man walking free, using his name, was an impostor. *Stefan Gotti.*

Acting swiftly, the task force took Gotti into custody—and brought in Marcy for multiple rounds of intense, controlled interrogation. Each session grew sharper, colder, and more aggressive. Every answer she gave seemed to raise more questions than it settled. When Marcy was finally cleared of suspicion, the truth of her husband's identity shattered her. The confident, composed journalist who once commanded newsrooms now stood hollowed by betrayal. Once grounded in routine, bylines, and the reliable hum of daily life, her world

had imploded. She hadn't just lost a partner; she'd discovered she never truly knew him at all.

Photographs of the families involved were prohibited, but the media storm found other ways to infiltrate: drones, headlines, and speculative exposés. The scrutiny turned the survivors into prisoners inside their own homes. At the request of L.A. Times management—and without protest—Marcy resigned quietly. There was no press conference. There was no op-ed. (opposite the editorial page) She left for New York within days, seeking shelter in the anonymity of her family's embrace.

Eva, Dominic's mother, had long harbored a vague unease about her son's life, but nothing prepared her for this. The truth was a blow so devastating it barely felt real. Still, she found the strength to testify in court, her reluctant voice becoming pivotal in unraveling the stunning vendetta of Stefan Gotti. But the price was steep. The global fallout was relentless—news cycles, conspiracy theories, death threats. The Renaldi name became a warning whispered in legal halls and security briefings. Eva and her husband, weary and frightened, sold their home and disappeared into a quiet, unnamed town where no one asked questions.

Weeks later, I received a letter from Marcy. The handwriting was shaky, uneven, like someone learning how to speak again after surviving a storm. She'd found a cottage in a quiet Connecticut suburb, tucked behind trees and far from headlines. It wasn't much, she wrote, but it was hers. A space to grieve. To breathe. To begin again. She was now using her maiden name. Hoping that, in time, she might return to journalism in New York. But for the moment, she was focused on something more vital: *recovery. Piecing together a life no longer defined by a lie.*

A sliver of good news broke through amid the storm of headlines, hearings, and courtroom drama. Maggie Clarkson called with unexpected news—the owners of the Rose Haven house had accepted my offer. For a breathless moment, joy

surged through me. A ray of light pierced the gloom. But I was so immersed in the unfolding prosecution—so riveted by every motion and testimony—that I forgot to call Claire. Of course, Maggie had told her. And Claire, knowing me as she does, understood the silence.

The drama had swallowed me whole. Later, we made plans to celebrate, finally thrilled at the thought of becoming neighbors. But that joy was short-lived. Celebration halted abruptly when Commander Graves initiated a search for Joel and Ciara. My stomach turned to stone. Everyone knew we were friends. If they pressed hard enough, they'd come to me. And I wasn't ready. The secret I'd sworn to protect—that I *had* protected—now loomed over me like a guillotine. I told myself Ciara would understand. She always had. Yet, the mere thought of testifying against her cut like a blade, threatening to shred the trust that bound us.

Fighting for my sanity, I turned my thoughts toward Rose Haven. I still had one month left—one final stretch of time tethered to Los Angeles by my agreement to Tulsi. The days dragged. I buried myself in observation, note-taking, and anything else that might keep the questions at bay. But every hour I stayed, the weight of divided loyalty grew heavier. Would I ever find the path that led to the truth about Daniel? The question haunted me. It surfaced in my sleep—or rather, the absence of it. Every night, I tossed beneath sheets twisted by dread, the shadows whispering what I refused to admit: that something was closing in. And then, the knock. Firm. Relentless. It struck like a gunshot through morning silence. My breath caught as I approached the door, heart pounding in my throat. I opened it and froze. Detective Blanding stood there. She stepped onto the threshold like she belonged, her eyes unreadable, her presence taut with control.

"Good morning, Molly. May I come in?"

Her tone was neutral. Unpleasantly neutral. I nodded, stiffly stepping aside.

"Would you like some coffee?" I asked, my voice barely steady.

She moved like a predator—slow, sure, assessing. Her eyes scanned every corner of the room, noting what I couldn't hide, what I hadn't even thought to conceal.

"Yes," she said. "I could use a good cup of coffee."

Not until her silent inspection was complete did she sit at the kitchen table, spine straight, gaze unwavering. She took a sip, set the cup down, and locked eyes with me again.

"That stuff at the precinct is awful," she muttered, almost casually. Then, with zero pretense, she dropped the hammer.

"Listen, Molly. I need to ask you about Ciara and Joel Conway. Do you know where they are?"

Her voice wasn't a question—it was a command. Her eyes drilled into mine, unrelenting, dissecting every micro-expression—every twitch of hesitation. I lifted my mug, trying to stall. The coffee burned going down. My mind scrambled, but the truth loomed large between us—silent, heavy, impossible to hold back much longer.

"Yes. I do," I finally said, my voice barely above a whisper.

I gave her the location. Just the facts. Nothing more. The words tasted bitter, like betrayal wrapped in obligation. They stuck in my throat, clinging to my conscience like a stain I knew I'd never thoroughly wash away. The rest of the conversation was painfully polite, both clinging to a strained façade of normalcy. Blanding finished her coffee, thanked me with practiced professionalism, and left.

The door closed with a soft click, but it echoed like a gunshot in the stillness. And with it, a heavy weight settled across me. I had betrayed Ciara. I stood in the silence, numb and breathless, then reached for the burner phone David had given me. My fingers trembled as I dialed. Ciara answered after two rings. Her voice was tense, but steady. I began to explain, already stumbling into apologies, but she cut me off.

"Molly, I understand."

Her calm stopped me in my tracks.

"I knew this day would come," she continued. "Joel has to face what he did, even if he didn't understand it then. And I can't keep living like this, looking over my shoulder. Don't feel bad. I took an oath, too. And I need to think beyond my love for Joel."

Her words, though gentle, hit harder than any rebuke. She was trying to make peace with something that refused to be simple. I listened, hollowed by guilt, as she told me she had already called a trusted officer at the precinct. She and Joel were coming in voluntarily that afternoon. The officer had accepted her call, relieved to hear from her, and relayed the message to Detective Blanding. Blanding's initial response was all suspicion. She wanted to send a team to bring them in officially. But after reviewing Ciara's record, her character, and her forced leave of absence, she backed down—reluctantly. She agreed to let them come in on their terms. I had given up their location. That couldn't be undone. But Ciara had chosen integrity over fear, and now the cost was coming due. My hands trembled as I reached for certainty that wasn't there. But I still had one thing left. I would face the storm, even if I had helped unleash it.

The Fourth Silence

From a quiet bench just outside the precinct's sally port, I watched Ciara's aging silver sedan pull up to the gated entry. She drove, her knuckles white on the wheel, Joel silent beside her. I kept my distance, not wanting to interfere or draw attention. But my eyes were fixed on them as they stepped out—Joel walking with quiet resolve, Ciara close beside him, her expression unreadable. There was no dramatic confrontation, no resistance. Only the heavy silence of two people moving toward the inevitable.

Detective Blanding met them at the door, flanked by two officers. Her interrogation skills were legendary within Internal Affairs. And from the moment she spoke to Ciara, her sharp intuition went to work. It didn't take long before she saw what I'd suspected—Ciara had forced herself not to know, loyalty blinding her to the danger at her doorstep. She'd held the storm at bay, never daring to face its full strength. But Joel wasn't so fortunate. He was led to a holding room, then processed without ceremony. By late afternoon, he was formally charged with *compromising national security.* The words rang in my ears, surreal and suffocating. Still, the question that haunted Blanding—and me—remained unanswered: *Who had removed the top-secret files?*

As the officers placed the cuffs on him, I saw Ciara's face through the observation window. Pain etched deep lines into her usually composed expression. Their eyes locked as Joel was led away, the weight of their love and loss compressed into that one final glance. His lips moved, barely perceptible. *It's okay.* The silent message, filled with acceptance and quiet bravery, shattered her. Her mouth trembled—the heartbreak unmistakable. Not just from watching the man she loved vanish behind a steel door, but from knowing that as an officer, she should have dug deeper—confronted her suspicions. She'd trusted too blindly. Now, she'd done the right thing—too late—and the price was painfully high.

Later, as she drove north, Ciara's mind reeled with worst-case scenarios. Sentencing. Isolation. Regret. She reached Big Bear long after dark, the lake house offering only a thin veil of solace. The silence was vast and overwhelming. It echoed Joel's absence. She stayed long enough to pack up what they had left behind. When she returned to Los Angeles, the phone was already ringing.

"Hello, Ciara. It's Chief Bates. I understand you're back in town. Are you ready to return to duty?"

The sound of his voice sent a jolt down her spine. *How did he know I was back?* She hadn't told anyone outside of a text

to the precinct officer. The thought lodged in her like a splinter.

"Chief. I wasn't expecting your call," she said, surprised. "Yes, I'm ready to come back."

"Tomorrow?" he pressed.

"Yes," she answered, her voice barely masking her unease.

"Good," he said. "We'll ease you in. Let's see how you handle it. Fair enough?"

"Fair enough, Chief."

But the moment she hung up, the pressure slammed into her, like a weight she wasn't yet strong enough to carry. By evening, her back throbbed, her limbs heavy with fatigue. Pain flared beneath the surface, and exhaustion pulled at her bones. Searching for comfort, she reached into the cabinet and pulled out a bottle of her favorite whiskey—something she and Joel had once savored in rare, quiet moments. She poured a generous glass, added ice, and retreated to bed.

A stack of pillows, an ice pack, and the slow warmth of whiskey were all she had left to soothe the ache. She opened a book—an old favorite—but the words drifted past her. Sleep eventually pulled her under, but her dreams were disjointed and dark, haunted by what-ifs and echoes of Joel's final look. She awoke just before dawn, her head pounding, her mouth dry. The remnants of last night's whiskey clung to the back of her throat, a bitter reminder of everything she was trying to push down. Still, she took a cautious sip from the bottle—just enough to steady herself—and managed a modest breakfast. The day ahead loomed—a quiet reckoning. And the question lingered: could she pass the test?

The drive through her old L.A. route felt surreal. Everything looked the same—same gas station, same traffic light, same jogger passing the same hydrant—but none of it felt familiar anymore. Her world was strangely different. Joel was gone. And she was walking back into the lion's den. When she pulled into the precinct lot, she spotted them

immediately—her colleagues, gathered in the morning sun, chatting and sipping coffee from mismatched mugs. The moment they saw her, the group broke into spontaneous cheers. Her heart squeezed. She stepped out of the car, face flushing with relief and embarrassment.

"It's good to see you all. Thank you," she said, her voice hoarse with emotion.

Kyle, ever the quick wit, grinned.

"Finally, we get to enjoy good coffee again!"

Laughter followed. The warmth was real, tangible, and unexpected. It pierced her armor. For a fleeting moment, she allowed herself to feel... welcomed.

"Oh, so that's why everyone's so thrilled to see me," she teased, her tone light despite the throb still pulsing behind her eyes. Applause followed, playful and full-hearted. Mugs were raised like toasts. Someone whistled. A few officers jokingly bowed as she walked past.

"Yes, the coffee's been a shadow of its former self since you left!" Kyle added, dramatically lifting his cup and pretending to gag. The banter was infectious. It didn't erase what had happened, but dulled the sharp edges. As the officers surrounded her like schoolkids awaiting recess, their enthusiasm broke something open inside her. Ciara couldn't help but laugh.

"Alright, alright—I'll make the coffee!"

Cheers exploded as they made their way to the coffee station inside, Ciara ignoring the pounding in her head and the tension tightening her back. As she measured out grounds and flipped the switch, exaggerated expressions of anticipation filled the room—mock suspense, crossed fingers, exaggerated prayers. She turned, raised her hands in a mock victory pose, as if she'd lassoed a wild steer. The room erupted in laughter, whistles, and applause. And that's when Chief Bates emerged. Drawn by the commotion, he stood in the doorway of his office, arms folded as he surveyed the scene. His eyes lingered

194

on Ciara, surrounded by adoring teammates. He smiled, easy and bemused, and strode forward.

"Back where she belongs," he said warmly.

On the surface, it was perfect. But something in his gaze lingered a little too long. Yet in that moment, surrounded by laughter, the clink of mugs, and the rich aroma of fresh coffee, Ciara felt something she hadn't in weeks: calm. The chaos of her personal life momentarily retreated. In its place was the warmth of camaraderie, the grounding sensation of belonging. For one fragile instant, she could breathe again.

But as she returned to her desk, a strange chill slid over her shoulders like mist—an invisible fog of dread. The moment of comfort had passed. Reality was waiting. Chief Bates approached with a neutral expression, returned her firearm, and offered a firm handshake. His eyes didn't smile. Then, taking a long sip from his cup, he raised his voice to address the room.

"Alright, everyone. Caffeine up—then back to business. Officers Ciara and Kyle are on light duty today. You're assigned to the Drug Abuse Awareness Program over at Hollywood High."

Ciara paused, caught off guard. Bates continued smoothly.

"It launched while you were on leave. Kyle will get you up to speed. We're focusing on youth outreach—steering kids away from destructive behavior. So far, it's been... successful."

His tone was too rehearsed, and his cadence was too even. Something about it scratched at the edges of her intuition. Still, she forced a smile.

"I look forward to being a part of it, Sir."

"Good." He nodded, then lingered a gaze a beat too long, again.

"And thanks for the coffee, Ciara. It's good to have you back."

He turned as if to leave—then stopped abruptly, like a man remembering an afterthought too necessary to forget.

"Oh, and Ciara—don't visit Joel right now."

She froze.

"I spoke with him," Bates continued casually. "He was glad to hear you're back on duty. He understands the situation and doesn't want you worrying. He's in maximum security. Well-guarded. Give yourself a few days to settle in."

Why were his words chilling? Although the request was framed as caring, even protective, it felt more like a command. She nodded, masking the building unease.

"Understood, Chief." *But I don't,* she thought. She wanted—*needed*—to see Joel.

Maybe a few hours at Hollywood High could help her think more clearly. The days that followed blurred into routine. The outreach work was noble, distracting, and even therapeutic in brief moments. But Joel's calls—when they came—were clipped. Empty. Strained. Each conversation grew shorter. The pauses between words became longer. Something was missing. Something vital. Ciara's gut twisted. One night, unable to take it anymore, she asked him directly.

"Did the Chief visit you?"

"Yes," Joel said. "He told me you were back. He said he wanted to make sure I was okay. He was... kind."

The words echoed Chief Bates's version exactly. Strangely perfect. A warning bell rang in her mind. The investigation had moved fast. Joel's arraignment turned into a full-blown federal trial within weeks, the prosecution building its case on a growing web of classified data leaks and confidential informants. And now, the courtroom had become a crucible—one where every truth, lie, and every silence would be tested. Though she wasn't on the case, Ciara couldn't stay away.

On a rare afternoon off, Ciara slipped into the back of the courtroom, unnoticed, concealed in shadows. She needed to see him. To know the truth in his eyes. When Joel was escorted in, his gaze drifted across the room, then landed on hers. The connection was instant. A jolt shot through her. He

tried to look away, but it was too late. The tears had come. She watched him lower his head, trembling. Today, he would take the stand.

His testimony under direct examination was strong, measured, and composed. But the cross-examination was a different beast. The prosecutor bore down, ruthless and unrelenting, unearthing new evidence—alleged ties to a broader espionage network, encrypted files, secret accounts. Joel stood firm. He refused to name names. The courtroom crackled with tension. The defense objected, citing a lack of direct evidence and the speculative nature of the questioning, but the prosecutor pressed on. And through it all, Ciara sat frozen in the back row, her heart fracturing with every passing second. Joel was protecting someone. And whatever truth he was shielding—it might be the key to everything.

Hours passed, and Ciara could see the toll it took on Joel—his face pale, his eyes unfocused, each answer slower than the last. He was unraveling in real time. When the judge finally called for recess, suggesting they resume after the weekend, Ciara felt a chill crawl down her spine. Something was wrong—terrible wrong. Whatever it was, she sensed they were running out of time to uncover the truth.

She slipped out of the courtroom with quiet precision, moving like someone who had learned to survive in the shadows. Once outside, she crossed the parking structure quickly, checking her rearview mirror as she pulled into traffic, just in case. Later that evening, we met for dinner at a quiet, out-of-the-way restaurant. The normalcy of it—the soft movement of candlelight, the murmur of other diners— offered a fragile comfort. It was the first time we'd talked in weeks. Ciara sat across from me, her expression composed, but her eyes revealed the storm hiding a beat behind them. She confessed this had been the most challenging year of her life. Her voice was steady, even thoughtful, but the exhaustion clung to her mercilessly.

"I need moments like this," she said softly, "to remember who I was before everything started to unravel."

We caught each other up on cases, on emotions we hadn't had time to process, on the ache of living two lives: the one we were surviving, and the one we used to have. There were pauses between our words, long silences filled with more truth than speech. Ciara never complained. That wasn't her style. But I could see the wear. It lived in the curve of her shoulders, the tightness in her jaw, the way her fingers trembled slightly as she sipped her water. And yet, she spoke with clarity about growing through the chaos—becoming a stronger officer and a more empathetic friend. I admired her in that moment more than she knew.

But while we savored the warmth of friendship and tried to pretend, for just one night, that life was steady again, a squall was mounting on the other side of town. The next morning, it slithered onto the streets. An unarmed man was stopped for driving while intoxicated. When he resisted arrest, the situation spiraled into something darker—something cruel and sinister. Years of buried bias, frustration, and rage detonated in an instant. Backup arrived. Two more officers. Then a third. Four men. One suspect. The line between law and vengeance vanished when the man fell to the ground. Three officers unleashed a brutal assault, striking the man over and over. Kicks. Fists. Batons. One officer watched—motionless, silent—as if seeing in the man not a citizen, but a symbol of everything they'd ever resented.

While the travesty continued, someone watched, in quiet terror, unseen on their balcony, filming the horror. The footage was sent to the news by midday. And by nightfall, the city was trembling. Chief Bates appeared on television, composed and commanding. He promised swift discipline and said three of the officers would face criminal charges. But one name—one face—was never mentioned. The fourth officer. The one who watched. No charges. No suspension. And the silence around him grew louder with each passing day. Months

198

later, another storm broke: the trial ended in a deadlock. The jury couldn't agree. Justice, once again, had slipped through the cracks.

The city burned. Sirens never stopped screaming. Plumes of smoke rose like funeral veils over buildings that had once been filled with laughter and routine. Military tanks patrolled intersections where kids used to ride scooters. The streets were choked with rage, tear gas, and unprocessed grief. Inside my home, the noise outside was a distant roar, like the sea during a storm. I couldn't shut it out, but I had learned to move through it.

That morning, as I scanned the headlines—*Trial Delayed Indefinitely. Death Toll Rises to 47. Guard Units Extended Through Next Week*. I thought of Joel. Of Ciara. Of Daniel. And then I thought of the fourth officer—the one no one would name. I reopened Daniel's files—not just the digitized records, but also the physical notes I had boxed up and nearly packed away. The paper was creased, and some pages almost fell apart from repeated handling. They were scribbled with codes, initials, and time stamps. But Daniel had a method to his madness.

His notes weren't just documentation. They were *patterns*. In one manila folder labeled "Internal/IA Corruption – Restricted Leads," I found a yellow legal page folded in half, tucked beneath an envelope I'd somehow missed. My heart raced as I unfolded it. Daniel's handwriting—quick, jagged, unmistakably his.

"Watch the watcher. One officer never signed the log—same man from the Westfield sting." "Initials: C.B." "No bodycam. No badge scan. Always present, never documented." I stared at the letters. *C.B.* Chief Bates? My hands shook as I checked the log number. I'd seen it before, and it was referenced in an early conversation with Tulsi. She had mentioned a botched operation involving stolen biometric data and a suspect who walked due to "clerical errors." But now it looked less like a mistake and more like a *cover-up*.

If Daniel had suspected Bates was tied to the Westfield sting—the same sting connected to the biometric leak and now possibly Joel's betrayal—then the fourth officer in the recent beating might not have been anonymous by accident. He might have been *protected*. Daniel's following note was scribbled hastily, almost unreadable. *"Badge pulled after informant leak— resurfaced on rotation via fake ID/pass—M.I.A. two years. Why now?"* Could that be the link? Someone had disappeared, scrubbed from records, then reappeared during the recent arrest. Daniel had chased someone and maybe died because of them. And now, Chief Bates might've brought them back. Daniel's handwriting cut deep into the page and into my mind. Not Bates himself. Someone working for him — a ghost who vanished after the sting, reappearing only when the ground was safe again. Bates never needed to disappear; he had others to do it for him. A shadow figure who could step through walls of red tape, erase witnesses, leave nothing but questions. And now, that shadow was here.

I wanted to run it by Ciara, but she was already fighting a private war. Her once-clear sense of duty was clouded now, blurred by fear and worn thin by frustration. I couldn't bring myself to add more to the battlefield in her mind. She felt like she was combating an unseen enemy that was as much within her as outside. But through the haze of despair, a glimmer of hope appeared. Joel's new trial date was set for the end of the month, and Ciara allowed herself a small sigh of relief. Perhaps this time, she thought, the process would move forward. Maybe now she could finally visit him. However, each attempt was stonewalled with vague excuses, *claiming "security concerns."*

It didn't add up. Growing desperate, she reached out to Chief Bates, only to hear the same response every time: "The Chief was *unavailable*." Frustration morphed into a gnawing worry. None of us knew that Joel was quietly relocated to another prison on the outskirts of Los Angeles—allegedly for his protection. It wasn't until the following week, while Ciara and Kyle were out on patrol, that a fellow officer pulled them

aside for coffee. His face was pale, his voice gentle but shaking as he delivered the news: *Joel was dead.*

Ciara gasped, spilling her coffee as the words landed. Her shock gave way to disbelief, then a desperate need for details. The explanation followed like a cruel echo: Joel had been transferred—and, unthinkably, had taken his own life. The room spun. She collapsed. When she came to, fury replaced disbelief. Joel would *never* have committed suicide. She knew him. This-this was a defining moment. Would she stay within the system? Or would her pursuit of unyielding justice take her beyond it?

She didn't hesitate. Ciara stormed into Chief Bates's office. He met her with that familiar, polished calm, like reading from a prewritten script. He explained the transfer process, the necessary precautions, and the protocols. But his reassurances only stoked the fire inside her. Even then, Ciara's heart wouldn't allow her to pursue justice at any cost—not even when everything she believed in had been shattered. She removed her badge and service weapon with measured grace and placed them on his desk with quiet finality. The moment felt ceremonial. Her calm and controlled voice held a power that silenced the room.

"I quit," she said. "I will not work for someone like you. We both know what happened. And I believe you know the reason for the city riots."

Bates didn't move. His expression was stone. But something slipped by in his eyes—*fear, maybe. Or guilt.* Ciara didn't stay to find out. She turned and walked out of the precinct for the last time. From that moment on, the truth became her sole focus. I helped her close the house in Los Angeles, room by room. It was the quietest move I'd ever assisted with—no small talk, no distractions: just boxes, tape, and the finality of what had been lost. As Ciara packed her suitcase, I noticed the bottle of whiskey she slid into the corner, tucked between sweaters and case files. It was unlike her, but I said nothing. Some grief asks for silence. Some pain rewrites

the rules. She needed space, and Big Bear offered solitude. But I knew she wasn't retreating. She was regrouping.

That night, after she'd driven away, I sat at my desk surrounded by Daniel's old notes. His handwriting looped across the pages like a voice echoing through time—quiet, precise, unresolved. I studied them as I imagined a detective would, tracing lines between names and codes, departments and directives. And then I remembered Miss Jane Marple. She had no gun, no authority, just her intuition and the audacity to believe that evil, no matter how polished or protected, always left a trace. She listened more than she spoke. She saw what others dismissed. And she understood something most never did—*that the truth, once glimpsed, refuses to stay buried.* I wasn't Miss Marple. But I understood her. And like her, I'd keep watching. Because someone still wasn't telling the truth. And I was no longer afraid to find it.

Back in our fractured city, Detective Blair had quietly resumed her investigations. Her return to the force was like the re-lighting of a signal fire—small, steady, and impossible to ignore. The hunt for justice wasn't over. I called Ciara to tell her the news and asked if I should give Blair her number. Ciara agreed. Her voice even brightened for a brief moment before she abruptly hung up. Grief still held her in its grip, but the beginning of purpose was returning.

I visited Detective Blair that afternoon. Seeing her back at her desk—alive, focused, and upright—was a surge of relief. I brought her coffee—her favorite—just a small gesture of normalcy in a city barely clinging to it. She smiled as I approached, then wordlessly handed me a folded note. *"Keep the conversation light,"* I arched an eyebrow. She smiled again, tired, but subtly signaled that the room was bugged. We casually discussed my house sale, Rose Haven, and the fog rolling in along the coast. Our words danced around the truth like actors in a play without a script. When the meeting ended, she walked me to my car. Once outside, I shared Daniel's

information on the Westfield Sting. Detective Blair's voice dropped to a whisper.

"Molly, this is gold," Tulsi said, her voice low but electric. "Westfield wasn't a dead case — it was the blueprint. I'm convinced Bates ordered Daniel and Joel's murders, and I'm almost certain which ghost he's been using to keep his hands clean. I can't nail Bates in court yet, but I've got enough to rip the badge off his chest and shove him out of that office. And once he's off the throne, we can hunt him in the open."

Her words landed like a gust of cold wind. Heavy. Icy. The kind of truth that cuts deep, lethal in every sense.

"One bad cop can undermine a hundred good ones," she continued. "One corrupt chief can bring down a city. The anger that fueled the riots was already here—Bates just poured gas on it. We're building the case. Quietly. But it's delicate work. Daniel refused to bend, refused to stay silent. That's why they took him out."

I felt the chill run up my spine, and my throat threatened to close with emotion, but I kept my voice steady.

"What's the plan?"

She glanced around, then leaned closer. "I need you and Ciara to meet me at six sharp—Catalina Island ferry, Wednesday morning. You'll blend in with the commuters. We're back by 7:30, and I'll be at my desk like nothing happened. Perfect cover."

I nodded. "I'll be there. It's been years since I've ridden that ferry."

We walked toward our cars. Her voice dropped just above a whisper.

"Oh—and I overheard Bates calling you a 'snoopy sleuth.' Keep your head down, okay?"

I gave a dry laugh. "Coming from him? I'll wear it like a badge."

But the laugh didn't last. If Bates knew what I was doing—what Blair was risking—then we were walking a razor's edge. He reminded me of Goliath. Towering. Ruthless.

But even Goliath had a weakness. And I was already holding the stone.

The Crossing

Where secrets surface and power expands

I rose before dawn with a mission burning through me. At 5:15 a.m., the world wasn't asleep—it was mine to outrun. Streetlamps buzzed faintly above the empty sidewalks. A single dog barks in the distance. I slide behind the wheel, adrenaline sharp beneath the stillness. The freeway is mine—wide open, a ribbon through the dark. It feels like chasing the sunrise. As the sky begins to warm with color, salt air sweeps in from the sea, crisp and invigorating. San Pedro signs flash past. Five exits later, I veer off, just as a golden orb crests the horizon. Morning breaks with a swell of birdsong, and the city awakens. For a fleeting moment, I forget the danger. The road, the sky, the light—everything feels possible.

Then the Catalina Express appears, sleek and still at the dock, waiting like a sentry. Inside, the lower deck buzzes with commuters—nurses, teachers, laborers—sharing coffee and quiet laughter. Their ease feels foreign. I remind myself: today, I can't be noticed. Detective Blair boards without a glance, her movements fluid, focused. She heads to the top deck. A moment later, I follow, slipping into place on her left. Ciara appears next, silent and sure, taking Blair's right. We stand like strangers watching the water, our triangle unspoken.

The boat lurches into the Gulf. Wind rips across the deck, hurling salt and spray into our faces. The sea lifts us higher with each surge. The rhythm is almost meditative—until it isn't. Nausea punches me without warning. I stagger below, reaching the nearest head just in time. When I return, breathless and hollow, the spell is broken. I'm no longer invisible. Blair and Ciara exchange the smallest of smirks, their gazes never leaving the horizon.

"Are you okay, Molly?" Blair's voice is a whisper against the wind.

I nod, ashamed of the flush in my cheeks.

"Yes. Mostly."

Blair tightens her grip on the rail. Her hair snaps around her face like a warning.

"Good," she says. "Because what I'm about to tell you—won't sit any easier."

"Keep looking toward the horizon," Blair murmured. "It helps."

I steadied myself against the rail, knuckles white, eyes fixed on the place where sea met sky.

Her voice carried in fragments on the wind—sharp, urgent, undeniable.

"Gates is tied to General Ridley Baffington—GRB. The power behind Hampton Fife Aeronautics. He's not just a defense contractor. He's wired into the top: a judge, a senator, and a billionaire with White House access. We believe all three are eyeing the presidency. Their ambitions go far beyond power. Offshore accounts. Hidden assets. Shadow deals."

I shielded my eyes against the sting of sea spray, but her words blurred my vision.

"Joel was their golden goose. His facial recognition software is next-generation. Smarter than anything on the market. He created a backup, probably sensed the danger. But it vanished. They framed him to cover the theft. Then they killed him. And Daniel? He got too close to the truth."

A sharp pain bloomed behind my ribs as the puzzle pieces fell together. I couldn't speak. Could barely breathe. The deck beneath me felt like it might give way.

"The file's being processed offshore now," Blair continued, voice hard. "Our cyber team linked one breach— personal banking data—to a flagged location. This is global, Molly. One crack in the system and entire populations are exposed. We're standing on the edge of a weaponized future."

The bile returned—not from the sea, but from the sickening truth. I steadied myself, eyes still fixed on the

horizon. It offered no peace now, only the illusion of distance. Blair's voice dropped.

"You and Ciara must stay invisible. Play the role. Smile. Grieve. But keep digging quietly. We're dealing with machinery far more complex than what's visible."

The wind howled around us. For a long moment, none of us moved. Then, almost in sync, Ciara and I exchanged a glance—silent, resolute. Without a word, we melted into the press of passengers at the exit ramp. Catalina shimmered ahead, sunlit charm and postcard beauty that felt almost cruel against the chaos burning in Los Angeles. The island held its calm, a fragile bubble of peace, while everything else waited, unresolved, beyond the horizon. Detective Blair lingered briefly near the lower deck, blending with ferry staff as she prepared to return to the precinct under cover. Playing our part, Ciara and I merged seamlessly into a group of unsuspecting tourists, twenty in total, led by a silver-haired guide with an encyclopedic knowledge of the island and a voice that soothed my frayed nerves. We followed winding trails as he spoke of wildlife, shipwrecks, and Catalina folklore. I nodded and smiled when prompted, but my mind drifted miles away, tangled in offshore accounts, stolen data, and names now heavy with consequence.

The tour was refreshingly lovely, with gorgeous views, fragrant breezes, and enough space to think. I needed that. Something soft to balance the steel of what Blair had given us. During lunch, Ciara slipped away quietly, catching a small commuter plane back to the mainland. No goodbyes. No sudden moves. Just enough silence to keep her invisible. If anyone was watching, I prayed they didn't notice. I followed suit after the tour, booking a ride on Catalina's family-run helicopter service—quiet, discreet, and fast. The island held its peace, a bright bubble untouched by the chaos chasing us. But as the mainland grew closer beneath the rotors, I braced myself—the real fight was still ahead.

Back home, the stillness felt loud. Blair's revelations echoed like a warning bell, but Miss Marple's voice steadied me. Her world was different, but her methods—rooted in observation, intuition, and quiet resolve—felt essential. I remembered one of her lines as if whispered just for me: *"Listen to your heart; it's smarter."* She knitted to still the noise—to let the answers rise. So I lit a candle, boiled water for tea, and began working on the soothing puzzle I'd started weeks ago. If I were going to face this storm, I'd need every ounce of stillness I could summon.

10

Smoke and Mirrors

I took Tulsi's preliminary advice to heart and temporarily set my investigation aside. Any digging must be subtle. With her assurance that leaving the city at the end of the month was safe, I shifted my focus to the move to Rose Haven. Yet, embarking on a new chapter without Daniel felt surreal. An unexpected wave of vulnerability surfaced as I thought of Rose Cottage— the remembrance of familiar perfume clinging to the air. And then, there was the locket. Its significance troubled me in countless ways. It couldn't be ignored. I picked up the phone and called Tulsi. She was out of the office, but that's when I learned the news: Bates had left the force. His office was wiped clean, erased as though he had never existed. A man with blood on his hands rising to such prominence was never addressed. No charges were filed against him, and there was no hint of ties to Daniel's death. Instead, the media was handed a polished statement about his "retirement," crafted to perfection, leaving nothing but questions and shadows in its wake. The next day, Bates reappeared—not as the disgraced officer he should have been, but as a man with ambition. He sat under the harsh glow of studio lights, smugly announcing his plans to write a memoir, promising to "help" where he could. His words dripped with the hollow authority of someone untouchable who could play the game. But to me, it was a fresh wound. Watching him parading this false persona—this supposed philanthropist whose compassion now extended to the lives he had destroyed—was unbearable. He had escaped justice, and now, he stood in front of the world, cloaked in lies, daring us all to believe him.

Many were convinced he was not culpable and that the media was behind the accusations of brutality. Yet, his removal was a small victory in a much larger war—a battle won, yet an elusive enemy loomed in the shadows. The perfume and locket

mystery hung in the balance. There were more nagging dots to connect, and I prayed that Tulsi, Ciara, and I would piece them together. In the meantime, I sent my resume to several papers around Rose Haven, eager to dive back into work. But just as Bates's shadow began to recede, something unexpected happened. Janet, Mr. Takahashi's assistant at the L.A. Times, called with an important assignment. My heart leaped with excitement, but confusion quickly followed. It had been two months since our awkward conversation, and I had assumed my position had been filled.

"Janet, I thought someone else took my position."

"No. He's given a few minor assignments to other reporters, but your position is still open."

"Is it possible to speak with Mr. Takahashi?"

"He's out of the office. Can I give him a message?"

"Yes. Please ask him for a letter of recommendation. I'm interested in what he thinks of my work."

"Really? Are you leaving us?"

I sidestepped her question, asking if the letter could be mailed or ready for pickup by tomorrow. She agreed and pressed me for an answer regarding the assignment.

"Can you give me until tomorrow to decide?"

"Sure, Molly. But please say yes."

The following day, a glowing letter of recommendation arrived by special delivery. I held it like a lifeline—tangible proof I hadn't imagined the stonewalling, the sudden silence, the walls closing in. At lunch, I passed it to Tulsi across the table. She skimmed it, then looked up, her expression tight.

"Molly," she said carefully, "I found out why you weren't getting assignments. It was Bates. He asked for your dismissal. Mr. Takahashi refused."

I paused, stunned. "You're serious?"

She nodded.

My breath caught. "He tried to bury me—*from inside the Times?*"

Disbelief hit first, followed by anger.

"Before assignments on fashion, I've written about warlords, corporate corruption, and offshore black sites. But this? This was personal." I shoved my plate aside. Nerves frayed. "He was willing to ruin my career—just to shut me up."

The weight of it settled like smoke in my chest. There it was. Not imagined. Not paranoia. *Proof.*

Tulsi nodded. "He can still make things difficult, but with the investigation ongoing, I doubt he'll push it. For now."

His absence felt less like a relief and more like a silence waiting to be broken. He wasn't gone. Just reorganizing.

Tulsi softened.

"A few more connections are about to crumble. You'll be in the clear soon. Molly, getting that letter was a smart move."

Her words brought some relief,

"I've decided to take the *Times* assignment," I said. "It's at Twentieth Century Fox. It'll be my last one before I move."

"You're not telling them you're leaving?"

"No. Just that I won't be available for future work."

She arched a brow. "You sure you don't want to apply for I.A.?"

I laughed. "Me? Internal Affairs?"

"Why not? You're tenacious. Snoopy, but effective."

Before I could answer, she changed gears. "How's the packing going?"

"Halfway there."

"That's progress. And speaking of moving forward, Ciara's slow return is going well. She's started with the Intervention Team and should be back full-time soon. We're thrilled she's finding her footing again—and yes, we're all looking forward to her great coffee."

I smiled, grateful for some good news. In a war full of shadows, even small victories felt like light.

"Thanks for that," I said. "And for helping Ciara ease back in. These little steps… they mean so much." I paused. "Is there anything I can do for you?"

She shook her head. "This is a solitary job, Molly. For security reasons. But your friendship means a lot."

"As yours does to me," I said. "I know justice isn't always guaranteed. But I believe in your fight. I always have."

Tulsi looked away, visibly moved.

"I'll keep doing everything I can, Molly. But knowing you've got my back—it helps more than you know."

That afternoon became a pivotal moment, etched into memory like sunlight through stained glass, warming every fiber of my being. The following morning, I awoke with a rare and radiant sense that life was, somehow, good again. The beauty held until it became believable, but was momentarily shattered by a loud knock rattling my door. My breath caught until I heard laughter and a familiar voice shouting my name. Ciara stood on the porch, flanked by five off-duty officers, each carrying coffee, donuts, and flattened moving boxes.

"Good morning!" she called. "We're here to help you pack!"

I stood frozen as they poured into the house, turning my chaotic living room into a buzzing hive of energy and care. By noon, every box was filled. Then they whisked me away for lunch, treating me like an honored guest instead of a woman with a trail of grief behind her. It was a whirlwind of support, a vibrant moment of connection—a welcome gift.

Two nights later, that glorious light was obliterated. Ciara called. Her voice was low, almost hollow.

"Blair's dead."

The words didn't register.

"She was shot. Drive-by. They got her on her way home last night."

I sank onto the edge of the bed. An ice-cold wind swept through me like a torrential wave.

"She took every precaution," Ciara continued. "But we think they planted a tracker on her car. Then they removed it after the hit."

I covered my mouth, as if it might stop the rising scream.

"They've arrested one suspect. The rest? Ghosts. This wasn't random, Molly. They hunted her."

The call ended in silence. I sat there in the dark, stunned, barely breathing. Then my phone rang again. Mr. Takahashi. I let it ring to voicemail. He called back. Then again. On the third try, I answered.

"Ms. Cleary," he said, clipped and formal. "Apologies for the timing. But I need you to write an article on Detective Blair's shooting."

His words landed like a furious blow—swift, cold, and clinical.

"I'm not the right person for that," I said, my voice brittle. "You have reporters with more experience in criminal investigations."

"You knew her," he replied. "Your voice matters. If I have it by tonight, it'll run on the front page."

There was no condolence. No space for grief. Just business. My stomach turned. How did he even know about Blair and me? Had Tulsi told him? Then, through the searing pain, came the words I'd once spoken over lunch: "Is there anything I can do for you?" What was once a quiet kindness now echoed as a raw, helpless offering—my last reach toward her. Swallowing the fury rising in my throat, I forced the words out.

"You'll have it in an hour."

I ended the call and let the tears come. Grief and rage collided in every part of my being, choking me. But I could write. I had to. I brewed my strongest tea, sat at my desk, and began. A 500-word tribute poured out of me—sharp, clean, and pulsing with heartbreak. One of the best pieces I'd ever written. But it still felt impossibly small compared to what Blair

had given. After one last edit, I hit send. The article vanished into the digital void—my final dispatch, Tulsi's truth, and the closing signature on my life at the Times.

Meanwhile, under the cover of darkness, Ciara and Kyle launched their covert patrols—tracking shadows, retracing Tulsi's last moves, chasing any thread that might lead to her killer. By day, Ciara led the planning of a city-wide memorial in Tulsi's honor. The meticulous logistics were a brilliant smokescreen, masking the deeper operation underway. Then came the break.

Just days after Tulsi's death, Ciara discovered that the FBI had sealed all of her investigative files. No warning. No explanation. But something about the timing was too precise to be a coincidence. Then, the next domino fell. Ciara's findings about the Senator's direct connection to Chief Bates reached Congress. And this time, it couldn't be buried. Proceedings were launched under Article I, Section 5, Clause 2: *"Each House may determine the Rules of its Proceedings, punish its Members for disorderly Behavior, and expel a Member with the Concurrence of two-thirds."* The Senator was forcibly removed from office for misconduct. But no criminal charges followed. Not yet. The official line: "Insufficient evidence." Detective Tulsi Blair was posthumously awarded the Medal of Valor.

The moment the news broke, her final words to me echoed like prophecy: *"A few more connections are about to crumble, Molly; that should put you in the clear."* It was a hollow triumph. Justice had limped across the finish line—too late to matter for the one who deserved it most. The day of her memorial arrived. Hundreds gathered—citizens, officers, family, friends—all standing beneath a sky that looked just a shade too calm for what the day demanded. The ceremony was solemn and beautiful, but there was a shadow in the air that no Medal of Valor could lift.

When Ciara stepped up to the podium and announced the award, polite applause followed. But I saw it in the

crowd—etched on weary faces, locked behind tired eyes: resentment, frustration, and unspoken questions.

As Ciara descended the steps, her posture straight and her face composed, something within her cracked—her smile faltered, she couldn't quite catch her breath. She reached the empty chair beside me and sank into it slowly, like the world's weight had finally found her. Her voice was low, trembling, barely above a whisper.

"Molly… we need to talk after the memorial."

I turned to her, concern rising.

"Okay," I said gently. "Are you alright?"

She didn't answer right away. Just stared ahead, holding back the storm. Then, she nodded, but the lie was written across her face. Her composure was a crumbling mask—one breath away from shattering. The pain in her eyes was louder than any scream. I glanced past her to Kyle, seated on her other side. Quietly, I asked,

"Can we meet at my place after the service?"

He gave a solemn nod, his jaw tight with concern. As the memorial ended, we slipped Ciara out a side door, flanking her like guards. She didn't speak on the drive—just silence. She made it through my front door before her legs gave out. Kyle and I caught her mid-fall, easing her onto the couch as her body finally surrendered to what her spirit had carried alone.

"Water." She barely managed a whisper.

Then the dam broke. Her sobs came like a storm unleashed—violent, full-bodied, unrelenting. The kind of grief that doesn't just escape, but erupts. It tore through the silence, rattling the walls, clawing through the air like something alive. We sat within her torment. No words.

As Ciara began recovering, Kyle stood, gently touching my shoulder.

"I'll cover her shift for a while," he said, voice hoarse.

The front door clicked shut behind him. I turned back to Ciara, still collapsed on the couch, her body limp with exhaustion.

"Ciara, what can I get you?" I asked softly, knowing full well that nothing could make this right. She didn't respond right away. Just stared at the floor, her breath ragged. When she finally spoke, her voice was barely more than air, so low I had to lean in.

"Molly..." She paused, her hands trembling. "Stefan arranged the Taxine for Tulsi."

My breath caught.

"We're piecing it together," she continued. "Bates knew about Dominic's death. We believe he ordered Stefan to eliminate Tulsi. When that failed, he manipulated an ambitious officer from another precinct—fed him false intel, knowing it would leak to one of the gang leaders. Bates publicly praised Tulsi for orchestrating the drug bust that brought down the city's most violent street gang. Their leader got life. In retaliation, they killed her."

The words slammed into me.

Ciara looked up at me, eyes hollow but steady.

"We've arrested two of the shooters, and we're closing in on the one who coordinated the attack." She hesitated, then added, "There's more."

Of course, there was.

"After Stefan was locked away, he got word that a relative of Joel's was tied to his father's death. What looked like a suicide—it wasn't. Joel was murdered. We've detained two suspects, including the officer involved. We're building a case against Bates—linking him to the leak."

She paused again, this time longer, lying motionless on the couch, her face pale, her breath shallow. She gripped my hand suddenly, her fingers ice-cold.

"There's something else," she whispered. "We know who the locket belongs to, and why she was in your garden. Maybe even at Rose Cottage."

A sharp breath escaped me—I wasn't ready. I needed the truth... but feared what it might destroy. A darker part of me wasn't sure I could survive it. She didn't say the name.

Maybe she saw in my eyes that I wasn't ready to hear it. Not yet. The room closed around me, the air suddenly hot and humid. The silence between us was filled with what-ifs and half-formed fears I hadn't dared name out loud. Then, without warning, her eyes closed. Her body sagged against the cushions, her hand slipping from mine.

"Ciara?" I leaned closer. "Ciara—"

No answer. She'd passed out. I sat back, pulse pounding. The name stayed unspoken, suspended in the room like a storm cloud threatening to break. I have to face the truth, the entire truth—to speak the question I wasn't sure I wanted answered. An hour later, Kyle returned. And when Ciara opened her eyes again, her edges were hardened. The detective was back. She insisted she was ready to return to duty. But as I watched her walk out into the fading light, a tight coil of dread wound in my stomach—a slow, relentless knot refusing to loosen. I grabbed a cup of strong tea and went over each scenario while preparing my heart for the unspoken name.

Stefan Gotti was serving life. Bates had been forced out—the Senator, disgraced and expelled. On the surface, it looked like justice was finally turning our way. However, there were still missing pieces, such as a picture that hung slightly crooked. The scales weren't balanced yet. Something vital still lay hidden in shadow. Then the thought returned—sharp, uninvited. *How did Mr. Takahashi know about my connection to Tulsi?* And why did that knowledge feel like a thread—thin, frayed, and leading somewhere darker? Frustration simmered. But then, as if on cue, Miss Marple's voice echoed in my memory: *"Anger clouds the judgment, my dear, and leads to foolish decisions."* I breathed deeply. Let it settle. I had come too far to fall for fury.

Before sunrise the next morning, I drove to Bobby's Café—a quiet little spot Daniel and I used to visit on slow weekends. I reached for the door handle, half expecting to feel his hand over mine. The memory palpable—Daniel holding the door open, his heartwarming smile. Inside, the smell of

bacon and fresh coffee brought a familiar comfort. I slid into our booth. For a few precious moments, I pretended everything was the same. The coffee was hot, the eggs perfect. But he wasn't there. And he never would be again. The grief didn't vanish. It settled deeper, quieter, no longer crashing through me—but present all the same. That quiet resolve carried me through the morning, out of the cafe, and straight to the precinct.

The first rays of sun stretched across the parking lot as officers trickled in—crisp uniforms catching the light, faces weathered but resolute. Nods. Small smiles. Silent gestures that spoke volumes. Even in grief, we endure. The station hadn't changed. Same chipped paint. Same creaking floorboards. But Tulsi's absence followed me down every hallway. Detective James Franklin stood quietly in what used to be her office. The new title sat heavily on him—he wasn't just Officer Franklin anymore. The badge on his chest looked too new—the weight behind his eyes, too old. Life never asked if we were ready. It just came. Ciara was brewing her infamous coffee, each movement unhurried, sure. The aroma rose around us—sharp, grounding. She passed me a mug. The heat steadied more than just my hands.

Chief Paul Bertrum, Bates's replacement, moved with quiet authority. Steady and soft-spoken, each word to his officers was as a conductor guiding a symphony—subtle, composed, and in command without needing to prove it. Then his calm eyes caught mine and motioned me to join the morning briefing. Despite the solemn undertone, the room pulsed with a sense of hope—a quiet, purposeful energy. Each conversation was a small attempt to mend what had been torn. The sure voice of their new Chief rose above the hum, a steady comfort that reached everyone, softening the edges of the morning. As the meeting closed, he stepped toward me.

"You've still got family here, Ms. Cleary. Stay in touch," he said, offering his hand.

I shook it, grateful. "Thank you, Chief. And you've got family in Rose Haven. I've got extra rooms, Ciara-worthy coffee, and gardens with a view of the stars. Come anytime."

Their smiles said more than words. There were no heavy goodbyes, no tears, just the easy rhythm of shared jokes, warm laughter, and promises that felt real. Together, we stepped into the morning sun, the echo of camaraderie lingering in a warm embrace, locked within our souls. Their cheers faded as I shut the door. I gripped the wheel, caught between gratitude and the hollow tug of goodbye. I pulled out of the lot, stealing one last glance in the rearview mirror. Their faces—smiling, steady, framed in sunlight—burned into my memory as they slipped from view. I raised my hand in a quiet farewell, knowing that turning that corner meant leaving a piece of myself behind.

Trial by Fire

As I locked the door to my Brentwood home for the final time, the recollection of Daniel's death still haunted the threshold—that moment those terrible words had split my life in two. Now, I closed it for good. Following the moving van toward Rose Haven, I drove in silence, Daniel's memory strapped beside me—an invisible passenger—our love intact, untouched by time.

My thoughts drifted to Agatha Christie's *At Bertram's Hotel*. Miss Marple had always been the epitome of quiet certainty, cutting through lies with grace. I hadn't attained that gifted strength—but I was trying. Today, I felt more like the other Jane—the maid, a fan of Miss Marple herself. Still learning, still finding my way. She was eager, observant, but stumbling in the shadows of something far greater. Maid-Jane had misread the red herring. She'd tried to mimic Miss Marple's instincts and faltered. Yet even in that mistake, she'd grown. Miss Marple, with her soft smile, had said, *"Just get older, Jane."*

Not a dismissal. A truth. Wisdom came with time… and humility.

I held the wheel tighter. That was what I needed now. Not certainty. Not perfection. Just the courage to keep going. Daniel's case wasn't a mystery with clean edges but a tangle of lies, missteps, and hidden truths. And I had already tripped over my share of red herrings. But if I could learn from them and stay grounded in what mattered, I believed I'd find my way through.

As the hills of Rose Haven came into view, stress slowly loosened. Fragrant, invigorating ocean breezes carried a faint hint of roses as I turned the corner onto my new street. Then a burst of unexpected joy caught me off guard. Waiting at the curb—champagne in hand—stood David, Steven, and Claire. Steven popped the cork with a triumphant grin the moment I stepped out of the car. Ever the strategist, David pulled champagne flutes from his coat like a magician.

"We thought you deserved a proper welcome," Claire beamed.

Just as we raised our glasses, the unmistakable roar of a low-flying helicopter split the air. I glanced up as it descended toward the street, whipping wind into our faces. Seconds later, Ciara jumped down with five grinning officers in tow, waving like it was a reunion tour.

"Surprise!" she called out.

She sauntered over, wind in her hair, grinning like the ringmaster of a spectacle.

"We're here to help—I pulled some strings. LAPD's news chopper. We've got until tomorrow before it flies us back."

I laughed—really laughed—as astonishment gave way to joy.

"Wow, what an entrance."

The blast of wind swept us all closer, lifting laughter into the sky as the helicopter powered away. The movers, now wide-eyed, flung open the back of the truck and got to work.

Boxes began to vanish into the house, carried by officers and friends alike. The storm wasn't over. But here, in this moment, I had sunshine. And better still, what I'd assumed would be a quiet move-in became an instant celebration—a welcome so full of life and light it felt orchestrated by destiny.

Claire had stocked the refrigerator with farm-fresh eggs, herbs, cheeses, and jams. David brought crates of provisions from his market—enough to last a week, maybe more. Every box was unpacked in a whirlwind of laughter and love, each room transforming before my eyes as Claire expertly directed the furniture, much like a seasoned set designer. It was magical.

Steven left to relieve their babysitter as night deepened, but the rest of us—Claire, David, and the L.A. six—claimed spots on couches and sleeping bags scattered across the living room. It felt like college again—the kind of night where you talk until sleep steals your words. In that stillness, surrounded by steady breaths and soft blankets, I realized this wasn't just a new beginning. It was *the* beginning. A second chance. A softer chapter built on trust, truth, and the wisdom I was just beginning to uncover.

The Stillness Before the Shatter

As I entered the kitchen the following morning, Ciara and the five officers greeted me in strange unison. Smiling and stepping aside, they revealed a gorgeous, state-of-the-art coffee machine that took center stage, flanked by a sleek grinder, a bag of dark French roast, and ten police-themed mugs lined up like a tactical unit. My breath caught. The tears came instantly. Ciara, ever prepared, handed me a tissue, but her eyes shimmered too. She began to grind the beans, and the rich scent of her signature brew soon filled the kitchen, mingling with the aroma of breakfast and sounds of birdsong outside—comfort itself.

We gathered at the table, and for a rare, fleeting moment, peace settled over me with the warmth of sunlight on warm stone. I wanted to ask her about the case, but couldn't bring myself to break the spell. Ciara leaned back in her chair, her feet up in that familiar, thoughtful way. As if reading my thoughts, she said gently,

"Molly, I'll update you later in the week."

I exhaled with a slight giggle.

"Thanks. That would be great."

Just then, David, Steven, and Claire appeared in the doorway, sensing something in the air.

"Should we leave you two to talk?" David asked, always perceptive.

Ciara shook her head. "No—better saved for another time."

But something shifted in her eyes as she turned to David—a flicker of recognition… or suspicion.

"David," she said, almost offhandedly. "Your clearance is impressive."

He smiled, unusually calm. "Aye, that's a longer story."

Ciara smiled back—layers beneath it—and didn't push. The moment was acceptable for now. Steven clapped his hands together, eyes twinkling.

"Well, we were thinking—before we take the officers to the pickup site, maybe a quick detour to the farm? Fresh eggs, goat cheese… Molly, what do you say?"

I grinned. "Absolutely yes."

Steven's suggestion was met with eager agreement, and just like that, the air was threaded with anticipation.

David added with a smirk, "The pasture's been cleared already. Chopper's due tae land there round three."

I laughed, imagining the officers being airlifted out from a field full of goats. Claire, Steven, and David went ahead in David's truck, promising to meet us by the pasture. A few minutes later, the rest of us—Ciara and the five officers packed into my SUV. The car vibrated with laughter until we reached

viewing distance of the Moore cottage entrance. A sudden hush fell. Ciara gasped, her hand flying to her mouth.

"Stop the car," she whispered.

I braked instinctively.

Before I could ask why, the officers were already climbing out—silent, wide-eyed. Even Ciara, usually composed and unflappable, moved as if entranced. Just ahead, the wooden footbridge stood beneath a canopy of trees, its arched frame casting long shadows in the morning light. There was something reverent about it—something still and knowing—it held whispers of lifetimes past. They stood there, taking it in.

"Molly," one of the officers said softly, "the town, the lane, the bridge… It's just as magical as you described."

Ciara nodded. "It's incredible. I can see why you came here."

With that, they crossed the bridge slowly, capturing every detail. As they reached the other side and started through the gate, I called out, half-teasing:

"Wait! Let's ensure Effie, their Holstein, doesn't greet us unannounced."

That broke the spell, ushering child-like laughter to echo off the wooden beams, complete, spontaneous, the kind we hadn't shared in far too long. Beyond the gate, Steven, Claire, and David stood near the pasture, each holding loads of the Moore's signature touches: freshly baked bread, leafy greens, jam jars, and goat cheese wheels glistening in the sun. It felt surreal, like stepping into a dream that had, for once, decided to come true.

"Is it safe, Steven? Is Effie still roaming free?" I called out, feigning boldness.

Steven's grin widened, his eyes dancing with mischief.

"She's safely harnessed, but she's been waiting for you, Molly Cleary."

Laughter bubbled up again as the trio approached and handed out baskets to everyone—a simple gesture that felt

deeply profound. We were invited to share in their harvest, to gather fruits and vegetables of our choice. The garden pulsed with color—vibrant reds, deep greens, sun-warmed yellows—carried on air thick with the scent of ripe tomatoes, sweet basil, and rich soil. It didn't take long before my friends returned, faces flushed with delight, their baskets brimming with nature's bounty. In Claire's sunlit kitchen, Steven added a wheel of his prized lavender goat cheese to each basket before they were wrapped in cellophane and tied with twine. Ciara labeled them in her clean, looping script. Claire slipped handwritten notes of thanks between the jam jars. As the L.A. six reached for their baskets, a quiet sense of belonging stirred—something I'd only glimpsed in the city. The weight of the week, at last, was lifting.

Out in the distance, the low hum of rotor blades stirred the stillness. We stepped outside just as the news helicopter swept over the hills, its shadow skimming the goat pasture David had cleared for this moment. The wind from its descent kicked up swirls of golden dust, tousling our hair and rattling the trees. The officers climbed aboard one by one, waving through the haze with tired smiles and full hearts. There were no grand farewells—just a look, a nod, and the wordless recognition that this place had given them something they'd carry forever. Ciara paused at the steps of the chopper, then turned and pulled me into a fierce hug. Her voice was steady.

"You're not alone, Molly. We've got your back—no matter where this leads."

Her eyes held something more—something unsaid. I nodded, committing it to memory. As the helicopter lifted into the sky, I shielded my eyes against the glare and watched until it became a speck, then disappeared behind the ridge. The quiet that followed was heavy, but not hollow. It was *pregnant* with possibility. With danger. Claire came to stand beside me.

"You think it's beginning, don't you?"

I didn't answer—not with words. My eyes were locked on the phone I'd left on the porch railing. It had just buzzed. A text. From Marcy.

Court date moved. You were right about Chief Bates. Be careful.
—M

A chill slid down my spine. I hadn't told Marcy *everything.* Which meant someone else had. I should have felt fear. Maybe I did. But so did something else—a quiet courage, born not of certainty, but of love. As I stepped off the bridge to Abbey Lane, a grand love escorted me through the exquisitely marbled sunlight—I skipped like I was twelve again. Only this time, I knew absolute freedom as I reveled in the vibrant sweetness of nature, carried on the breath of its wings. When I reached my front steps, twilight had settled in— the golden hour fading to a soft lavender wash. I unlocked the door, still smiling, and stepped inside. And froze.

The scent hit first—chemical. Wrong. My hand froze on the light switch. The kitchen light was already on. I knew I'd turned it off. Then it hit my tongue—sharp, acidic. A cold coil tightened in my chest. I set the basket down, silent. Then stepped toward the hallway, each footfall louder than the last. The study door was ajar. That door had been closed. I pushed it open slowly, and the air shifted again. Not just disturbed. *Violated.* My desk drawers had been pulled open. Not ransacked—*searched.* Purposefully. Every file was still there—every folder. But the old shoebox I had kept hidden beneath the bottom drawer—the one that held Daniel's last journal and notes about the locket—was gone. Gone. My breath caught in my throat. And then I saw it. Taped to the edge of my computer screen, barely visible against the white monitor frame. A single Polaroid photo—The image: Daniel and I, from years ago, standing on a cliff near Big Sur. But in thick black marker, someone had circled my face. And beneath it, scrawled in block letters: STOP DIGGING OR YOU'LL JOIN HIM.

When Ghosts Walk In

My calm was fractured. The following day, amid the chaos, the burner phone rang—the line reserved only for the most urgent, dangerous truths. Dread began its ascent as I reached for it. Ciara's voice was steady, but I knew her too well. Beneath her calm exterior, something was amiss.

"Molly, James Franklin—the new lead investigator—has uncovered something," she began. "Dina McFarland, Sharon Bates' childhood friend, has been having an affair with Harold Bates for the past eight years."

The room chilled, sunlight dulling around me.

"And the locket?" she continued. "It belongs to Dina. We should know soon why it ended up in your garden—and if it was her perfume you noticed in Rose Cottage."

The news sliced through the afternoon like a blade. My mind reeled. Sharon Bates—poised, elegant, always in control. Had she been tangled in Daniel's life, too?

"Eight years?" I whispered.

"Sharon suspected something five years ago," Ciara said, her voice heavy. "But she never dug deeper. She was too afraid of Harold to confront him. So she drowned her suspicions in daily cocktails. Numbed herself."

My mind reeled as I listened. *And now the locket. Why had it ended up in our garden? What else did Dina destroy? And if it was her perfume, she was here too.*

Ciara's voice dropped lower.

"Molly, are you okay?"

"Yes, I'm good. What else?

"Detective Franklin thinks Dina may have been watching Daniel. Acting under Harold's orders. And if Dina was the one in your garden, Molly... she knows where you are."

I stared out the window, but the colors of the garden seemed drained, warped.

"How long have they known?" I asked.

"Not too long. Franklin only pieced it together after pulling Sharon's archived files. Dina kept an encrypted surveillance log. But Daniel's name was in there. More than once."

My grip on the phone tightened.

"So they were tracking him. And now they're tracking me."

"Molly," she said gently, "Franklin thinks the locket may have been planted. A warning. Or bait."

A sharp knock rattled my front door. Shocked, I stiffened, tears flooded my eyes as fright overtook me.

"Ciara—someone's here."

"Don't answer it," she said quickly. "Can you see who it is?"

I crept toward the window and peeled back the edge of the curtain. A silver sedan idled at the curb. A man in a dark suit stood at my front door. Sunglasses. Earpiece. Hands folded. Not LAPD. Not a delivery driver. Too still. Too precise.

"He's not FBI," I said. Looks private. Professional."

Ciara's voice sharpened. "Private security, maybe. From Bates. Molly, *do not* open that door."

I stood frozen. An envelope slid through the mail slot. Without hesitation, the man turned and returned to his car, then drove off. Thirty seconds passed before I moved. I pulled on gloves from under the sink and crouched to retrieve the envelope, which had no return address. Inside: one sheet of paper. White. Typed. *You're stirring ghosts, Molly. Some things are buried for a reason. Leave them there.* At the bottom, in red ink, two block initials: C.B.

I sat sequestered in a paralyzing moment, the letter trembling in my hands.

"Molly?" Ciara's voice called faintly through the phone. "Are you there?"

I swallowed. My voice came out as a whisper as I read the letter aloud to Ciara.

226

"Ciara, What about Sharon Bates? Is she involved?"

"When Detective Franklin questioned her, there was no evidence of involvement. Sharon collapsed when she learned the other woman was Dina—her best friend. She's been sent to a medical retreat. They're hoping she'll recover, but... It's not looking good."

I closed my eyes, the image of Sharon—so composed, so carefully polished—fracturing under the weight of betrayal. For a moment, an ache rose in me, an urge to reach out, to offer comfort. But Ciara's following words shut that door before it opened.

"Molly, any contact with Sharon is unwise. Harold still has a long and destructive reach, as you've just witnessed. It's safer for everyone if you keep your distance."

I nodded silently, the ache hardening into something else.

"There's more," Ciara said, her voice now edged with urgency. "Detective James is also convinced Daniel's death wasn't an accident. He believes Daniel kept track of clandestine meetings—times, dates, names. Possibly even coded links to Bates' operations. Have you found anything like that in his notes?"

I hesitated. "Daniel was alluding to those possibilities, but I think someone else is worried."

"What do you mean?"

"A few days ago, I came home and realized something was off. My study had been searched—not ransacked, but... *inspected*. Carefully. Deliberately. Nothing obvious was missing except one thing: a box of Daniel's private notes. It had old journals and references about the locket. I'd hidden it. But someone knew exactly where to find it."

There was a pause on the line. Then Ciara spoke, her voice tighter.

"Did you report it?"

"I couldn't. Not without exposing myself to local law enforcement—I don't know who's clean anymore."

"Molly…" Her tone softened, but the undercurrent was sharp. "This is escalating. If someone came inside your home, they're not just watching you—they're already *in it*. Be careful."

"Can I tell anyone?"

"I wouldn't advise it," she said. "But I trust your judgment."

The call ended, but the unease lingered—a dull fog rising inside me. I had combed through Daniel's papers weeks ago, desperate for answers—but now that instinct, which I trusted most, rose again with a quiet insistence: *Go back. Look again.* And so I did. I made my way to the garage and began to sift through the final four unopened boxes I hadn't had the heart to unpack. Each item I pulled out felt heavier than the last, suffocating in its potential. A life in fragments—his sketches, his notations, and his whispers, tucked between lines and margins. Then, in the last box, stuck beneath a stack of travel receipts and dog-eared manuals, I spotted a faded bank slip. A safe deposit box—my heart stopped. How had I missed this?

I sealed the boxes in a daze and ran back into the house, rifling through drawers for Daniel's key ring. Nothing. I searched the nightstand, coat pockets, every corner of the study—still nothing. The bank was no help. Without the physical key, ID, marriage certificate, and Daniel's death certificate, I was locked out. Frustration boiled over. I stood in the middle of the room, fists clenched, wishing I could scream the truth into the walls. I needed a break—a moment to breathe. I made tea and tried to steady my thoughts. The scent of brewing Provence tea leaves filled the room, but clarity didn't come. Miss Marple would knit, I reminded myself— some repetitive motion to tease out the knots in a case. I didn't know how to knit, but I could find something like it. Something that might help reset my mind. I thought *I'd buy a new, more intricate puzzle. Perhaps the pieces of this mystery will also fall into place.* Just as I reached for my coat, the phone rang again. David.

"Molly," he said without preamble, "I'd like to take you to lunch. There's been a discovery—quite amazin'....and it could change everythin.'"

His tone was measured, but the urgency beneath it was unmistakable. He had information, possibly about Daniel, Bates, or both. We met near the harbor and walked to Hanna's Café, our quiet local favorite. Despite the noon bustle, David had secured a booth far back, away from the windows and ears. As we sat, he leaned forward, his voice low and deliberate.

"I received confirmation of my ancestry. But that's not why I brought ye here." He hesitated, scanning the room before continuing.

"What I found... links Chief Bates to somethin' dark., ancient, that most people would rather keep buried."

He handed me a letter, his hands trembling slightly. As I read, the room seemed to tilt around me. The letter detailed how Prince Edward and his brother, Prince Richard, had escaped would-be assassins only to fall ill with a pandemic. Richard had died, but Edward, in a weakened state, was given a new identity: *Michael Carey*. Smuggled into Ireland, he recovered and was later moved to Scotland. There, he changed his name to *Maoilios Ogilvy* and married *Esme de Brus*, with whom he had six children. David looked at me, his voice barely above a whisper.

"I'm the great-great-grandson of their eldest son. The only living member of the line."

The air left my lungs.

"And Chief Bates?" I asked, afraid to hear the answer.

David nodded solemnly. "His ancestry traces back tae the men responsible for the assassination attempt."

The implications crashed over me like a tidal wave. History wasn't distant anymore—it was here, staring me in the face, tightening around the present like a noose. The connection between the corruption I was chasing and this centuries-old truth wasn't just symbolic—it was *blood-deep*.

"David," I asked quietly, "what will you do? Will you stay in Rose Haven?"

He sighed. "Ah dinnae ken."

"I don't understand."

"Sorry, Molly. It means 'I don't know.' If there's no publicity, aye—I can stay. But if the media gets hold of it..." He trailed off, then shrugged. "Ah dinnae ken."

He looked as weary as I felt. The emotional and legal ramifications were overwhelming. To be quietly reinstated into the monarchy's lineage, to carry a title, and receive a royal inheritance—it read like fairy tale prose. But the Royal Family had only offered him their best efforts to keep things private. No guarantees.

"Are you bothered by the injustice?" I asked.

He stared into the middle distance, silent. A moment later, he offered a faint, cloaking smile.

"It was a long time ago. Doesn't bother me now."

But his hazel eyes told the truth. Behind them, I saw centuries of struggle, betrayal, and pain. His ancestors had survived assassination, and now he had to endure the legacy.

"David," I said, reaching across the table, "what can I do to help?"

"Be a friend tae me, Molly Cleary," David said, his voice low and urgent, "and keep this quiet as long as ye can."

"I will," I said, my throat tightening.

Just then, the café door opened. The bell jingled softly. I glanced up and felt the air drain from the room. It was Dina McFarland. Her red Hermès scarf caught the light, elegant and unmistakable, fluttering wildly as she entered the room. Her sunglasses perched atop her head, and a faint smile played at her lips as she scanned the tables. She hadn't changed since that afternoon at the fashion show, still poised and disarmingly beautiful. Except now I saw a lurking danger in her eyes. Our eyes met. She tilted her head slightly, acknowledging me.

"Molly," she said smoothly, walking closer. "What a surprise."

230

"Dina. I didn't know you were in Rose Haven."

"I wasn't," she said, her smile tightening. "But it seems we're both full of surprises these days."

Her eyes shifted wistfully to David, a curious look on her face. "And you are?"

David stood slowly, guarded.

"A friend."

She extended a hand, but David didn't take it. After a beat, she lowered it with grace, but her word was acidic,

"Charming."

The tension between us crackled like static.

"Well," she said with a silky shrug,

"I won't interrupt. Just wanted to say hello." She turned back to me. "We should catch up sometime."

Before I could answer, she was gone—vanishing into the afternoon as if she hadn't just dropped a spark into a dry forest. David exhaled slowly.

"That... wis her?"

I nodded, pulse pounding.

"Yes. That was Dina McFarland."

He shook his head.

"Then whatever we thought we knew... it's aboot tae get worse."

We lingered in silence for another moment, the warmth of the café now strangely at odds with a growing chill. We said our goodbyes, and as David walked off toward the market, a driving determination settled over me. I needed to stay two steps ahead of whatever storm was brewing—and hold fast to the few people I could still trust.

Unready to return home, I wandered down the street and slipped into Jenn's bookstore. The comforting scent of old pages and wood polish grounded me, wrapping around my nerves like a reassuring balm. As I browsed the shelves, my eyes caught on a thousand-piece puzzle titled *"Miss Marple and Mr. Stringer: The Mystery of the Manor House."* I smiled. It felt like a gift from Miss Jane Marple. Clutching the box, I left the shop

with a hint of lightness, a reminder of the cleverness and clarity I'd always admired in Miss Marple—and the calm I needed to keep. Back home, I set the puzzle on the dining room table, my hand hovering over the lid. Had Dina been here? In my new home? Her sudden entrance at the café. That knowing look. The timing. It all knotted in my thoughts. I grabbed the burner phone and dialed Ciara. She answered on the first ring.

"Molly?"

"She's here, Ciara," I said. "Dina. I just saw her at Hanna's Café."

A sharp intake of breath. "What? Are you sure?"

"She came right up to me. Said we should catch up sometime." I paused. "Ciara, she was calm. Almost... expectant. Like she knew exactly what she was doing."

"She's not supposed to be anywhere near you," Ciara said, her voice low and urgent. "Rose Haven wasn't on our radar. We thought she was still under surveillance near L.A."

"She's not," I said. "Not anymore."

A pause. Then: "Stay vigilant. If she made that move, expect something else. I'll alert Franklin and send covert help."

We hung up. I stared at the puzzle box again, then slowly opened it, watching the pieces spill out like fragments of a mystery still waiting to be solved. As I sorted the edges from the corners, I couldn't help but wonder: Was I still putting things together? Or was someone else carefully pulling them apart? Then, as I found a matching piece, a calming thought surfaced—I hadn't heard back from the *Rose Haven Gazette*. I picked up the phone and dialed. Andrew Clayborne answered on the second ring.

"Cleary? I was just about to call you. We've had an opening come up. Can you come in this afternoon?"

The timing felt too convenient, but I said yes anyway.

11

The Paris Lie

When Andrew Clayborne offered me a job, I didn't hesitate. It felt like a small, sharp light piercing the encroaching fog. I said yes before I even asked what the job entailed. Two weeks later, I had a regular byline in the *Rose Haven Gazette* and a column that locals were reading. The comforting rhythm of routine settled around me—a well-worn sweater—familiar, protective. But constantly vying for attention, unease still threaded through the edges of my day. No barrage of headlines or looming deadlines could silence the deeper mystery still tightening its grip.

Each evening, I turned to my puzzle—methodical and deliberate. With every configuration that clicked into place, I felt a quiet sense of control return. It helped—for a little while. Then, almost accidentally, I stumbled upon the two legal documents I needed—Daniel's death certificate and our marriage license—tucked inside a file box I'd nearly given up organizing. It felt like a nudge from the universe. Or perhaps, as Miss Marple might say, "A clue always shows up when you're paying attention to something else."

That weekend, I resolved to visit our old bank in Los Angeles. The thought of what might be inside that box—the secrets Daniel died protecting—left my stomach in knots. Would it be answers? Or something closer to Pandora's box? When I arrived in Los Angeles, the city hit me like a furnace—105 degrees and a layer of smog thick enough to chew. It was the one thing I hadn't missed. The pressure only mounted with a phone call from my former boss, Jason. His gruff voice was filled with feigned surprise and wariness.

"You're in town? Let's meet for lunch."

I froze. How did he know I was here? I offered a flimsy excuse and said I'd meet him for coffee later. He paused—followed by a clipped, almost grudging *fine*—sending a sharp

prickle through my nerves. But once inside the bank, the marble lobby offered a sanctuary: cool air, spotless floors, and the kind of silence that buzzed beneath your skin. Mr. Pridmore, the bank manager, greeted me with a courteous nod and reviewed my paperwork without a word of doubt. Moments later, I was led to a small, sterile room and left alone with Daniel's safe deposit box.

"Please let me know if I can be of further service, Mrs. Cleary," he said, closing the door behind him.

"Thank you," I murmured, though my voice barely sounded like mine.

I sat across from the box, staring at it like it might stare back. My pulse thudded in my ears. The metal lid felt heavier than it should've been. I opened it slowly, the hinges creaking through the stillness. Inside: Daniel's old police notepads, letters, and two sealed envelopes. I didn't touch anything right away. My chest tightened as I stared at the contents—each item he had chosen to leave behind. His handwriting. His secrets. His last, silent trust. I wanted to scoop it all up, shove it into my purse, and make a run for it. Save the unraveling for later. But fear and logic don't always walk hand-in-hand.

I closed my eyes, drawing in a slow, deliberate breath. *Lord, give me the strength to face whatever I'm about to find.* Finally, with trembling hands, I opened the first envelope—two open-ended plane tickets to Paris. My breath caught. For a moment, my mind went blank. Paris—the dream Daniel and I had always talked about but never realized. Had he been planning to surprise me? Or was this something else... something tied to Dina? The tickets were dated only weeks before his death. This wasn't the time to dwell.

The second item was a large manila envelope labeled Vacation in Daniel's handwriting. My pulse spiked. I opened it—neat stacks of one-hundred-dollar bills. Thousands—maybe tens of thousands—banded tightly, silently accusing. The weight of it was staggering. Where had he gotten this money? And why hide it here? Tears welled in my eyes, blurring

the lines of the truth as dread settled over me like a shroud. This wasn't just a surprise trip. It wasn't romantic. It was preparation. Escape. Or payoff.

My worst fear had returned with a vengeance: *Was Daniel part of something I never truly understood?* Hands shaking, I shoved everything back into my purse and stood abruptly. I needed answers. Now. I found Mr. Pridmore just outside the vault. He turned, startled, but before he could speak, I blurted,

"Are there any open accounts in either of our names?"

He blinked, then recovered, gesturing for me to follow.

"Let's check in my office."

A few quiet keystrokes later, he nodded.

"There's one remaining account in your husband's name. A small savings balance—three hundred dollars. You're listed as the beneficiary. Would you like to close it?"

"Yes," I said, struggling to keep my voice steady. "Can I see the transaction history?"

He hesitated, reading the desperation in my eyes.

"One moment."

When he returned, he handed me the printout. There had been sparse activity. The last deposit had been made six months before Daniel's death. There had been no transfers or withdrawals—just... stillness.

"How would you like the funds?" he asked.

"A check, please. And thank you, Mr. Pridmore."

He nodded with polite finality, and I took the enveloped check with mechanical precision. The realization of three hundred legal dollars in one hand and thousands of secret ones in my purse felt like two lives colliding—one I knew, and one I had never been meant to see. I was moments from devastation. The short walk to the car was endless. Every step was pounded with questions. *Was Daniel trying to protect me... or was he hiding from me?* As soon as I slid behind the wheel, I grabbed my phone and canceled the coffee meeting with Jason. I couldn't face him—not like this. We agreed to meet

tomorrow instead. Then, without another moment, I started the engine and drove straight to my hotel.

Once inside the safety of my room, I dropped my bag and locked the door behind me. Only then did I allow my hands to tremble. I spread Daniel's documents across the bed like puzzle pieces. Slowly, I began calculating the deposits. The account had been opened a few years before we were married, with quiet, consistent deposits. No flags. Just... secrecy. Why hadn't he told me? The total came to $120,300. A pang of light-headed relief fluttered in my chest. *Could this have been just savings?*

One withdrawal stood out—a large one, made exactly one week before he died, just days before our tenth anniversary. I sank back onto the pillows, heart aching. Could it have been a gift? A surprise trip to Paris? The idea shimmered with everything we'd once dreamed about but never done. Tears streamed down my cheeks as I whispered to the ceiling,

"Oh, my Daniel. Please tell me you were planning to take me to Paris..."

The thought warmed me—but it didn't erase the shadows. Not the locket. Not the surveillance. Not Dina. Too tired to untangle it further, I carefully gathered everything and slipped Daniel's notes into the lining of my suitcase. Carrying that much cash felt reckless, so I drove to a nearby branch of a bank affiliated with Rose Haven. Within minutes, I opened a temporary savings account and deposited every dollar—it was one layer removed from panic.

Afterward, I sought solid ground. My car found its way to the only place in Los Angeles that still belonged to us—Le Chariot Bleu, the shadow-lit French bistro where we'd toasted anniversaries, fought in whispers, and dared to dream. The restaurant's warmth hit me when I stepped inside—soft lighting, golden wood, and garlic and wine sauce hanging in the air. A violin hummed quietly beneath the soft clink of silverware. For a moment, I could almost feel Daniel beside

me. Almost. Henri, the owner, spotted me instantly and rushed over, his face a mixture of warmth and gravity.

"Molly," he said, his French accent wrapping my name in warm chocolate tones. "It is so good to see you."

His eyes searched mine as if measuring how much I could bear. After a gentle expression of condolences, he hesitated. "May I sit with you for a moment?"

I nodded, brushing the corner of my eye with a napkin. "Of course."

Henri eased into the seat across from me, hands folded.

"There's something I think you should know."

I nodded, already sensing Henri had something important to share. As I sipped a glass of my favorite red wine, he began to speak, his voice low and tender.

"Daniel made reservations here," he said quietly. "For your tenth anniversary."

The words cut through the fragile calm I'd been clinging to like a gentle knife.

"He also arranged a month in Paris. He was going to surprise you."

Tears welled up instantly. There was no stopping them now. Henri slid a crisp linen cloth across the table, his eyes reflecting the same ache I felt blooming in my chest.

"Molly... je suis tellement désolé. I'm so sorry. But I've never seen a man more in love. He was so excited to see your face when he told you. He couldn't stop smiling."

My throat tightened. "No, Henri. Thank you. You've no idea how much this means to me—truly."

"Oh oui, ma chère Molly, I hope so. He was... a man extraordinaire. We all miss him." He hesitated. "But I am glad to see you well."

As if on cue, my meal arrived—perfectly prepared duck à l'orange, a favorite Daniel had always insisted on ordering for me. The familiar aroma settled something of

weighty consequence in my bones. Henri stood to leave as the waiter retreated.

"Eat. Rest. Come back soon. Your meals will always be on us."

I reached for his hand. "You're an exceptional friend, Henri. Thank you."

He placed his other hand over mine with a warm smile, then returned to the kitchen. I ate slowly, letting the flavors and memories blend into something bittersweet but nourishing. The wine, the food, the kindness—all blended into a strange calm release. Daniel had planned it. He'd wanted to take me to Paris. That was real. That was true. And somehow, that truth steadied me more than I expected. After dinner, I returned to my hotel room, slipped into a long, hot bath, and let the warmth wrap around me like a silk cocoon. For the first time in weeks, I slept without dreaming.

The following morning, Frank, the author, unexpectedly came to mind—how effortlessly charming he'd been, the way he'd read Miss Marple aloud at the *Bookstore and More*. There'd been a look in his incredibly gorgeous eyes, something unspoken. I hadn't told him I lived in Los Angeles, too. Maybe I wasn't ready, or afraid of what might happen if I let myself want a relationship again. But even now, his voice echoed in my mind like a promise not yet made. If there was still a next chapter waiting, maybe Frank belonged in it—a quiet hope flickering in the shadow of everything.

But morning light cut through that hope with cold precision. I was meeting Jason. The boutique café smelled of strong coffee and worn leather. I spotted Jason waiting, his gaunt frame leaning heavily on a cane. His eyes—sunken and sharp—held the weight of exhaustion and bitterness carved deep by time.

"Jason," I said, startled, "are you okay?"

He waved me off irritably. "Just get me a coffee. Black. Sit down. I don't have time to chat."

We settled at a table. I handed him his drink, noting the tremor in his hand. Something was off—not just physically, but emotionally.

"I need a favor," he said, without preamble. "Get me a job at the *Times*."

I hesitated. "Jason, I'm not at the *Times* anymore."

His eyes narrowed. "Then, where are you?"

I didn't answer. His tone felt too pointed, too invested. I wondered why it mattered so much. Guarded, I offered instead,

"I'll reach out to a few people. But no promises."

He scoffed, muttering under his breath. He looked like a man unraveling—yet, there was a sharpness beneath the desperation. Was this staged? Our meeting ended awkwardly. I watched him limp away, and that gnawing question returned: *Was this a setup?* Back at the hotel, I dropped my purse on the bed and saw the phone blinking —a new message from an unknown number. *Still think Paris was the plan? Look closer.* My breath caught. Whatever Jason wanted, whatever Paris might have been... I was no longer sure it had anything to do with love. I sat down hard on the edge of the bed, pulse hammering, the words crashing through my mind—a brutal warning shot. Who had sent it? And what else did they know? I tried to shake it off, at least for the hour ahead.

My next stop was lunch with Ciara before catching my plane home. As I stepped back into the hotel lobby, still rattled from the message, I spotted her waving from across the room. Her bright smile breezed through the fog in my mind, lifting me—if only for a moment. We embraced, and with arms linked, made our way into the elegant dining room. The soft clink of china and murmur of quiet conversation enveloped us, a gentle embrace that pressed against the sharp edge of my unease. Over crisp salad and warm artisan bread, I let my breath steady, though beneath the calm, the weight of what awaited still lingered.

"Reading about detectives is infinitely different from being one," I confessed, half-laughing, half-weary.

"Molly," Ciara said, her voice steady, "detective work is about getting to the truth. It's not always easy, and it's agony when you can't get there."

"Yes, that's true, isn't it?" I sighed as I shared the message with her.

Ciara leaned in, lowering her voice. "We're watching several suspects, and still certain Bates was behind Daniel and Joel's deaths. But getting proof?" She shook her head. "He makes Capone look like a novice."

She looked around the restaurant, her eyes scanning for anyone listening.

"He's not just covering his tracks, Molly—he's rewriting the map. People who ask questions disappear, get reassigned, or suddenly forget how to talk."

Her jaw clenched. "And that message? That wasn't a warning. It was a breadcrumb. Someone's trying to help you— or trap you."

She dropped her voice to a whisper.

"Look closer. At what? At who? And why now?"

Leaning in, urgency sharpened her words. "Molly, whatever you've stepped into, goes deeper than Daniel's case. Way beyond him... and far above Bates. You need to be smart—and fast."

She glanced over her shoulder before whispering, "But we've got a lead on the driver of that car."

My heart skipped. "Who is it, Ciara?"

"It's just a lead," she cautioned. "But I'll let you know the moment it's confirmed."

"What about Bates?"

"IA and the FBI are watching him closely. Every account, every move. He's writing memoirs, and apparently, his health's deteriorating."

"I knew about the book," I said softly, "but not his health." Guilt and something darker shot through me.

"What about Dina? Is she still with Bates?"
Ciara's expression tightened. "We don't think so. She's disappeared. Saks said she stopped showing up about a month ago. No one's heard from her."

"Sounds like she's under investigation," I ventured.
Ciara paused, then nodded. "She is. But before you ask— *that's* all I can say."

I nodded, absorbing the silence between her words. As we wrapped up lunch and I prepared to head to the airport, I found myself balancing two realities: the warmth of a shared meal with someone I trusted, and the cold blast of a message from someone who wanted to rattle me. Pieces of the puzzle were falling into place. But the picture forming was far from comforting. As I stepped out into the blinding afternoon light, the city seemed louder, faster, more dangerous. I hugged Ciara one last time on the curb, her grip firm, her eyes filled with the kind of fear only someone inside the machine could understand.

"You sure you want to go back alone?" she asked.

I nodded. "I don't have a choice."

Slipping something into my hand, she said, "A flash drive—encrypted. A name came up—someone tied to the car that hit Daniel. I haven't confirmed it yet, but it's someone unexpected. Be careful. If I go dark, wait three days, then open it."

Before I could protest, she turned and disappeared into the crowd, swallowed whole by the city she once believed in. I boarded the flight to Rose Haven with a stomach full of dread and a head full of questions. The message. The flash drive. A possible lead on Daniel's killer. Everything pointed toward a final reckoning. And now, it was hurtling toward me.

The plane lifted off, banking west. Below me, Los Angeles shrank into a puzzle of shadows and secrets. Above, clouds closed in, a heavy curtain drawn across the sky. When I landed, dusk was already bleeding into the hills of Rose Haven. The town looked unchanged, but I wasn't. Not anymore. As I

pulled into the gravel drive of my new home, headlights flared in the distance—too far to make out, too close to ignore. I slowed the car. Someone was watching. And they wanted me to know it.

What Comes with Recognition

My phone rang early the following morning.

"Molly, have you heard the news about David?" Claire's voice crackled with excitement.

"No, what happened?" I asked, my heart quickening.

"He received confirmation from Queen Elizabeth's office. He's been formally recognized as part of the royal line. They've invited him to a private dinner at Buckingham Palace. He'll receive his title... and an inheritance."

I sat up straighter, stunned. "Oh, Claire, that's incredible."

"Molly, he's accepted the invitation. They've already prepared rooms for him inside the Palace. But he wants this kept quiet. Only the three of us know."

"I understand. What should I do?"

"Nothing, for now. Let him come to you."

"All right. Thanks for calling, Claire. Talk soon."

Later that afternoon, David called. His voice was measured and calm.

"Lunch at Hanna's?"

I agreed without hesitation. When I arrived, he was already seated by the window, a beam of sunlight catching in his hair. He rose to greet me, and for a moment, I glimpsed an unguarded rest behind his eyes. As we sat, he quietly dove into the details. I listened, spellbound, delighted for him, and couldn't stop staring. Still, I continue wondering how this could be the same gruff, prickly man I first met in Claire's kitchen? The transformation was increasingly elegant. Then came the part that left me breathless: he was now a direct heir to King Edward IV, a royal bloodline that had been verified

and validated. After the waitress left, he leaned in, voice shifting lower, the trace of his Highland lilt threading through each word.

"Aye, I still cannae prove Richard didn't kill the lads," he said, eyes now shadowed with frustration. "That mystery runs deeper than I ever imagined—twists and turns like the moors back home. But mark my words, Molly... I'll no let his name rot in the mouths of those who never knew the truth."

He paused, put down his fork, and met my eyes with a quiet intensity, and with an edge of vulnerability in his voice stark against his usual confidence, he whispered,

"Molly, I'll be leavin' for England in a few days. Stoppin' in France first... then on to London. Would ye come with me, Molly?"

The offer stunned me into silence. I wanted to say yes. Every part of me did. But the more we discussed the logistics—the inevitable media attention, my separate accommodations at the Resident Victoria Hotel—the more the fairytale unraveled into something far more complicated. It was too clandestine. It was too risky. One wrong photo, and the world would make assumptions we couldn't take back.

Nevertheless, David didn't pressure me. His understanding was more persuasive, more compelling than any plea. I asked if there was anything I could do for him while he was away. He smiled, warm but resolute.

"Steven will mind the place. Best ye keep a bit o' distance till this all settles."

An unspoken current pulsed between us, charged with possibility, the rising tension just before a rollercoaster drops. We shared a silent smile. Then David returned to the market, and I headed to the Gazette. The days before his departure blurred by, but time seemed to freeze on the morning of his flight. Claire called early, asking for help preparing a celebration breakfast. David was expected to swing by hungry before loading his market order and heading to the airport. It all felt achingly familiar, yet like a river that never flows the

same way twice; the steady turning of the seasons meant I barely recognized David now. A quiet reminder that grace and time can transform even what once seemed unchangeable. David was now a man of distinction. Jacob toddled through the house, a wonder in motion. And I, once an outsider, was a working resident of Rose Haven. Steven and Claire's farm had flourished, bringing fresh produce, dairy, honey, and poultry to town. Like David's, my life had shifted into something I never could have predicted.

When it was time for David to leave, we said our goodbyes in the kitchen, where he quietly asked for a last moment with the people he now considered family. Insisting on taking the airport shuttle himself, he determined not to involve us further in what lay ahead. Claire and I stood at the window, watching as Steven helped him load the truck. The two men shared a wordless embrace—brief but filled with a kind of masculine grace, a silent vow of respect. Then David climbed into the driver's seat.

The engine rumbled to life. Claire and I stepped outside, waving as he pulled away. We lingered there in the cool morning air, watching until his truck vanished down Abbey Lane, leaving only dust and the stillness of a new chapter taking shape. Holding Jacob on her hip, Claire broke the silence.

"Those we care about can affect our lives in ways we could never have imagined. I wonder what it'll be like... the next time we see David?"

Scenarios tumbled through my mind, each one demanding attention. Later, as water ran over the breakfast dishes, I let slip that my instincts were already sharp, alert for trouble. We laughed at the irony, but beneath it, a thread of unease wove silently through the room.

"No one would believe it," Claire said, "even if you did write about it."

"You're right. But if the story is ever told—if a photo surfaces of him beside the Queen—people will believe in the miracle he's living."

She nodded. "Yes. But most will never know the cost of getting there... or the price of such recognition."

Her insight was profound as usual, yet it carried a hint of something distant. I glanced at her.

"Claire... are you worried for David?"

She looked down at Jacob, smoothing a wisp of hair from his brow. "A little, yes, Molly."

Much to my surprise, I realized I was, too.

The Line Goes Dead

Ciara's warning still rang in my ears as I left the Gazette later that morning. The flash drive in my satchel felt heavier with every step, its presence almost humming against my side. I'd covered fashion today—polished, safe, forgettable. But my pulse hadn't slowed since the moment she'd said, *Be careful. If I go dark, wait three days, then open it.*" The cobblestone streets of Rose Haven were postcard-perfect, but my thoughts kept slipping back to Los Angeles—runway shows, studio tours, Daniel's hand warm in mine. I was living my dream, or so I thought. I believed that having a child would complete the picture. But Daniel was murdered. I knew it in my bones. My perspective on life has widened. My view is more encompassing. And now, whatever's on that drive might be the proof I've been chasing—or the thing that gets me killed.

I texted Ciara. No response. I called her direct line—voicemail again. Maybe it's nothing. Perhaps it's standard procedure. But something in me, an intangible I've learned to trust, says otherwise. The fog hangs low tonight, curling around Rose Haven like a breath held too long. The distant clang of the lighthouse bell echoes through the mist, a sound that somehow stirs both comfort and warning. As I reach my front door, I pause—one hand on the key, the other brushing against the flash drive in my bag. I won't break my word. Not yet. But if Ciara stays silent much longer...I may have no choice.

I escaped into my enchanted garden, letting the blooms of my private bit of Paris wrap around me, smoothing the ruffled edges of my worries. The tension in my chest softened as fading sunlight spilled across the cobblestones, and with a delicate cup of spiced Darjeeling in hand, I curled up on the sofa with Agatha Christie's *The Murder at the Vicarage*. Miss Jane Marple—sharp, unassuming, relentless. Just like her creator, who was dared by her sister Madge to prove she could write a mystery. Maybe I'm being dared, too. Dared to push forward. To unearth the truth, no matter how deeply it's buried. Halfway through a particularly clever chapter, my phone rang. *Ciara.* Her voice was low, urgent.

"I'm in D.C. Still on assignment. Molly, something's happened. Dina McFarland resurfaced."

I straightened. "Where?"

"Saks Fifth Avenue. She showed up as if nothing had happened, reinstated as their lead buyer without a single question. They assigned her to the Winter Collection in Paris. But after the show, she detoured instead of returning to Beverly Hills. She's here now. In Washington."

I tightened my grip on the phone.

"So what's the play? Why surface now, and why is she in Washington, of all places?"

"She didn't just reappear, Molly—she was *escorted*. A long black limo met her at the airport, bypassed baggage claim, and took her straight to the most expensive hotel in the city. Top floor, directly across and facing the White House. Less than thirty minutes later, Harold Bates walked in like it was all prearranged."

My pulse quickened. "The Hay-Adams" hotel?

"Yes."

"Are you saying they might've had business across the street?"

"I don't know," Ciara replied, her voice tightening. There was a pause. Then: "Molly…we believe Dina was driving the car that hit Daniel."

246

"What?"

I stood without realizing it, the book tumbling from my lap. "It was a man. That's what everyone said."

"We thought so. But now it looks like it could've been a woman disguised. I'm still running it down. I don't want to move until we close every hole a defense attorney could crawl through."

"And Bates?"

"I don't know yet. But this isn't just about Dina. I wanted you to know before the precinct leaks it. Officially, no one knows—just me and my lead. Keep your distance, Molly. Seriously."

"Thank you. Thank you for trusting me." My voice cracked. "And Senator Randolph Warren?"

"Nothing solid yet. Only whispers. I'll call when I know more."

"Be careful, Ciara. Please."

"I will." Her tone softened. "I promise. I'll be in touch soon."

But when the call ended, a hollow ache filled the quiet. I tried to shake it and push its weight aside, but dread clung tightly to me. I went still. The Hay-Adams wasn't just a luxury hotel—it was a front-row seat to the most powerful office in the world. If Bates walked through this hotel lobby, there was a reason. And if he'd crossed the street? That wasn't a coincidence—it was a strategy. Whatever they were planning wasn't just personal—it was political. Restless, I grabbed my coat and headed out for Hanna's Café.

The clatter of plates and the low hum of conversation brought immediate comfort, a fragile shelter against the news still pounding in my head. Lobster chowder thickened the air, rich and briny, daring me to forget why my hands still trembled. Margot waved me over; her husband and Jenn from the bookstore leaned forward, eyes bright with questions I wasn't ready to answer. We raised chilled champagne glasses, the cold biting into my palm. The chef called out the evening's

catch, drawing laughter that tried to pull me under its warmth. For a heartbeat, I let it. But beneath the clinking glasses and easy chatter, the storm gathered, waiting to break.

Days passed. No word from Ciara. And that's when the unease hardened into something darker. Something that told me—she was in trouble. The tension strained every nerve, leaving no room for sleep. I brewed a cup of chamomile tea and queued up an old noir film, hoping for a distraction. But the images on screen blurred. My phone rested beside me on the couch, silent and foreboding. Somewhere between sips and shadows, exhaustion claimed me. But sleep offered no peace. In my dreams, I saw Ciara trailing Dina through the teeming streets of Washington—then vanishing into a swell of shadows and noise. I woke with a start, my heart pounding, as the early morning light cut across the room in sharp gold lines. For a fleeting moment, the sounds of seagulls and barking seals from the harbor brought comfort. Then it hit me. No call. No update. Had Ciara gone dark?

I reached for the phone but froze mid-dial. Calling the precinct now could raise suspicions. It could ruin whatever operation she'd been running. I had no proof—just fear. Maybe it was time to review the flash drive—no, not yet. So I shoved it aside and moved on autopilot, preparing for work at the *Gazette*, clinging to routine like a lifeline. When I arrived, Maryanne Lumley stood at my desk, fidgeting with her glasses. Her face was pale, her expression stiff.

"Mr. Clayborne wants to see you. Right away."

My heart seized. *Please, God, don't let this be about Ciara.*

I followed her to his office, forcing down panic. Maryanne closed the door behind me, and I braced for the blow.

"Good morning, Mrs. Cleary," Mr. Clayborne said, surprisingly composed. "I've been following your work. Your column has become one of the most-read in the city. Reader response has exploded."

My body exhaled before my mind did. This wasn't about Ciara. Not yet.

"Mrs. Lumley is leaving us," he continued, "and I'd like to offer you the lead position in the fashion section. You've earned it."

Caught between gratitude and dread, I managed, "Thank you, Mr. Clayborne—I'd be honored."

He smiled. "Call me Andy. We're informal around here."

Maryanne walked me to what would soon be my new office, detailing the transition. I took notes mechanically, nodding when appropriate, but my thoughts were nowhere near fashion. They were in Washington, tracing Ciara's last known steps. By the end of the day, her silence had turned deafening. I called. No answer. I paged her. Nothing. The panic I'd been staving off surged like a tidal wave. It was all over the news the following day: *Police Officer Missing—Last Seen in Washington, D.C.*

My hand trembled as I dialed the precinct. A fellow officer recognized my voice and transferred me to Detective James Franklin. One breath was enough to tell me the truth.

"She didn't check in Friday night," he said, voice grim. "We sent two of our best to D.C. to find her. There's no sign yet."

The weight dropped on me like a stone slab. I thanked him, barely able to speak, and hung up. When at the *Gazette*, I wore the mask of professionalism. Though I burned to report the story, I couldn't risk the fallout—not with so much at stake. Secrets were piling up, and each one squeezed the breath from me. That's when my special phone rang. David. His voice cracked like splintered wood.

"Molly... I heard what's happened. It's Ciara, aye?"

When I confirmed his fear, David went silent—a pause heavy with dread. Then, his voice returned, quieter now, edged with something darker.

"I'll be in touch," he said. "Soon."

The line clicked. He was gone. My hands trembled as I set the phone down. Panic dismantling my self-control, begging to be let in. I couldn't afford it. Not now. I grabbed the notes I'd taken on my first day with Maryanne—mundane, methodical, mercifully precise. They became my lifeline, keeping my mind tethered while the world spun faster around me. But something kept whispering... The worst hadn't happened yet.

A Higher Law

Waiting for David's return call was unbearable. What could he possibly do from London? When the phone finally rang, his voice cut through with a sense of urgency.

"Molly—I asked Detective Franklin tae have his men search the basement of that inheritance property in D.C."

Relief and horror crashed over me like a wave. I reached for Ciara's flash drive and held it tightly as if holding on to her. The basement? Why? What had David uncovered? Before I could ask, he said with commanding accuracy,

"During the war, there was a master carpenter—Harry—who worked at the White House. Brilliant lad, but crooked. Caught skimming government materials. They showed him the door, but no' before he made a few... valuable connections."

He drew a breath, then carried on.

"Not long after, Harry took a job just a block from 1600 Pennsylvania Avenue. The owners—a wealthy Scottish couple—wanted something grand. Safe. So, Harry teamed up with a general contractor named Pete, and the two set about building a secret basement, one meant to rival the one beneath the White House. Private access. Hidden rooms. Then, columns and facade were fashioned to mirror the real thing up the street."

I sat frozen, adrenaline coursing through me as he went on.

"Back then, the place turned into a kind of underground salon. Politicians. Power brokers. Even Senator and Mrs. Randolph Warren. They'd host covert gatherings—chess games, aye, but played wi' real stakes. Then one day, an MI5 agent vanished. Last seen steppin' into that house. Never came out."

David paused, his words horrifying me.

"That house, Molly—it's the one I've just inherited."

A chill shot through me. "David... do you think Ciara's there?"

"I dinnae know," he said quietly. "But they're runnin' out of places tae look."

The silence between us crackled with what neither of us dared say aloud. Then, his voice softened.

"Listen, meh bonnie lass," his accent thickening with emotion. "Investigative work's come a long way since the days o' that MI5 lad. Ciara's no' just sharp—she's a fighter. She'll no' go down easy."

I closed my eyes, clinging to the thread of reassurance, still gripping the flash drive.

"Thank you, David," I whispered. "You're right. I'll keep the faith."

But the image of that missing agent, swallowed whole by history, refused to let go. I couldn't voice the darkest thought pressing in. So I shifted gears, my voice barely steady.

"So, David, how are things in London?"

David's tone lightened, but only slightly. He spoke of the old monarchy's relentless efforts to erase his lineage—how they buried ties to a castle in Devonshire, a manor in the South of France, and the grand home in D.C. His identity had been kept secret for decades. I could hear the fatigue in his voice—the kind that only comes from years of injustice. It would take time for the scars to heal—to soften.

"The end's nearly in sight now, Molly," he said, his voice low but steady. "Maybe then, I'll be able to breathe easy... for the first time in years."

The news broke the next evening: the missing officer had been found alive, dehydrated, disoriented, but safe—no location given. Relief washed over me, sharp and unexpected. My instinct was to call David and Ciara to share the news and hear their voices. But it was four in the morning in London, just shy of midnight in Washington. I let the silence settle. Instead, I stepped into my garden, drawn by the stillness of the night and the scent of jasmine thick in the air. Overhead, the stars sparkled in endless constellations. My best friend had been found. David helped make it happen. I sank beneath the mimosa tree, its blossoms sweet and heavy above me, and let the tears fall—tears of gratitude, release, and something deeper I couldn't yet understand.

When Ciara returned to Los Angeles, she stayed with me in Rose Haven. The first thing I did was return the flash drive. For a reason that escapes me, I couldn't open it. Seeing her in the sunlight again—unharmed, alive—was a gift I hadn't dared to hope for. We spent long hours beneath the trees, warmed by filtered light and the safety of silence. Then one morning, over coffee and birdsong, Ciara told me everything. She'd gone to Washington to finalize the evidence against Dina. But what she uncovered was far more damning.

"Dina wasn't just tangled with Bates," Ciara said, her voice quiet. "She was involved with Senator Warren, too. They used that house, a block from the White House—the one no one talks about, and now belongs to David. Access was gained through a key provided by the previous owner. But Dina and the Senator never entered through the front door."

I froze.

"What do you mean?"

"There's a tunnel," she said. "Underground. Hidden. They came and went unnoticed—until one day, everything changed."

She looked out across the garden, her eyes distant.

"Dina left first. Routine. But Warren stayed behind. I watched him press a code into a device mounted on the west

wall—something subtle, invisible unless you knew where to look. The wall shifted. Quietly. And he stepped through."

"What was inside?" I asked, barely breathing.

"I waited. Ten minutes. He never came back. So I went in—just a flashlight and my nerve. The passage was narrow, stone-lined. Then it opened into a chamber, about twenty feet across, with stone benches circling the walls. The kind of room built to outlast governments."

A cold ache moved through me. "I searched every corner," she said. "There were signs someone had just been there—blueprints, folders, maps. But Warren was gone. Vanished."

She looked back at me. "This wasn't just a tryst or a conspiracy, Molly. This was infrastructure. Hidden. Protected. Possibly sanctioned. And we've only scratched the surface."

Ciara's voice faltered, the strength she'd held onto cracking at the edges—eyes clouded by memory.

"I stepped forward, searching for another way out—then the wall slammed shut behind me. No handle. No seam. Just cold stone at my back. The lights died. The air went black. No power. No water. No food. The dark pressed in until I couldn't tell if I was standing or falling. Minutes blurred into days—or maybe it was the other way around. I lost count. And then came the sound. Soft. Precise. Mechanical clicks in the silence, like something was keeping score. Watching. Waiting."

My pulse quickened. I gripped my mug tighter, the steam curling between us like a ghost.

"And then?" I asked.

Her voice hushed. "Then came the light. The hiss of the door sliding open. And faces—uniforms. Hands reaching. I remember the air first, the oxygen hitting my lungs. I didn't even cry. I just... inhaled."

We were beneath the mimosa tree, sunlight dappling the earth around us, but the shadow of what she'd endured lingered like a threatening storm cloud. And then she dropped the match.

"Molly," she whispered, eyes locked on mine, "I saw Detective Tulsi Blair."

Everything inside me stilled.

"What?" I gasped.

"It was only for a second," she rushed on excitedly, "as the door opened, just before the others stepped in. She was standing in the corner. Watching. And then—she was gone."

My breath caught.

"You're the only person I've told," Ciara said, her voice trembling now. "What do you think?"

I stared at her, caught in a moment I couldn't resolve. Grief and reason collided in my chest like two freight trains.

"Ciara... you were in rough shape. Exhausted. Alone. We both miss her more than we're ready to admit."

"Maybe." She looked down, then back up with that rare, steel-eyed focus. "But our eyes locked, Molly. I *saw* her."

I wanted to tell Ciara she was wrong. That hallucinations under duress were common. That Tulsi Blair was gone, buried under facts and folded flags. But the words refused to come. I reached for her hand instead, grounding us both in something real.

"Maybe," I whispered. "Or maybe it was the shock."

We let it go—but not really. The question hung between us, trembling like a string pulled too tight. Ciara turned her gaze back to the trees, the breeze shifting the leaves into murmurs.

"They've charged Dina McFarland," she said, her voice steadier now. "With vehicular manslaughter. She was driving the stolen car that hit Daniel."

A chill laced its way down my spine. I swallowed hard.

"That gives us motive," I said. "But what about Warren? There's still no direct tie."

"Not yet," Ciara said. "But we're circling the fire now, Molly. The smoke's getting thicker."

The weight of her words was a frightening, icy wind slicing into me. Dina's arrest, the locked basement, the

impossible glimpse of Detective Tulsi Blair, and now a senator's name whispered in the shadows. I shifted my gaze to the wildflowers beyond the porch, their delicate forms bending and twisting in the restless breeze. Their fragile dance echoed the uncertainty coiling in my chest. Maybe we weren't chasing shadows anymore. Maybe the shadows were chasing us. The unrest that had simmered in Los Angeles—the fraying trust, the simmering anger—felt as if it had seeped quietly into Rose Haven. The storm wasn't just on the other side of the country anymore. Its stifling presence was closing in.

Yet, Detective Franklin was determined to chase the darkness lingering over Los Angeles, one truth at a time. He believed the public needed to see justice not just served, but earned. With the judge's consent, the proceedings would be televised, a bold attempt to restore faith in the nobility of policing. Within the department, quiet forces were at work. Covert efforts had begun to root out any officer unworthy of the oath they once swore: "While doing my best to control crime, I will do everything in my power to do no harm to the communities I serve and protect." As Ciara wrapped up her account, I finally found the courage to ask the question that had haunted me since the very beginning.

"The locket," I said quietly. "How did it end up in our garden?"

She didn't hesitate.

"Molly, Dina was targeting Daniel. He was her next conquest. That night, she was watching him—watching both of you—from the shadows. Waiting for a weakness. She thrives on control. On seduction. And when Daniel wouldn't play her game, she turned venomous."

I swallowed, the nausea rising.

"She's brilliant, no question," Ciara continued. "But greed, entitlement, and a thirst for status blind her. She's like a Black Widow, Molly. When investigators questioned her, she became livid at the mention of Daniel's name. And, when she saw the locket you gave us, there was a momentary flinch—

she wanted to take it. She bragged about sending the flowers. About slipping into Rose Cottage. That perfume you caught? It was hers."

Relief, disbelief, and fury surged all at once, colliding in my being. I felt lightheaded. My fists clenched at my sides as I tried to contain the tide.

"She watched Daniel like prey," I muttered. "And I was next. But why didn't he tell me? Why keep that from me? I could've—" I stopped, the words choking off in my throat.

Ciara reached for my hand.

"Because he was protecting you," she said gently.

"He knew you, Molly. If he told you what was happening, you would've stepped into the fire for him. And that's exactly what they wanted. Dina started asking questions. She became curious about what you might know. And with Bates, Dina, and political figures all fighting to protect themselves... silence was Daniel's only defense."

My breath slowed. The knot in my stomach loosened, just enough.

"These people," Ciara whispered, "they would've kept going. They would've buried it all. But Daniel stopped them."

I looked down, desperately trying to focus. As I recalled Daniel's frantic scribble, the pieces clicked together. Ciara confirmed that The Westfield Sting wasn't just a faded case in dusty files—it was the key to everything unraveling now. If Bates had pulled strings to protect the fourth officer—the one who vanished after the informant leak and slipped back into rotation under a false identity—then that officer was no accident. He was a ghost brought back for a purpose. Daniel had been chasing a shadow from that sting, someone scrubbed clean but never truly gone. And now, the very same forces behind Westfield were tightening their grip, with Joel's betrayal as the latest move on their chessboard.

I closed my eyes, letting the truth settle as the ever-present weight on my shoulders began to lift.

"Thank you, Ciara," I said. "Finally knowing the truth… letting go of the doubts... It's more of a relief than I can explain."

She nodded. "We were lucky in a way, weren't we? To have men who fought for something greater than themselves. Men who gave their lives to make the world better."

"Right," I said softly, holding back the tears. "We were."

Ciara returned to work not long after, and her strength was restored by purpose. I, still gathering mine, agreed to testify if called. It was what we had all hoped for—to see justice take the stand. However, as the trial unfolded, a new fear began to take hold. Every word was televised, dissected in the headlines, and echoed in foreign broadcasts. My anonymity—my safety—was unraveling thread by thread. I read once that justice demands sacrifice. But as each day passed, I wasn't sure if I was ready to be the one offered up. I held my breath every time the phone rang or a knock came at the door. My eyes stayed glued to the television as the trial played out like a slow-burning fuse. At any moment, I knew I could be summoned. And if I were... There'd be no hiding from the truth. Not anymore.

Dina's trial was short, sordid, and nothing short of a media circus. Controversial papers spun it into tabloid gold, twisting the truth into something grotesque. On screen, the courtroom looked polished and composed, but every word that left Dina McFarland's mouth was a dagger, cutting deeper than the last. I watched, my body drawing tight as a bowstring, as she took the stand with that icy poise she wore like armor. The lies flowed effortlessly, her tone detached, her expression unreadable. She made my husband, Daniel, a strange distortion before the world. She claimed she had "borrowed" Senator Warren's car without permission, claiming she only meant to follow Daniel, to "gather evidence" on behalf of her "dear friend," Chief Harold Bates. The courtroom didn't flinch. But

I did. Then came the words that ripped through me like a dagger:

"Daniel Cleary was suspected of causing controversy in the Black and Hispanic communities," she said, her voice smooth as ice. "He was the reason behind the violence in L.A. He spread false information about Chief Bates, and everyone thought it was criminal of him."

I couldn't breathe. Every fiber in my body rebelled against her twisted script. Daniel was the opposite of everything she claimed—a bridge-builder, a quiet force for justice. The idea that *he* had incited violence, that *he* was the villain—it was obscene. My hands curled into fists. Fury and disbelief crashed in tidal waves. Still, Dina went on, spinning herself as the calm, impartial observer. She wasn't a stalker. Not a conspirator. No, she was just "concerned." And then, as if it were a footnote, she said it.

"Yes, I hit him. Accidentally."

Accidentally. Like that single word could erase the horror of what she had done. As if intent mattered now. As if "accident" justified fleeing the scene, leaving Daniel to die alone on that cold, blood-stained street. But what tore at me most wasn't the impact. It was her refusal to look back. No remorse. No regret. No explanation for why she didn't stop. No humanity. Just cold, clinical evasion—followed by the final, unthinkable twist: She implied *Daniel was to blame. He* had caused the incident. *He* had brought it on himself. My throat burned. The bile rose. This wasn't testimony. It was an execution by narrative.

And as the camera panned to Dina's face—still stunning, stoic, untouched by consequence—I felt something shift inside me. A surge of resolve. Pure, steady, and absolute. No. This wasn't over. They could rewrite headlines, distort facts, and flash falsities across a million screens. But I would not let them bury the truth. I steadied my breath. My pulse slowed. The anger sharpened into clarity. There was still work to be done. Daniel's name would not be the last word on her

tongue. I would not rest until the real story was told. They had taken him from me. But they would not take the truth. Not now. Not ever.

The following days of the trial were a crucible—raw emotion clashed with public fury, and tension hung in the air like toxic smoke. Angry picketers lined the courthouse steps, their chants ricocheting off stone walls, demanding the truth. Security remained on high alert as whispers of violence crept closer with every hour. Inside the courtroom, the tide began to shift. Ciara and the other officers took the stand. Their voices carried unwavering conviction—but their faces remained concealed, obscured from the cameras, shields against the inevitable fallout. Their testimonies didn't just contradict Dina's—they dismantled her entire narrative, piece by piece, exposing the web of deceit she had so carefully constructed. Then came the community.

One by one, local shopkeepers testified, offering something no prosecutor could manufacture: *truth from the people Daniel had served.* Gasps rippled through the gallery when Maria, the founder of Maria's Flowers, now in her nineties, was helped to the witness stand by her daughter. Her voice trembled, but the fire in her eyes had never dimmed. She spoke of Daniel Cleary with fierce, tear-streaked pride. Of kindness. Of courage. Of a man who had stood between her and danger during the riots, who once fixed the back door to her shop with his bare hands because he "didn't want her to feel unsafe." The courtroom fell into reverent silence.

When the jury finally withdrew, the air thickened with unbearable anticipation. Hours passed, and then, just as my nerves threatened to unravel, an unexpected letter arrived. David had extended an invitation. A private luncheon. At Buckingham Palace. The irony was jarring. From a courtroom drenched in grief to royal gardens and silver trays? At first, I couldn't imagine it. But David's note was clear: *We need air, Molly girl. Somewhere to breathe. Come.*

Claire and Steven urged me to go, reminding me that grief, when carried too long, becomes a chain—and that honoring Daniel meant stepping into the light he believed the world could still hold. Their words didn't lift the weight all at once, but they stirred something in me—a quiet willingness to move again, if only inch by inch. So, slowly, preparations began for a surreal escape that felt more like a dream than a destination. But reality had no patience for dreams. My mind kept snapping back to the courtroom, to the jurors locked away with Dina's fate. Even at the Gazette, the words on my screen blurred, replaced by the image of twelve strangers deciding if justice would hold. Fashion felt frivolous, distant. The days dragged until the verdict came in. Guilty. Of murder. The judges' sentence landed with a heavy finality—clean, cold, and irreversible. Life without parole. It wasn't dramatic. It wasn't emotional. But it was justice. And in that clinical moment, my every fiber began to settle. The ache remained, but the chaos quieted. A space opened within me—not yet peace, but something close. A beginning. But not all villains were caught.

Senator Warren and Chief Bates, slippery as ever, had sidestepped implication. The system let them slip through. I felt the bitterness rise, but I knew I couldn't allow it to stay. Possibly, with time, forgiveness would come. Maybe healing would follow. And perhaps, somewhere beyond this world, a higher law would finish what our courts could not. Ciara, relentless as ever, wanted to keep going and bring Warren and Bates down once and for all. However, the new chief wanted to focus on attending to the needs of the good people of Los Angeles. The city needed stability. Cases were piling up. Closure had been declared, and repair commenced while tragedy lurked.

Senator Norman Scott's voice was barely audible over the hum of the private club. Warren hadn't been the same since Dina's arrest—angry, erratic, pickling himself in whiskey. Two nights later, the headline detonated: "Senator Randolph Warren Killed in DUI Crash—Family of Four Also Lost."

Drunk, he'd drifted across the center-divide—smashing head-on into their car. The carnage was absolute. He died before they reached the hospital. Scott quietly confirmed that Mrs. Warren—shattered and pale—likely never knew: her husband's long affair with Dina McFarland. Warren would never face a courtroom. But his legacy still could. At a press conference, his son stepped into the strobe of cameras. Stoic. Crisp suit. A gaze that lingered a fraction too long on each reporter, as if weighing their usefulness, and said,

"My father's vision for this country will never be realized," his voice smooth, measured. "But I will carry it forward. I will run for Congress—as Randolph Warren Jr."

The weight of bloodline coiled around every word. And as the flashes popped, I saw it—a flicker in his eyes. Cold. Calculating. And I knew then: the shadow wasn't gone. It had simply chosen a new face.

Between What Was and What Could Be

I heard about Bates finishing his autobiography while visiting Claire and little Jacob. The buzz was impossible to ignore—literary agents circling like vultures. Rumors of his declining health only added urgency. Olivia, a relentless New York agent with a talent for repackaging villains, swept in with glossy promises. Bates signed without hesitation. A staggering advance. A major publisher. A media blitz. Suddenly, he was everywhere. Pre-orders flooded in as if the world had forgotten who he was. Olivia called it "sizzling" and "world-shaking." Maybe it was. But to me, it felt like vindication he didn't deserve. His crimes hadn't vanished. He had rewritten the ending.

Meanwhile, across the Atlantic, another story was quietly unfolding. David—brash, brilliant, impossible-to-ignore David—had been granted a private audience with the Queen. Rumors turned to reality when the announcement came: he'd been named a Duke, placed in line to inherit the

title of Duke of York. A private royal luncheon followed, reserved for a select circle of family and a few carefully chosen guests. Then, just as swiftly, David returned to Rose Haven. No press. No ceremony. He stepped behind the market's meat counter as if nothing had changed.

"David's always been a Duke," Claire said lightly. "If not for history, he might have been King."

I stood at the door, watching him slice smoked ham with the same relaxed precision. He looked up, caught my gaze, and smiled—the same familiar, grounded smile. The title hadn't changed him—it had only confirmed what had always been true. In the following days, he arranged everything— flights, hotels, high tea in Mayfair, even a potential Paris fashion show. With calm ease, he carried us forward, helping me to slip further out from grief's cloud. I emerged into what once were the exciting days of planning a splendid vacation. At times, I could almost feel Daniel beside me in the quiet moments. Not pulling me backward anymore—but urging me on. Life, I was beginning to see, was not something to solve. It was something to step into.

Ease accompanied us like an old friend as we quietly embarked on the journey David had so carefully arranged. Claire, Steven, and I flew beside him across the Atlantic, each of us still processing the incredible, transformative weeks behind us. David wore his new title with a quiet dignity, but this time, he wasn't guiding us as a friend—he was leading us into a world few ever glimpsed. I quickly learned that luxury wasn't about wealth. It was about clarity of purpose—the unflinching confidence of integrity. Claire and Steven had once hinted at this. Now, I understand. What separated ordinary lives from the extraordinary wasn't status. It was a commitment. Daniel had lived by it. But David... David embodied it.

When we were introduced to the Royal Family, I saw it mirrored in them as well. Loyalty—unspoken but palpable— guided their every move. Claire, Steven, and I exchanged

glances. We could feel it: the same pulse, the same purpose, alive in David's eyes. A line I'd once read returned to me with piercing clarity: *To whom much is given, much is required.* It wasn't a motto. It was a reckoning. Their lineage, silence, sacrifices—the weight of it lived in the spaces between words. And yet, they carried it with grace. The luncheon was flawless—the garden divine. Even the birds seemed in on the secret, their wings slicing the air with reverent stillness. With her effortless magnetism, the Queen drew us in with warmth and quiet command. For a fleeting hour, we belonged to that world I had only ever read about. As the meal ended, I wished we could stay in that suspended beauty. But David, ever attuned, leaned closer and murmured,

"There's still more to see."

His timing nudged me forward, and by the following morning, we were swept into the vibrant elegance of a Paris fashion show. My heart was still catching up when David stopped short of the entrance. From his coat pocket, he drew something out—his hand closed tight, deliberate. Then, like a magician with his final flourish, he opened his palm. A lanyard. A press pass. My name was printed neatly beneath the Gazette's insignia. He smiled.

"I thought ye might want front-row access—with a purpose."

Emotion surged. I couldn't speak. I felt the future was mine to claim. Tears welled in my eyes and spilled freely. Claire, beaming, wrapped me in a hug.

"We'll be up front," she whispered. "Come find us after."

I nodded, overwhelmed. And just like that, they disappeared into the crowd. I turned back, dazed. I was seated among the world's press, camera in hand, notebook ready. In Paris. At the show of my dreams. Flashes lit the room. Cameras clicked like castanets. The energy was contagious. The models emerged onto the runway from behind a floor-to-ceiling movie screen of ocean waves on the French Riviera, sun-drenched

vineyards, grand châteaux, and candlelit riverbanks. Each scene matched the fashion—elegant, defiant, bold. And then the finale. Every wall erupted with a synchronized display of dazzling fireworks. Gasps echoed. Models emerged through the glittering bursts like deities in motion. The audience surged to their feet, euphoric. I pressed through the buzzing crowd until I reached the front row. We embraced, laughter spilling above the fading hum of wonder.

"Shall we continue this over lunch on the Champs-Élysées?" David asked.

I was too breathless to answer. Steven and Claire shared a quick, knowing glance.

"Perfect idea," Claire said. "We know just the place."

They led us to their favorite café—discovered on their honeymoon, with its red canopy swaying in the breeze. Glasses clinked, conversation rustled, and the pulse of Paris beat around us, framed by centuries-old stone. Then my phone buzzed. A message from Ciara: Confirmed. "T" is alive. Will explain later.

My breath caught. Alive. I stared at the message, reading it repeatedly, as if repetition would make it real. Looking up in disbelief, my voice barely above a whisper.

"Tulsi's alive."

Claire gasped. "Are you serious?"

Steven leaned in, his brow furrowed. "You're sure?"

I nodded slowly, still reeling. "Ciara just confirmed it. Tulsi's alive. After everything..."

For a moment, none of us spoke. The café hum faded beneath the weight of the impossible made real. David lifted his glass, his voice quiet and reverent.

"To Ghost protocol.".

Claire's eyes glistened. "To survival."

Steven added, "To truth—and the ones still standing."

As I raised my glass, "And to those who never stopped believing.".

As we toasted, the shadows loosened their grip. The past didn't vanish, but it softened. The warmth of now reclaimed its space as conversation resumed. Those few days had done more than expand my view of the world. I gained a new perspective on life. A dream had come true—not the way I'd expected, but the one I sorely needed.

While the plane climbed into the night, Paris fell away—a scatter of lights against the dark. The glass was cool against my forehead; Claire and Steven slept, and David read in silence. My thoughts drifted homeward. Daniel would have loved this view—the calm above the storm, the way distance made everything small. By the time the captain announced our descent, I wasn't thinking of Paris anymore. I was thinking of Rose Haven, and the life waiting there. We caught the shuttle into town, agreeing to meet for dinner at Hanna's Café. After freshening up at Rose Cottage, the walk through the scented air to the café felt electric, magical. Hanna greeted me with a knowing smile and led me to a quiet corner booth, where Claire, Steven, and David were waiting. David's eyes met mine first—steady, searching—as he reached for my hand, inviting me closer. Before our fingers touched, a sudden fragrance of orange blossoms and honeysuckle drifted past. My heart leapt, carrying me back to that intoxicating spring night with Daniel. I was suspended in the fragile space between what was and what could be. David's voice, low and gentle, broke through.

"Molly, lass, would you like to sit down?"

In the quiet certainty of an unspoken blessing from Daniel, I released a breath I hadn't known I was holding and, with a trembling kind of peace, answered,

"I do believe I would, David."

To Be Unraveled

Author's Note

Thank you for joining Molly on this journey through loss, resilience, truth, and discovery. This story began as a whisper, a quiet echo of questions about justice, legacy, and the secrets we carry. As it unfolded, it became deeper: a search for peace, purpose, and the courage to begin again.

Molly Cleary is, at her core, a seeker. She seeks truth in the world, but more importantly, she seeks truth within herself—and I believe we all do, in our particular way. This novel is dedicated to those who have loved deeply, lost significantly, and dared to move forward.

To you, dear reader: thank you for turning the page.
If Molly's story resonated with you, I'd be honored if you shared your thoughts in a brief review. Your voice helps others discover the journey, and is ever so encouraging.

With gratitude,
Carolyn Haynes

About the Author

Carolyn Haynes, a mother of four beautiful and talented daughters, has captivated readers with two critically acclaimed memoirs: *The Lloyd Haynes Story: A Remarkable Journey to Stardom*—hailed by the *Tribune* as "Superbly Written"—and *Bewitched: Secrets from Comedy Genius Sol Saks*, praised by the *Los Angeles Times* as "First-Class." A proud member of the Screen Actors Guild, the American Federation of Television & Radio Artists, the Authors Guild, and a vibrant writing and poetry community, Carolyn brings a rich creative legacy to her writing. Her background includes studies at the American Film Institute, CBS Workshops, and the Pasadena Playhouse, as well as an invitation to the prestigious Royal Academy of Dramatic Art in London. She assisted comedy pioneer Sol Saks in developing books, plays, television productions, and university-level writing courses for many years. As the wife of Samuel Lloyd Haynes, she also contributed to his screenplays, short stories, and photography.

Now turning her talents to mystery fiction, Carolyn invites readers into the gripping world of *Molly Marple Mystery*—a psychological thriller laced with history, suspense, and an unforgettable heroine. More addictive and thought-provoking stories are sure to follow.

- **The Lloyd Haynes Facebook Page:** https://www.facebook.com/lloydhaynesroom222/
- **Blog:** https://thelloydhaynesstory.wordpress.com
- **X:** https://twitter.com/carolyngrace505
- **Instagram:** https://www.instagram.com/chaynes5050/
- **LinkedIn:** https://www.linkedin.com/in/carolyn-haynes-author-14752a100/

Made in the USA
Columbia, SC
17 January 2026

a3ddb999-4457-4f01-94e9-b11431e5f770R01